THE ATONEMENT

BONNIE POIRIER

CHAPTER 1

"I heard some talk that you were coming back home. Is that right?"

My pulse raced. Why would Sandra Morton be worried about me returning? Surely after this long, I could come home without any trouble from them. "Yes, ma'am, it's true."

"That's fantastic. I have a huge favor to ask. I need a wedding planner. Now I know you haven't settled in, but this is urgent."

"Thank you for the opportunity, but I haven't made it to town yet."

"Well, perfect. You might as well swing by here first. What time can I expect you?" She was matter-of-fact, and there was no arguing with her. Once she made up her mind, there was no changing it.

I glanced at the clock on the dash. "I should be about half an hour."

"Okay, see you then." There was no goodbye, just the deadline.

I didn't need to ask for directions to the Morton ranch. They were burned into my brain. Almost as deeply as the bittersweet memories from the time I'd spent there.

What had I just agreed to? Who was getting married? Surely, she wouldn't have asked me to plan Rob's wedding. That would be weird. Gavin, maybe? He was in his early thirties. Mom hadn't mentioned Tyler getting married, but she never talked much about the Morton family. Jessica, get it together. Stop making a mountain out of a molehill. My mind was spinning. I turned the music up, hoping to drown out my thoughts.

The peacefulness of the drive was shattered, and I was now a bundle of nerves, which only increased as I got closer to the ranch turnoff.

The grand gates loomed ahead of me. At one time, this had been a place of comfort It had felt like my home. I had ruined all that by leaving.

There was a new road off to the right, and I wondered if one of the boys had built a home away from the prying eyes of their father.

The Morton Mansion rose from the earth as I climbed the slight hill into the yard. It was a magnificent home. Windows covered the front of the house, and the large stone columns looked like they were holding the entire weight of the structure.

Seeing the home for the first time in many years gave me the same inadequate feelings it had the first time Rob had brought me here. I would never be good enough for this lifestyle.

Sandra Morton stood outside the massive home, smiling from ear to ear. She hadn't aged a day. Her blond hair was perfectly styled, her clothing immaculate. I parked my car and took a deep, calming breath. It didn't help at all. My palms were wet, my heart was racing, and I was completely freaking out. No part of me ever thought I would be here on this ranch again. The last time I left, I'd been crying, my life falling apart around me.

Sandra walked over and pulled me in for a tight hug. "My

goodness, Jessica, it's wonderful to see you again." The hug was familiar and calmed my nerves slightly.

"Mrs. Morton, it's nice to see you too. Thank you for this opportunity." My hands were shaking, but I was proud to say my voice never wavered.

"Nonsense, dear. I needed the best wedding planner, and that's you. It's not every day an event planner from the Big Apple is right here to call upon. Besides, it's a shame about what happened to you. You were a scapegoat." Sandra laced her arm through mine, gave it a pat, and led me into the house. I had forgotten how much like my mom Sandra was. When one of her own was in trouble, there was no force that could compete with her.

The family photos on the wall had changed since I'd seen them last, but the feel of the house was the same. Sandra led me through the house and past the beautiful stone fireplace. It had always been my favorite part of the house. Whether lit or not, it made the home warm and inviting. I followed Sandra into a cozy office with overstuffed furniture and a large family portrait taken when Rob was likely in his early thirties

Looking at the picture, I wondered how much he had changed in the last seven years. Was he still as fit? Did he have salt and pepper dotted through his jet-black hair? Did he still wear it a little longer? The slight wave in his hair was irresistible, and I never could keep my hands out of it. Would I recognize him if I ran into him today? What if I ran into him today? I tried to smooth out the wrinkles of my travel-worn shirt. I hoped I didn't see him while I looked like this.

"Please have a seat." Sandra walked behind her desk and motioned for me to sit in the chair in front of her. "Thank you for coming on such short notice. This wedding needs to be discreet." She lowered her voice, and I had to lean over the desk to hear her. "Tyler and Kate Patterson are getting married. It's a business deal gone wrong set up by my husband."

My stomach lurched, and my blood ran cold. Brian obviously hadn't changed his ways over the years. Sandra crossed her arms over her chest and had such a sour look on her face she could have easily just bitten into a lemon.

"I could just throttle that man. I don't know what on earth he was thinking. Kate is far too good for Tyler. I love my son, but his choices in women leave a lot to be desired." She leaned forward, resting her elbows on the desk. Her gaze flicked toward the door before she continued. "I knew you would understand how discreet this needs to be."

"Sandra, it doesn't matter to me how a couple gets to the altar as long as the day goes off without a hitch. I assure you, gossiping about the couple isn't how I work."

Sandra nodded and continued, "We want to keep this within the family if we can, and you were the only person I felt I could trust, since you were almost family once."

When I felt my face flush, I knew I needed to change the subject. My onetime position in this family wasn't something I wanted to talk about. "Did you or Kate have a vision in mind for the wedding?"

"It needs to be a small, intimate setting. Fifty guests max. The wedding will take place here, so I'll show you around soon. We'll hold the reception in the event barn, and if we could transform it into a romantic setting, that would be fantastic. After talking with Kate, I think a late afternoon wedding would be perfect."

I was frantically jotting down notes in my planner and mentally wrapping my head around the fact that I no longer had a team to help me get all this accomplished. "And when are you planning to hold the wedding?"

"This weekend." Her face didn't change. This had to be a joke, but her demeanor was the same, no smirk, no grin, and no backpedaling on the timeline.

If I said yes, I would have to plan, organize, and pull off a wedding in six days. No team, no vendors, just me. How was this going to work? Could I actually pull it off? It wouldn't get done sitting here. I needed to make a plan. Now.

"This all sounds lovely, Mrs. Morton. For this to work, I'll have to be in and out of the area almost daily. I hope that won't be any trouble." I folded my hands on my notebook as I sat back in my chair. "We should also discuss my fee."

I had no idea what an event like this in Texas run, so I did a few mental calculations. I considered the fact that I would be working basically alone and that the event was being held on the ranch. So, I would have to rent very little, and the wedding would be small. The price I quoted seemed to be okay because Sandra grabbed her pen, pulled her check book out of the drawer, and flipped it open. "Shall we say half now and half at the end of the wedding day?"

"That works for me."

"Now, let's take a walk. Leave your things here. No need to drag them all over the ranch." I grabbed my notebook and pen out of my bag and followed her out the door. She was as organized and as straight forward as ever.

We walked behind the house where the trees had grown up and arched together. It was the perfect backdrop for the ceremony. I could see it in my mind, but it wasn't Tyler and Kate standing in front of the crowd. It was Rob and me. "Sandra, where to next?" I had to get away from here.

"Let's go toward the event barn, and you can share your plan for decorating."

I looked for Rob around every corner. I wasn't sure if I was looking for him, or if I was trying to avoid him completely. Part of me thought I should just leave the past in the past and move on. But we'd had chemistry, and I needed to know if it was still there.

"Do you think there's enough time for you to organize all this?" Sandra stopped and turned to look at me, her eyes hopeful and pleading for me to say yes.

"Honestly, Sandra, no, there isn't. But I've never backed down from a challenge, so I'll do what I can."

She flung her arms around me and pulled me in for another hug. "You're a lifesaver. Thank you. By the way, he's single again."

I stopped on a dime, my entire body freezing in place. Had I heard her correctly? Brow furrowed, I looked up at Sandra and opened my mouth to ask a question, but no words came out. "I called you because I need the best event planner and so you two could see each other again." She shrugged and smiled. "Just call me Cupid."

"Sandra, I… um… I don't know what to say." Fumbling over words wasn't something I was used to doing. Panic rose from the pit of my stomach. The last thing I needed right now was to be forced into something that shouldn't happen again.

"Thank me later, dear." She chuckled and rested her hand on my shoulder, squeezing gently before she rounded the corner of the barn to walk back outside. I glanced around one more time, jotting down notes as I walked.

I wasn't paying attention to where I was going., and suddenly, I walked into a solid mass. I looked up, and there before me stood Brian Morton. The man who had crushed my life's dreams.

"Well, Jessica, what a surprise to see you here," Brian drawled. His arched brow was accusatory, and I felt the increasing urge to say to hell with this and run away.

"Mr. Morton." I nodded curtly. I lost sight of Sandra and looked around in quiet panic.

"Jessica, I don't need to remind you of the deal we struck, do I?" His size had never intimidated me, but his words were a different story. He knew what to say to make people question their position in life.

"No, sir, you don't. There is nothing further from my mind." I looked down at my notebook, avoiding his stare. Even at thirty-four years old, I was still terrified of this man.

"Good." As abruptly as he appeared, he was gone.

I peeked around the corner of the barn, looking for Sandra, and I headed her way when I spotted her.

"Let's head back to the office, and we can discuss the ideas you've thought of," Sandra said. When we finished discussing plans for the wedding, she walked me to the door. As it shut behind me, it felt like prison bars were clanking shut. Once again, I was on the outside looking in. Only this time, I had to return day after day instead of being banished.

Putting one foot in front of the other, I headed for my car. Out of the corner of my eye, I glimpsed the first man to break my heart, the one I thought I was going to spend my life with. He looked the same, like he hadn't aged a day. His smile spread across his face, making my heart race. Rob waved and walked toward me. No, I couldn't do this now. It was too soon, too abrupt, and I wasn't prepared. My day had been long enough. I couldn't face him now. He looked good, whereas I was tired, sweaty, and in wrinkled clothes from traveling all day, and that equaled trouble in my mind. I hurried the last few feet to my car and slammed the door. Tossing my things on the passenger seat, I backed away before he was close enough to stop me. The look on his face made me ache inside. The locked jaw, the frown, the wrinkled forehead from confusion. It was the same as the day I walked away eight years ago.

My hands shook on the steering wheel as I tightened them, my knuckles turning white while I drove the few miles to my mom's house. The last time I'd seen him played on a repeating loop in my head, and I barely paid attention to where I was going.

When I finally pulled into mom's driveway, she was sitting on the front porch swing, and I couldn't help but smile. That was her "waiting spot." Every time I came home from New York, she would be there waiting.

It was where she waited when I missed curfew, and it was where she waited when she told me my father had been killed in a trucking accident. We sat on that swing for hours that day. She wrapped me up in a hug and didn't let go until all our tears had been cried. I was eight. Dad had been the center of our world. He was on the road a lot, but never for more than one night at a time. He never missed a concert or a play. When he died, part of me died too. It was part of the reason I never let boys get too close.

Until Rob. I saw my father in him. He was a strong protector, a loyal friend, a man whose family was a priority. It was easy to think of settling down with Rob because of that.

I grabbed my purse from the passenger seat and walked to the porch.

"I wondered if you were ever getting out of that car." Momma chuckled as I walked up the sidewalk.

"Hey, Momma, just thinking about some memories." I climbed the three steps of the white covered porch and sat beside her on the swing.

"You were thinkin' of your daddy, weren't you? I see it in your eyes."

I smiled. She always knew when I was thinking about him. I nodded and rested my head on her shoulder like I did when I was little.

"I wonder how life would have turned out if he was still here." My voice trailed off, my heart aching as I thought about what he'd make of the crap that had happened in New York.

"Oh, honey, you can't think like that. I used to make myself crazy with the what-ifs. Our life is what it is. Sure, we've had a few downs, but we are fortunate to have had many more ups." Mamma turned and kissed the top of my head.

"Now, tell me, how are you?" She didn't beat around the bush. I was prepared for her frankness, but I wasn't ready for her to ask me how I was. Once a tear fell, it allowed the floodgates to open.

CHAPTER 2

$\mathcal{W}$hen I saw Jessica walking out of the main house, you could have knocked me over with a feather. I thought back to our last conversation all those years ago, which hadn't been pleasant.

She looked the same. Jessica Walshay, the woman I'd thought would stand beside me, the would-be mother of my children, and the love of my life. But it wasn't meant to be. After her exchange with my mother, she walked to her car.

Now was my chance to talk to her, to clear the air, so I headed toward her. "Jessica." Waving, I called her name. She looked up, and our eyes met, but she looked like a deer in the headlights, terrified and frozen in place. She didn't wave or smile. Nothing. All she could do was jump in her car and take off. Did she hate me so much she couldn't even say hello?

I watched once again as she left me in the dust, anchored in place until there was no sign of her car, just like all those years ago. I had hoped that when we did eventually see each other again, we could be cordial, but obviously I was wrong.

When I finally snapped out of it, my hands were clenched as hard as my jaw, and I forced myself to relax. I needed to figure out what was going on, and Mom always knew everything.

"Mom, was that Jessica?" I asked as I walked into her office.

"Yes, dear." She sat beaming. "I've asked her to plan Tyler's wedding. She will be in and out of the ranch for most of the week. Please tell the men to help her if she needs anything." Mom picked up a pen and started working on something. I just stood there, my body unwilling to move. She was going to be around. Back here on this ranch like she had been when we were younger. Suddenly, I felt like the shy younger version of myself trying to figure out if I should run away or deal with this.

"Robbie, is there something you need, or are you just going to stand there staring at me all day?"

"No, sorry." I walked to the door and placed my hand on the doorframe. "Mom, why Jess?"

"Because she's the best, son, and it doesn't hurt that you're both single again." I dropped my head and walked out the door. Of course, she would try to set us up. My mother had never wanted us to break up, and now she'd figured out how to get us back together.

I took some time to regroup while I walked back to my house. I was thankful Addison was at school today, so I could process things before she came home. My home was one more thing that reminded me of Jessica every day. We had picked this floor plan and had chosen this spot to build. Grabbing my phone, I sent a text to all the ranch hands.

ME: JESSICA WALSHAY WILL BE BACK TOMORROW TO SET UP for the wedding. Give her any help she needs.

. . .

I PLOPPED DOWN ON THE COUCH AS THE ACKNOWLEDGMENT texts rolled in as. One last text notification sounded on my phone. Grabbing it, I opened the message.

GABLES: THE JESSICA WALSHAY? HOW ARE YOU GOING TO help her out, boss?

NATE GABLES WAS OUR RANCH FOREMAN AND HAD COME WITH us when we moved from Montana. He'd wanted to leave the cold and snow, so he packed up and tagged along. That meant he was the only one besides the family who knew about Jessica around here. I chuckled and shook my head.

ME: GET BACK TO WORK.

I STOOD AT THE COUNTER GETTING A POT OF COFFEE STARTED. It was not in Nate's nature to leave things alone. He was a hard worker and the one I wanted with me while I was fencing or moving cattle. He managed the ranch hands so I could be hands-on in the daily operation of this place. Tyler sat behind the desk, and I did the hard day-to-day grind, so it did not surprise me when Nate knocked on the door.

He walked in and didn't even bother with small talk.

"So, Jessica? How did that happen?" He sat down at the other end of the table, and I slid a cup of coffee toward him.

Nate was ten years older than me. He happened upon me the night I ran away in a blizzard when I was a little boy, and when I couldn't talk to Tyler or Gavin, Nate was always there. We worked well together and were more like brothers than friends.

"From what I've heard, her life fell apart in New York, and

she had no choice but to come home. So, my mother, being my mother, hired her to plan Tyler's wedding."

"Well, I bet planning the wedding isn't the only reason your mother wants her around." Gables took a sip of his coffee and leaned back in his chair. "Like how bad were things in New York?"

"Business destroyed and divorced."

"Oh, like bad, bad. Well then, if that's the case, your mom is the one to help her business recover. And the heartbreak, I'm guessing, will be your department." The tough cowboy chuckled.

"Don't you have work to do?" I shot back at him.

"Nope," he replied as he took another sip of coffee.

"There's a whole lot to unpack there. I pushed her away. Might as well have driven her to New York myself." I grabbed my cup but didn't drink any coffee.

"I was working so hard to make my family happy and make extra money, and in the process, I made her feel like she was the last person on my mind. She must hate me. That's why she wouldn't talk to me. Should I even hope for something or just avoid the situation like the plague?" My heart raced as I for his reply. If he was smart, he would tell me to walk the other way.

"Don't know what to tell you, kid. She was always a nice girl. Her momma is respected around here. There are worse fires to rekindle. But don't forget, your heart isn't the only one on the line anymore. Anyone you bring 'round here will be involved with Addie. I don't envy your situation at all."

Staring past Gables, I looked out the window. I never thought I would see her again. Living my life as a single dad never seemed to be that bad, but suddenly, I was lonely for a companion, someone to share life with, to share struggles with when parenting was hard. When had that started? Hearing Jessica had come home opened up old feelings I had long ago put to bed. "I never thought seeing her would make me feel like this."

Gables didn't respond, just sat there, drinking his coffee.

"Well, I better run if I'm going to get anything done before I lose my guys to wedding prep. All I have to say is it could've been you roped into this marriage instead of Tyler, so be thankful." He walked to the door.

"Kate's a brilliant girl, and I think she will be good for Tyler. He needs a powerful woman to put up with him." We both laughed.

Gables left, and I was left alone waiting for Addie to come home from school. That meant I had a few hours to stew on how to approach Jessica without scaring her off. Flopping back down on the couch, all I could think of was how gorgeous she looked in those black pants and purple shirt.

CHAPTER 3

The week flew by, and I had been on and off the
Morton ranch probably fifty times, or at least it felt
like that many. It disappointed me every time I didn't see Rob.
He probably steered clear of me on purpose, and I wouldn't
blame him at all, but I couldn't deny I was disappointed each
time. I had run away and hadn't even said goodbye. No
wonder he was avoiding me.

I needed to prepare myself because seeing him that first
day had reminded me of all the horrible things, we'd said the
night before I left… And the horrible thing he didn't know
about. My ultimate betrayal when we'd broken up.

Parked in front of the barn, I sat in my car, mentally
preparing for the day and listening to the song playing. I
closed my eyes as George Strait sang "You Look So Good In
Love." Tomorrow, my time here would be over, and I was
thankful for that. I could rebuild my business and move on
from Rob.

Obviously, he wanted nothing to do with me, and as much
as I wanted to try again, it would be easier now that I wouldn't
have to watch for him around every corner. I took a deep
breath and readied myself to get out of the car. The passenger

door swung open, and someone sat down in the seat. When my eyelids fluttered open, I stared into Rob's eyes, five inches from my face.

I stopped breathing. My heart was pounding so hard I suddenly felt like it was going to burst out of my chest. So many thoughts ran through my head, but I couldn't think fast enough to make sense of them. I had wanted to see him, and now he was here, but I didn't have a clue what to say.

He smelled the same, like a walk in the woods. Cedar surrounded by lavender and the sweet scent of honeysuckle. It felt like coming home. I used to long for my clothes to smell like him at the end of the night. Smiling, I thought back to the pullover jacket I'd stolen from his room just because it smelled like him. It was the one thing of his I took to New York with me, and until I met Jeremy, I'd curled up with it every night.

"Is there a reason you run away every time I get close enough to say hi?" His smile was the same crooked one he always reserved for me. Others only got a quick smirk, but his face lit up for me. His eyes were a dark chocolate brown that danced when he looked at me.

My heart raced, and I thought of how easily I could get lost in those pools of melted chocolate. The last eight years had been good to him. "Don't be nervous. It's just me."

"I'm not nervous." I hoped I was convincing because I was sweating like a liar in church. If he kept looking at me like that, he would need to call an ambulance or start CPR. I licked my lips and tried to slow my breathing.

"You always bite your lip when you're nervous. I'm glad to see that hasn't changed. How have you been, Jess?"

"I'm good. How are you?" I fidgeted with my keys.

"Getting by. Are you going to answer my question?" He hadn't changed. Still relentless as ever.

"Well, the first day I was here, I was tired from my drive, and I didn't want you to see me like that. And since then, I haven't exactly been hiding, so who's fault is that?"

His warmhearted, full of joy laugh reverberated through my car, and my heart skipped a few beats. That laugh had haunted my dreams when I was lonely those first months in Manhattan. Then, when life crumbled with Jeremy, I started hearing it again. Now, sitting here beside him, I knew I was a goner.

"Fine, I will admit when you drove away without so much as a wave, I was hurt. I wanted to welcome you home. Talk to you and see how you were. I figured you were still angry with me, so I stayed away." Rob looked down. He brushed an imaginary piece of lint off his jeans before looking at me again, his eyes reflecting the same vulnerability I was feeling.

"I'm not mad, Rob. To be honest, I never was." I could feel tears filling my eyes. Being open with him had always been easy until our fight about me leaving.

He cleared his throat and changed the subject. It wasn't one either of us wanted to dive into at this moment.

"You've been busy. I'm not sure I've ever seen this place look so good."

"Ha, your mother has hosted so many events and has had famous planners and decorators over the years. I don't think this would even make the top fifty." I shook my head and stared out the driver's side window.

"Hey, look at me."

I slowly turned toward him.

"Talk to me."

I didn't know what to say.

"Jess, it's just me. Come on, we've never had a problem talking."

"No, that was something we were usually good at. Have you had a busy week?"

"Yeah, it has been busy. There's been so much to help Tyler with. How about you? Are you ready for this week to be over?" His face didn't match his calm demeanor. His eyes were searching, hoping I would give him the answer he wanted.

"I will be happy to breathe again, but I'll miss being here every day. I can't ever thank your mom enough for trusting me with this wedding."

"Why will you miss being here every day?" Rob's voice was low, and he almost whispered it.

"Because I won't have any more opportunities to run into you." Looking into his eyes, I knew those were the words he hoped I would say. How could I just have word vomited all of that?

Jessica, you're coming across as desperate. My internal critic was harsh but right. It appeared as if I was pining for him. Was I? Maybe I was. Did I want him to know that? No way.

"It was disappointing not seeing you." There was no way I could take the words back now. The thing was, I meant the words I had just said. He was the reason I took this job.

The tension was thick, and I needed to get out of my car before Rob and I went to a place neither of us needed to be right now. Flinging my door open, I climbed out and took a deep breath of cool country air. Rob had gotten out too and came to stand in front of me.

"Look, I know you're going to be busy today, but I would like to take you out next week. Supper in town? I'll pick you up Monday at six thirty." He placed a finger under my chin and lifted it so I was looking right at him. "Okay?"

All I could do was nod.

"I better go make sure Tyler isn't trying to run away."

"And I should make sure everything is ready." I needed today to go smoothly. Wedding days rarely went off without issues, but problems today were not an option. We both turned to go in opposite directions. "Hey, will you explain to me what this shotgun wedding is all about sometime? I've known Kate all my life, and this doesn't seem like her at all."

"Oh, it's a story." Rob arched his brow and chuckled. "I will fill you in on our date."

I turned and walked away first but was stopped by a whistle from behind me.

"You still look fantastic walking away, Jess."

I added a little extra sway.

"Damn."

If he could have seen my face, he'd have seen I was grinning from ear to ear. This would not be as easy as it seemed, I was sure, but it was nice to imagine we could just pick up where we left off.

CHAPTER 4

J wandered around the ranch, making sure everything was ready, obsessively re-checking the weather app, but all was clear. The day should go off without a hitch. Sandra came running out of the house as I was straightening chairs and turning on the battery-operated candles in the lanterns.

"Oh, Jessica, I'm so glad I ran into you. I can't believe how you've transformed this yard." She clasped her hands in front of her and slowly turned, looking at all the final touches. "When I called you, I never thought it could look like this. I followed your career in New York, but I never thought you could replicate that elegance here on the ranch."

Quickly, she gathered me up in a hug. Her hug was welcome, and for a brief moment, I felt like I belonged again. She let me go and looked around again. "My dear, you better get your business ready because, after this, I think you will have no shortage of work."

I looked at her, a little confused.

She smiled and squeezed my hands. "Jessica, I have connections, and everyone will hear about this wedding. I better go finish getting ready." As quickly as she had appeared, she was gone.

Standing in the middle of this beautiful ceremony space, I smiled. I couldn't believe I had pulled it off. The lanterns hung in the trees. The white folding chairs were lined up in short, neat rows. A sheer runner covered the grass and ran the length of the aisle. The trees that formed a natural arch at the end of the aisle were perfect. It felt good to see Kate's vision coming to fruition, to see a job well done and everyone happy with the big day. It didn't matter that it was in Texas and not New York. I wished I'd learned that lesson years ago, before I'd given up Rob, before I'd lost everything in Manhattan.

Suddenly, there was a tapping sound behind me. After one last glance over the seating area, I turned and looked at the house. A million scenarios were running through my head, and none of them good. A tapping foot was never a good situation form my experience. I had also been home for over a week and hadn't talked to any old acquaintances. When I turned, Rob was standing behind the glass French door. A grin spread across his face, and he started pretending to take his shirt off, mimicking a seductive striptease. He was giving me quite a show; I didn't mind, of course. It was a total Rob thing to do, but it still surprised me, and I shook my head in disbelief. Waving at him, I smiled and winked. I could hear him laughing through the open window.

I FOLLOWED TYLER OUT OF THE HOUSE AND ACROSS THE YARD to stand at his side in front of the crowd of people waiting for the ceremony to start. Addison looked like she was floating on air toward us with the biggest smile I had ever seen. You would never know these people weren't here for her.

I glimpsed Jessica flitting around the back of the yard, making sure everything was going smoothly. She made sure everyone was where they were supposed to be, and all was ready for Kate to walk down the aisle. I lost sight of her during the ceremony, and I was disappointed.

Since she was here in a professional capacity, she kept her distance, but that didn't mean I was going to avoid looking at her. Jessica moved easily around, giving orders, helping, and making sure things were perfect. As the evening drew to a close, I wanted to find her for a dance.

I spotted her across the barn. She was standing close to the wall, staying out of the way, trying to go unnoticed. She may have been invisible to most people in this room, but to me, she was the only one here. The black dress she wore wasn't flashy or fancy, but it hugged her delicate breasts and delicious hips. I needed to have her in my arms.

"Dance with me," I whispered in her ear when I walked up behind her. She turned and was only inches from my face, but I resisted the urge to kiss her. When I did kiss her again after all these years, and I would kiss her, I wanted it to be private, not witnessed by everyone we knew.

"I shouldn't be doing this, Rob," she whispered, and I saw concern in her eyes.

"Don't worry, the evening is almost over. Most of the guests have cleared out, and Tyler and Kate are leaving after this song. It's fine, stop worrying." We danced in silence. I looked into her blue eyes, they shimmered like the ocean on a summer's day where the sun's rays kissed the surface. Her lips widened, and she had that same sparkling smile I remembered. I sucked in a breath as my heart stopped for a second, and I pulled her even closer, feeling her body tremble in my arms. She was as nervous as I was. Pulling her closer to me, we slowly danced to "I Cross My Heart." Suddenly, I felt small arms wrap around my leg.

"Daddy, I'm tired." Of all the times for Addison to find someone else, this would have been the moment, but here she was. I looked up and sighed before I closed my eyes and looked down at my daughter.

"Hey, Squish." I took a step back from Jessica and picked up Addison. "I want you to meet an old friend of mine. This is Miss Jessica. She and I were best friends a long time ago." A little smile crossed Addison's face.

"You're the lady who planned all this? I think it's beautiful. When I get married, can you plan my wedding?" Her face was innocent, and I could tell she wanted Jessica to say yes.

Jessica's face never could hide emotion. Her eyes became sad, and her smile was pasted on. Maybe I should have told her in the car that Addison was my daughter.

Her eyes searched mine for a second, and then she looked to Addison.

"Miss Addison, I would be happy to. In fact, we will make it even better. I want you to have this little book." Jessica pulled a small notebook out of her back pocket and a pen out of the bun in her hair and handed them to Addison. "You take notes when you see something you like and want for your wedding. Then, when it's time, you bring it to me, and I will do it all." Addison threw her arms around Jessica's neck.

"Thank you," Addison squealed. Suddenly, her exhaustion was forgotten, and she ran off to start her notes.

I helped Jessica stand and took her back into my arms. "You're still amazing with kids."

She smiled up at me.

"They're so sweet." Her voice trailed off, and she suddenly felt different in my arms.

The song ended, drawing applause from the remaining the crowd. Tyler and Kate took their leave, and their guests started making their way to the exit too.

"Well, I should go find Addison." I didn't let her go, she still felt like she belonged beside me, in my arms.

"You're going to have to let go of me then." Her smile took me back to our youth.

"But what if I don't want to?" I felt her breathing speed up, and she started biting the corner of her lip. "I'm not going to let you go again."

Not running after her all those years ago haunted me almost daily. Life without her hadn't been a bed of roses, and although I wouldn't change some parts, I didn't realize until now how much I'd missed her.

"I won't argue." Her whisper shook me to my core.

I opened my mouth to say something when I was interrupted. "Rob, there you are. Oh, and you have Jessica. Good, I was going to send you to find her." Mom was beaming looking back and forth between us. "So, you two?"

"Mother, stop." I couldn't believe her, and I was firm as I spoke. She shrugged and smiled at me.

"Sandra, I hope you're happy with how things went today." Jessica stepped out of my arms and moved toward my mom.

"Gracious, dear, happy is an understatement. I don't know how you did it, and I expect you will need to sleep for a week, but I am ecstatic about today." She beamed at Jessica as they spoke, and I couldn't have been prouder. It was hard to explain. We'd been apart so long, but it felt like she had been here all the time.

Mom handed an envelope to Jessica and patted her arm. "It's more than we discussed. You have outdone any expectations I had for today. Now, you two, why don't you run along and have a nice evening?"

"Mother," I growled.

"As much as that sounds like a great way to end the day, I have a few things to get cleaned up so I can return them first thing Monday. Sandra, thank you again for this opportunity." I watched as my mother embraced Jessica before wandering off to find my father. "Can I help you clean up after I get Addison down? Or I can have mom take her home and get her to bed." I took her hand in mine.

~

I caught a glimpse of Brian out of the corner of my eye and slowly slid my hand out of Rob's grip. "No, you need to get Addie home. My Mom came back to help, so I will be fine." Looking over Rob's shoulder, I saw that his father had walked away. I let out the breath I had inadvertently been holding.

"You're exhausted. Are you sure you can't wait until tomorrow to clean up?" He took the sigh to mean I was tired, and that's what I needed. I also needed to leave here tonight without another Brian sighting.

"Night." I pushed him gently on the chest, a smile on my face.

"Good night, Jess." He squeezed my hand before turning to walk away. I let out a cat call whistle, and he laughed, sending a thrill up my spine.

"So, will this be our discussion for the drive home?" My mother walked up behind me and put her arm around my shoulders.

"I would expect so." I rested my head on her shoulder just as she turned her head and kissed the top of mine.

"Well, let's get this stuff into your car so we can get started on our talk."

I nodded, and we both turned and packed up. When we settled in the car, I took a deep breath. It felt like the first time I had sat down all day.

"Well, my little one, what's the story?"

I shifted the car into drive and headed away from the Morton Ranch.

"I haven't seen him all week. Well, no, that's not true. He tried to talk to me the day I came here to consult with Sandra, but I ran away like a coward." I made the left turn onto the highway and continued.

"Running into Brian that afternoon didn't help, either. He

reminded me of our deal. Oh mom, I don't know what I should do. Rob still has no idea that his father paid me to break it off with him, and I'm so ashamed." The dark night mimicked my future. My headlights illuminated the immediate road only. I wanted to see days, months, even years ahead of me, but all I could see was black.

"Baby, I told you then and I will say it now. You should never have taken that money. You should have gone to Rob. I know he would have made it right. There would have been other ways for you to get to New York. And you still would have had Rob. Maybe you wouldn't have gone at all if you had told him."

Her words stung. They always did when the subject came up.

"Why didn't you tell me he had a daughter?" We pulled into the driveway, and I turned off the car before shifting in my seat so I could look directly at her.

"Girlie, what good would it have done if I had told you? It wouldn't have changed the situation, and it would only have hurt you." Her eyes were soft and full of concern.

"Maybe I wouldn't have been taken by surprise tonight if I had known. I guess I just thought his life would have stopped when I left. How crazy is that? I moved on. Why didn't I think he would too?"

CHAPTER 5

I was a bundle of nervous energy on Monday. There was so much to clean up and return from the Morton wedding I thought it would keep my mind occupied for the day. I was wrong. Every time I tried to focus, I thought of Rob and our date tonight. I sat down at the desk in my father's old office and made a list of things that had worked well and things that hadn't from the wedding.

I was finally lost in thoughts of something other than Rob when my phone rang.

"Hello?"

"Hi, Jessica, this is Sally Dagnal. I heard all about the Morton wedding at church yesterday, and I was wondering if you only do weddings."

"Thank you for calling, Mrs. Dangal. No, I do all kinds of events. Were you wondering about something specific?"

I grabbed my pen and my day planner and waited for her answers.

"My husband is turning seventy, and I think a big bash is required."

"Goodness, ma'am, I never would have dreamed he was almost seventy. I would be happy to organize something."

We talked for about an hour, and I knew this would be easy compared to planning a wedding in less than a week. I hung up the phone and shot out of my chair.

"Mom, I booked another event." I ran into the kitchen where she was organizing her pie delivery for the diner.

"That's great, Jess! Help me take these to the car." She handed me a pie carrier, and I followed her out. "I hope this wedding leads to all kinds of events for you. This town needs someone who can plan things and stay organized."

I handed her the pies, and we went back inside for another load.

"I won't be long. Do you think you can stay occupied until I get back or do you need to come with me?" Her hands were on her hips, and she arched her brow.

I couldn't help but smile. As much as I thought I had changed, I was still that young woman who got nervous before a date. "No, Mom, I'll be fine."

She nodded and got in her car. "See you later, dear."

I waved as she backed out of the driveway.

I had a few hours before my date, but I was tired of pacing around the house. I should have gone with Mom, I kept thinking to myself. Giving the clock one last glance, I decided I might as well take a shower. I hated waiting to go somewhere. Morning coffee dates were more my thing.

Getting ready only took an hour, so when I was done, I grabbed a book and tried to read. Like I hoped I would, I got lost in a romance novel, and time no longer mattered. Before I knew it, the front door banged open, and I jerked my head up to see Mom walking in with groceries.

"Hello, girlie. Well, don't you look lovely." I hopped off the couch and took a bag from her, shut the door, and followed her to the kitchen. "What time is Rob supposed to be here?" She turned to look at me with a smile on her face.

"In fifteen minutes, I think. I remember him being punctual, and I'm sure that hasn't changed." My voice trailed off as I thought back to our past dates.

My head shot up when I heard a knock at the door, and I felt like my heart was going to burst out of my chest.

"Girlie, go answer that or I will." Mom stopped chopping celery and pointed the knife at me.

I took a deep breath and tried to calm my nerves as I stood from my chair and went to the door. Quickly, I turned the knob and swung the door open. He looked as good as he had the other night. A little more casual in his Wranglers, what looked like a new plaid shirt, and polished boots. I couldn't help but look him up and down.

"Jess, you look stunning."

"You're looking pretty good yourself." I moved out of the doorway. "Want to come in for a minute while I grab my things?"

He nodded and walked into the house.

"Rob, it's nice to see you again." My mom walked into the living room with my purse.

"Thanks, Mom." I rolled my eyes as I took it from her.

"I won't keep her out late, Mrs. Walshay." Rob smiled as we headed for the door.

"Oh, Rob, keep her out as late as you want. She doesn't need to be home until tomorrow morning. It's fine with me." Her little laugh mortified me.

I could feel my eyes bulge out of my head as I turned to look at her. Heat rose from my chest and up my neck, and I was sure my face was as red as a sunburned lobster.

"Mother," I growled through gritted teeth.

"I won't be waiting up." She patted me on the shoulder and turned to leave the room.

"I'm so sorry. That was slightly more than embarrassing." I tried to avoid eye contact with him until I could control my flaming red face.

Rob chuckled and looked at me as he gently placed his

hand on my lower back and guided me out the door and to his truck.

The epitome of a gentleman, he opened the truck door and helped me in before running around to his side. "I hope you don't mind, but I made reservations in Hammond. I just thought we could be away from any prying eyes that might take an interest in us." He turned the key in the ignition, and the truck roared to life.

"I don't mind a bit. Actually, I appreciate it." Smiling, I couldn't believe I was here with him again.

It didn't take long to get onto the highway, and the tension in the truck lifted. Rob kept his eyes on the road, but I could see he was stealing glances at me. My arm rested on the console, and Rob stealthily took my hand in his. I was worried my hand was sweaty or shaky, but it didn't seem to bother Rob if it was.

Looking over at him, I couldn't help but smile. He looked like the victor who had just received his spoils. Proud wasn't a deep enough word to describe his look.

The silence was enjoyable. I never felt like I needed to make small talk when we were together.

Rob pulled to a stop in the parking lot of a restaurant. He helped me out of the truck, and we walked to our table hand in hand. It was easy to talk to Rob, and we fell into a nice, paced conversation after ordering our drinks.

The restaurant was quiet. Music played softly in the background, and the lights were dim. It felt intimate, and while the room was full, I felt like we were the only people in the entire place. "Tell me everything about Addison. She seems so sweet." The smile that crossed his face when I asked about her was amazing.

We were interrupted by the waitress when she came to take our order. I had never been so perturbed about ordering food. I wanted to know everything about the last eight years, and I didn't want to lose any more time with this man sitting across from me. When our orders were placed, he continued talking as if he hadn't stopped.

"She is seven going on seventeen. I can't do anything without her being right on my heels. I don't remember what life was like without her." Rob put down his drink. "Jess, she's the light in my life I didn't know I needed. She's horse crazy and loves helping with the cows. I can't wait for you to get to know her. You two will definitely hit it off."

"I can't wait to get to know her. She seems like a great little girl." Quickly trying to do the math in my head, I figured that there hadn't been much time between our breakup and when Addison was conceived. It stung a little, but I had no right to question it. We had broken up, and I had run off to make a new life somewhere else without him.

"Where is Addison's mom?" Nothing like catching up on eight years in one dinner.

"Being a mom and wife wasn't her thing. She took off and decided an unattached barrel racer was more to her liking. Although I think she was more interested in chasing the steer wrestlers than competing in her events." Rob grabbed his water and downed it. I could tell from the vein that popped out of the side of his head he didn't really want to talk about it.

"She would be all lovey, dovey at home but would fool around with anything that wore a cowboy hat while she was following the circuit. When Addison was three, I went to surprise her in Abilene and caught her coming out of some guy's trailer. When she came back after that weekend, she packed her stuff and left for good.

Our food arrived at the table, and we were silent for a few minutes while we settled in with dinner. "What happened in New York?" His question shouldn't have shocked me, but it was the one I was getting every time I turned around.

"I had lined up a few events for one couple. Engagement party, bachelor, bachelorette parties, rehearsal, and wedding.

Little did I know my right-hand woman had met up with the groom in the coatroom during the engagement party." I took a sip of the wine in front of me and took a bite of the chicken parmesan that was finally cool enough to eat. "They carried on their affair until the night before the wedding when the bride snuck into the groom's room and found Haddie in bed with him. When the wedding was called off, the bride's family made sure to let everyone know who the mistress worked for. Her family is well-known and stated publicly that I had no control over my staff and that I ran a hack business. Slowly, clients started backing out, and I was having to issue refunds. Eventually, I couldn't even book birthday parties."

"Oh, Jess, I'm sorry. The entire thing had nothing to do with you, but you took the fall. And what happened to your employee?" He took a bite of steak and waited for my answer.

"Last I heard, she was engaged to that man and dealing with infidelity weekly." I sat back and crossed my hands over my lap, waiting for his response.

"I suppose it's appropriate for her. Losing your business and reputation isn't the way I wanted you to come home, but I'm glad you're here." He took the refilled glass of water in front of him and brought it to his lips and took a sip.

"And what happened with what's his name? Justin, Jordan, Jimmy?"

"Jeremy." I shrugged. There was no way I wanted to get into that story tonight, so I thought keeping it simple would be best.

"We drifted apart after my business folded. I found out he was fooling around, and I decided enough was enough. He filed divorce papers, and here we are."

I absentmindedly placed my hand on the table, and he reached out to place his on top of mine. I looked at our hands and then up to Rob, whose eyes were locked on me. The smile that crossed my face was completely involuntary, and I didn't try to stop it. Rob was good. He'd always known how to flirt.

When supper was over, we walked back to the truck.

"What should we do now?" Rob asked as he started the engine.

"I don't know. All I know is I don't want our evening to be over." I looked down at my hands, afraid to look into his eyes.

"That's good because I wasn't planning on taking you home yet." Reaching out, he gently grabbed my hand out of my lap, and we drove off. The worry eased in my heart.

I hadn't been paying attention to where we were going or how long we had been driving, so I was surprised when Rob finally pulled to a stop overlooking White Stone Lake. He flipped the console up, revealing another seat. I unbuckled my seat belt and scooted over.

"Wow, I haven't been out here for ages." Beyond the windshield, the moon shone off the lake and illuminated the trees that surrounded it. Over the years, they had installed lights around the walking path, but they didn't take away from the beauty of the night.

"Want to take a walk?" Rob asked quietly.

I nodded as I reached over to grab the door handle.

"Don't move." He jumped out of the truck and ran around to open my door to hold his hand out for me to take. It was warm in mine as he helped me out of the vehicle. He kept a hold of my hand as I stepped away from the truck before he closed the door. We were in the shelter of the truck, and he took a few steps toward me.

Instinctively, I backed up until I was pinned between the truck and Rob. Letting go of my hand, he brought his arms up and placed his hands on either side of my shoulders. My breath hitched and my heart rate sped up.

The moon outlined his gorgeous face as those dark eyes stared into my soul. He moved closer, his face inches from mine, and I felt as drawn to him as I always had been. Like a firefly drawn to the light… His hand lifted my chin, and his lips pressed against mine. All my nerves melted away with his tentative kiss filled with love and hurt.

That old spark ignited again, although I don't think it ever went away. Not for me. The kiss lingered, and the passion bubbling under the surface broke through as he deepened our connection. Our tongues danced in rhythm together. His lips were as familiar as they had been eight years ago.

I slid my arms around his waist and held him close.

CHAPTER 6

She felt the same in my arms as she had eight years ago. I slid my hand from her face to the back of her head. Running my hand through her hair, I couldn't help but grab it in my fist. She drew me in like a magnet, and her light floral perfume wafted toward me thanks to the slight breeze. Our lips met, tentatively at first, but the passion increased almost instantly. Her lips were pillowy soft, welcoming and familiar. They tasted like mint from the gloss she wore.

Jessica let out a sigh, and I broke the kiss. "Jess, I'm sorry I…" Searching her eyes, I worried I'd gone too far.

"You better not think of apologizing, Rob Morton. If I didn't want you to kiss me, you wouldn't have." She rested her head on my chest, and I held her tightly to me.

I smiled. Yep, that was my Jessica, she was still feisty woman I fell in love with. "Let's walk down to the water." I didn't want to let her go, but there was a more romantic spot than beside the door of my truck.

Holding her hand in mine was nothing short of heavenly. It was soft, but strong. The years of living in the city had been good for her.

We stopped at a bench by the water's edge and sat down. "I would like to kiss you again."

Jessica's smile was the first thing people noticed about her. It was impossible to miss, and I knew that was my go ahead.

Slowly, I trailed my hand down her neck and traced her collarbone with the tips of my fingers. Somewhere in my memory, I remembered this drove her crazy. Her perfume was inviting and smelled like peonies, oranges, and jasmine. I wanted more of her. Our passion increased as brought her as close to me as I could. She broke our kiss and let her head fall to the side, giving me access to nibble on her neck. Moving my hand to the top of her breast, I waited for a sign of hesitation, but Jessica didn't stop me. It was firm, and fit perfectly in my palm as I kneaded it.

Jessica let out a quiet sigh as she looped her fingers around my belt and pulled herself to straddle me. Her skirt rode up, and I moved my hands to her thighs. "Were you always this forward, Ms. Walshay?"

"No, but I have dreamed about you and this moment for eight years, and I'm not about to let you go now." She sank down onto my lap and made me moan before she attacked my mouth.

We were lost in each other. I had moved my hand underneath her blouse and worked my way under her bra. I was the one making her moan now as I pinched her taut nipple.

Suddenly, we heard the chatter of a group of kids coming down the walking path. Jessica quickly hopped off my lap, stood, and sorted out her clothes. "We should go," she whispered, looking around.

As much as I didn't want to agree with her, an indecent exposure charge wasn't what either of us needed. She weaved her fingers through mine, and we headed for the truck, passing the group of ten teenagers with just a nod. Jessica moved closer to me, and I heard her let out a giggle.

"We are thirty-six and thirty-four. Why do I feel like I was just caught by my mother making out with you?" Her voice was full of joy, and I could see her eyes dance as she looked at me.

"Do you remember when she caught us??" I asked when we got back to the truck.

She nodded and bit her bottom lip. "That's when you asked me to move in with you. Forgetting that you lived in your parents' house. It was that night we sat where you built your house, dreaming of a home together. I couldn't help but notice the house when I went back to the ranch last week. It looks as beautiful as I hoped it would." Her voice became soft, and her eyes gazed off into the distance.

"When I built the house, I was single, and hoped maybe if I built our dream, you would hear about it and come back." My voice trailed off as I looked into her eyes. "It was always so peaceful sitting there with you, but even when you didn't come back, I could still feel you beside me." I felt vulnerable in that moment, but also brave.

"Come on, it's getting chilly. Hop in the truck." I opened my door and gestured for her to climb in. Part of me worried that bringing up the past would drive her away again, but she slid past the steering wheel and stopped in the middle seat. That movement reassured me, but I couldn't stop there. I took a deep breath. "Can I say something that may ruin this moment?"

"You mean like I just did?" She looked at me with pleading eyes.

"You can't ruin anything. I should have asked you to marry me that night. I had a ring in my pocket. There was no doubt in my mind we belonged together." I ran a finger over the knuckles of her hand that rested on my leg.

I had shopped for weeks, trying to find the perfect ring. Jessica wasn't flashy and had never called attention to herself, so a big diamond wouldn't be what she wanted.

In what felt like the last jewelry store in Texas, I saw it. A gorgeous solitaire diamond with a band of channel-set smaller diamonds on a thin band. It was understated and beautiful, like the woman I loved. I had kept it safely tucked away in my safe-deposit box because I couldn't bear to part with it. It was the only thing from what was supposed to be our life I had left to hang on to.

A sadness engulfed the truck, and I wished I'd kept my mouth shut.

"I wish you had," she replied, her voice barely above a whisper. Jessica rested her head on my shoulder.

"You wouldn't have been able to chase your dreams then."

"Chasing my dreams didn't get me anywhere. I'm back home, alone, divorced, basically broke, and living with my mom again." Her voice caught in her throat.

"You will never be alone, because I'm still here, and it won't be as easy to get rid of me this time." I leaned over and kissed the top of her head.

We sat in the truck silently for a few minutes.

"It's still early. Would you like to go somewhere else?"

I could feel Jessica's face turn up in a smile. "Let's go to the diner. I need a banana split."

HE WALKED ME TO THE DOOR, AND WE STOOD ON THE PORCH. Mom had left the light on, and I stood there, as nervous as I had when we had gone on our first date.

"I should let you get inside. I have a busy day tomorrow, and we are down a man with Tyler gone." He took a step closer to me and grabbed hold of my hands. His smile was familiar, but it still sent goosebumps through my body to see it, especially when it was directed at me.

Rob gently pulled me toward him, and our lips met. I felt like I had gone back in time ten years standing here kissing him. The light above us started flickering, and I dropped my head onto his shoulder and groaned. "I'm so embarrassed." My voice was muffled by his shirt.

Strong arms wrapped around me, and his chest vibrated with a chuckle. From the other side of the door, I heard a laugh, which made it even worse. Not only was my mother monitoring my dates, but she was eavesdropping on us as well.

"I need to move." Lifting my head, I looked into Rob's eyes and searched them for disgust or the urge to flee, but they just sparkled in the light.

"I need to take you away. It won't be easy to get you alone while you live. There are things I want to do to you that I can't do here or at my place." He ran his hand up my arm, gently over my neck, and into my hair. "I've had a great evening."

"Me too." I smiled, but inside, I was jumping for joy. I felt like I would explode from excitement. "Honestly, Rob, tonight was better than great. I never dreamed we'd get to have another date, much less feel so comfortable spending time with you again."

His smile grew, and he leaned in to kiss me again. It was sweet and swift. "I need to go. I will text you when I get home, and we can plan our next date. Better yet, our weekend getaway." He wiggled his eyebrows and made me laugh.

I nodded. We kissed again, and he walked down the steps to leave. "Rob."

He turned to look at me.

"Thank you for tonight, drive safe."

He sprinted back up the steps, placed his hands on the sides of my head, and our lips met. This kiss was hungry and passionate, and I didn't want him to leave.

"Night," he whispered as he rested his forehead on mine.

"Good night."

I watched him walk to his truck and waved as he backed out of the driveway until I couldn't see his lights , just like I used to do. I leaned up against one of the porch posts and wrapped my arms around myself and smiled. Tonight was wonderful; I felt alive. It had been far too long since I felt happy. I stared into the darkness for a moment, then turned and prepared myself for the onslaught of questions I would get as I walked through the door.

"How was your date?" Mom was sitting on the couch, reading a book in her pajamas. "Sorry about the light, I thought it would be cute." She shrugged and looked back down at her book with a sly smile on her face.

I rolled my eyes and shook my head. "It was good, Mom." I headed to the hallway and looked back. "Really good."

"Have you thought about how you're going to deal with Brian? I would think the terms of his payoff are still in effect." I turned to face her.

"Wow, you can't just let me have a night of being happy, can you?" It hurt that she brought it up, but she wasn't wrong, and it hadn't been far from my mind.

"I'm sorry, sweetheart, but eventually there's going to be a thud, and you need to be prepared for it. Brian Morton isn't a man easily crossed."

"I know, Mom. It's been on my mind since the second Sandra called. I will think about it tomorrow."

"Okay, Scarlett O'Hara, but don't say I didn't warn you."

Giving her a half smile, I headed to my room.

My phone buzzed, and I looked at the clock on my dresser, knowing it was too soon for Rob to be home. Opening the phone, I had to smile when I saw it was Delaney texting to check up on my date.

I hadn't been close to Delaney, Kate's sister, in school, but during all the wedding preparation and setup, she helped me see Kate's vision for the wedding and we had hit it off.

DELANEY: WELL? I'M DYING TO KNOW!

Me: It was great.

Delaney: Like how great?

Me: Like make out in the truck great. Kissing on the front porch great.

Delaney: I told you it was going to be awesome.

Me: He wants to go away for the weekend.

Delaney: You better be packing your suitcase.

Me: You don't think it's too soon?

Delaney: If you had met him yesterday, yes, but you have known him forever.

Me: That's true.

Delaney: Lunch tomorrow? I need all the details.

Me: Yeah, sounds good. 12 at the diner?

Delaney: See you then.

I FLOPPED BACK ON MY BED, DROPPED MY PHONE BESIDE ME, and stared at the ceiling. He was the same, but harder. It was like his patience and understanding went only into his daughter. For everyone else, Rob was a brittle shell of the kind man he once was. His stare could stop a man in his tracks and gave my mom's evil eye a run for its money. He didn't seem to go with the flow anymore. Instead, he controlled every aspect of his environment, which might be why he made such a good boss on the ranch. The softness of his youth was gone, which made me wonder what he had been through in the last eight years.

The new Rob intrigued me.

We had both grown up over the years we been apart. He was still handsome—and a good kisser. Time had been good to him, and his body had filled out on his large frame. Bigger muscles, stronger arms, and his hands were rough from years and years of hard work.

I thought back to one of our last dates. Life was good then, great even, as I looked back on it. Rob was always a gentleman, always making sure I was comfortable and in control of the situation, no matter what we did.

Tonight, Rob was in control. He directed the way the date went; it was like he finally knew what he wanted. Finally over letting people tell him what to do, which was what I had always hoped for him. A life of his own, away from the dictatorship of his father, and away from always trying to gain the approval he so desperately sought.

My phone buzzed again, and I grabbed it as fast as I could.

ROB: I'M HOME AND I WISH YOU WERE WITH ME.

Me: Glad you got home. I would have liked to be with you.

Rob: So, are you free this weekend?

Me: You don't waste time, do you?

Rob: Too much wasted time already.

Me: Well then, I'm free.

Rob: Addison and my parents are going to Dallas, and I want to take you to the cabin.

Me: What time are you picking me up?

There was no use beating around the bush and playing coy. I wanted to find out if Rob and I were compatible now, and a weekend away would be a great way to discover each other again.

My phone rang, bringing a smile to my face. "Hello."

"Hi, I wanted to hear your voice. And I hate texting."

"Well, what would you like to talk about?"

"This weekend. I want you to know what I'm hoping for. Jessica, I want you. All of you. I've always had dreams of being back together with you, but I want more than just dreams." His voice was quiet and sent thrills through me.

Internally, I was in a complete panic. It had been a year and a half since my ex-husband walked out on me. It had also been longer than that since I had been with a man. What if I'd forgotten what I was supposed to do?

"Jess, did I lose you? Am I going too far too soon?" Rob's

voice had changed from sultry to concerned. He was always thoughtful and never pushed beyond what I was prepared to give to him.

"No, I'm here. You aren't pushing me. I want to be with you." I sounded more confident than I felt, but I wasn't questioning what I wanted. Because I wanted Rob. "I want nothing more."

"Well, I'm going to shower and head to bed. You can be sure I will be dreaming about you tonight."

"I have dreamed about you every night since I saw you the day I got home." I slapped my forehead. How on earth could I have said that? It was true, but why had I said it? He was going to think I was nuts.

"I'm glad I'm not the only one having dreams this week." Smooth as glass, he always knew what to say. "Good night, Jess. I'll talk to you tomorrow after I get home from rounding up cows."

"Good night. Be safe tomorrow." My words came out huskier than I intended. The line went dead, and I knew sleep wouldn't come easy.

CHAPTER 7

*H*aving girlfriends was an experience that had always eluded me. I made guy friends more easily, so when Delaney extended her friendship, I treasured it.

"Hey, lady, let's get some lunch." Delaney's head bobbed up and down as she jogged down the sidewalk toward me. She threaded her arm through mine, and we headed off to the restaurant.

"I want to know everything. Like, everything from the start of you and Rob. Every juicy detail." When we were seated, Delaney was almost bouncing off her seat.

"I have to warn you, it's a little boring, but you asked. We met at the diner where I worked shortly after they moved here."

"Are you ladies ready to order?" Again, overly attentive waitstaff irritated me as I was trying to get into my history about Rob. We placed our orders, and the server walked away.

"Okay, where was I? Right, the diner. We went out on our first date. We dated for a little over two years, hardly fought, and had a lot of amazing times together."

"Tell me he was a good lover. He just looks like he would be," Delaney leaned across the table and whispered.

"A lady never tells." I took a sip of my water and fiddled with the cutlery on the table. "He's the best I've ever had."

Delaney squealed and tapped her feet under the table.

"Our history isn't all that earth-shattering. We fell into a comfortable routine and were happy. We started planning a life together and had house plans. We were ready to build, but I started to feel overwhelmed.

"I wanted to see things, get out of this town for a few years, so I applied for a job in New York, spur of the moment. All of a sudden, I felt like I needed to live instead of settling down and doing what everyone expected of me."

Taking a bite, I waited for the inevitable question about whether I regretted leaving.

"Were you happy?"

"When?"

"Were you happy in New York?"

"Not at the start, but, eventually, I thought I was happy. Jeremy made me feel like a queen when we started dating. That all changed after we were engaged, and I should have walked away then, but—stupid me—I stuck around."

"Okay, but at least you didn't waste thirteen years hoping your scum of a boyfriend would propose, thinking that would make you happy." Delaney grabbed her glass and downed her water.

"Um, okay, let's discuss you for a second. I need to know about this." Stabbing blindly at my meal, I waited.

"I met him when we were students, and we started dating, moved into an apartment together right away to save on rent, and just kind of became an old married couple without being married." Delaney's voice trailed off, and I wondered where her mind was.

"Are you seeing anyone now?" I asked between bites.

Delaney shook her head. "I need a little time to reprogram my brain to small town life and being a principal. Also, he'll have to be a pretty strong man to put up with me." She laughed, but I thought she was selling herself short. She was too good for most men.

"What do you want out of this thing with Rob? Do you think you will get back together?"

I sat staring at Delaney for what felt like forever. It was a question I had asked myself a million times in New York, and now that I was home with the possibility of a future with him, I had no idea how to respond.

We finished our lunch and went our separate ways. It was so nice having a friend to talk to.

My phone rang in my purse, and I dug around blindly, trying to find it as I walked to my car.

I walked straight into the chest of a man and dropped my purse.

"Oh, my goodness, I'm so sorry. I wasn't watching where I was going." When I looked up, I stared right into Rob's familiar chocolate-brown eyes. "What are you doing here?" I was stunned as I stood back up.

"Well, I was here for a meeting and saw your car, so decided to see what you were up to." He grabbed my hand, and we began to walk along the street.

His hand felt like it was made for mine. I took a step closer to him as we passed a group of people, but I didn't move away when we were past them.

"What are you doing downtown?"

"I just had lunch with Delaney." Part of me wanted to tell him everything, but the other part wanted to keep the girl talk just between us.

"Ah, so she wanted the details of our date."

I looked up at him and smiled.

"No, she got those last night before you called."

His laughter was infectious, and I couldn't help joining in.

We walked together, neither of us saying much of anything, even though there were many things unsaid between us. Enjoying this moment was more important.

"Rob, Jessica, what a pleasant surprise." Sandra's voice rang out as we approached her and Brian.

Quickly, I let Rob's hand go and shook mine from his grip. He turned to me with a confused look on his face, but I looked back at his mom.

"Sandra, how are you?" She embraced me, and I glanced at Brian. He had a poker face that didn't give away his thoughts. I always assumed it was years of business dealings that made him that way. His eyes, on the other hand, were shooting daggers in my direction.

"Well, it was nice to see you all, but I really should be getting along. I have another event to find supplies for. Sandra, Brian, it was good to see you again. Rob, nice bumping into you. Literally."

I turned and dashed across the street to my car. Glancing in the rear-view mirror, I saw Rob staring at me with a frown across his face, like he had lost his favorite toy.

I backed out of the parking spot and sped away as my phone rang. It was Rob, and I was sure he would be relentless until I answered. I needed to come up with some sort of reason for escaping like I had.

The truth would have been preferable, but it wasn't worth the risk, not yet anyway. Someday, I would tell him, but not now.

SHE CONFUSED ME, BUT IF I WAS HONEST, SHE ALWAYS HAD. Jessica wasn't like other girls I dated, who let me know what they wanted on the first date. Most wanted marriage, a family, and my money. Not my Jess. She was thoughtful, always put others ahead of herself, and never once brought up that my family was wealthy.

I never knew what she wanted, but I guess all those years ago, she didn't want me. The wave of guilt for pushing her away flowed through me again. I didn't even think about it last night, but with her taking off just now, my mind went there again.

That's what made this afternoon so strange. She looked like she'd seen a ghost when we ran into my parents. We weren't teenagers who needed to sneak around. We were two mature adults who shouldn't have to hide their budding relationship.

The last few times my father had been around, she'd been jumpy, and that wasn't her either. She needed to get away from everything, and this weekend would be perfect.

I dialed her number for the second time and waited for her to pick up the call.

"Hello?"

"Hey, you good now?"

"Hi. Yeah, sorry, I must have eaten something funny. I just didn't feel good all of a sudden."

"Jess, you should have let me drive you home. Mom or Dad could have brought me my truck. How are you now?" I couldn't hide the concern in my voice.

"You're too sweet. Rob. I wouldn't have put you out like that. I'm feeling much better. So, what did you do with the rest of your afternoon?"

"Wandered around town and then waited for Addison to get off school. If I'm in town close to school letting out, I pick her up. It saves her almost an hour on the bus, and let's me visit with her about her day."

I worried it was too much when there was silence on the other end of the line. Addison was my life, and I couldn't be afraid to talk about her openly. In past relationships, I had done that, but it never served me well. When I would start talking about her, women always felt like they were the second fiddle, and they would walk away. In fact, they were the second fiddle. Addison would always come first in my life.

"I hope she had a good day. She probably likes not having

to ride the bus for an hour. I can't believe you are a dad. Sometimes that shocks me, but then I think about it, and I always knew you would be the best dad, Rob. When I used to think of our future together, I always knew our kids would have an amazing man to look up to."

Jessica's voice trailed off. It was the first time she had talked about us having a family since she had been back. Not that I had expected a grand declaration the second we saw each other, but we had a history, and that included plans for the future I ruined.

"Have I lost you?" she whispered.

"No, you will never lose me again." Ugh, why did I say that? Who says things like that?

"Well, I'm glad." Her voice was cheerful again, and I didn't feel like such a tool.

I had forgotten how compatible we were. There was no show with Jessica. What you saw was what you got, and she was the match to my soul. Or she was at one point in life. Only time spent together would prove if it was still true.

CHAPTER 8

$\mathcal{P}$acking a bag for a weekend away was almost impossible because I had no idea what our plans would involve. Rob was going to be here in thirty minutes, and I was spinning circles in my room. Every piece of lingerie I owned was splayed across the bed. I packed one and then took it out. I repeated the process so many times I didn't even remember what I had actually packed.

Mom had gone to her ladies' night supper, so I was home alone. I wasn't sad she'd left. It was awkward enough having Mom know that Rob and I were going to his cabin at the lake for the weekend. I didn't need her here watching this tailspin I was heading for.

I looked at the bag and shrugged. It was what it was. A knock on the door scared me, and I felt like I jumped ten feet in the air. Grabbing the bag, I walked to the door and took a deep breath, trying to calm my nerves. My pulse was racing, and butterflies danced in my stomach as I opened the door. "Mr. Radliff? What are you doing here?" The older gentleman looked like he was dressed for a date. He was a tall, slim man who had a full head of salt and pepper hair, and he looked sharp in his dress pants and button-down shirt.

"Well, Miss Jessica, don't you look lovely this evening. I came to call on your mother. I believe she's expecting me." Mr. Radliff was the same age as my mother, and suddenly, I realized he was here for a date.

"Oh, sir, I think she double…"

"No, Jessica, I'm right here," my mother called from her room. "Hank, please just wait in the sitting room. I'll be right out. Jessica, please come here for a second."

I motioned to the sitting room, which had always been the living room until now. I smiled, dropped my bag at the door, and dashed down the hall.

Opening her door, I saw my mother standing in front of the mirror. I hadn't seen her look this beautiful in a long time. Her face was glowing, and her smile was content. She held her arms out as she turned toward me. "Do I look okay?" Her eyes sought approval, and I could tell her hands were shaking.

"I don't think I've ever seen anyone look better than you do right now." Moving over to her, I hugged her gently, then quickly backed up to look at her again. "I thought you left."

She laughed. "I told you I was leaving so you wouldn't overthink your weekend. You may have been gone a while, girlie, but I can still read you like a book." She slid her earrings in and handed me her necklace so I could help her with the clasp.

"Mom, how long has this been going on?" I whispered, knowing Mr. Radliff couldn't hear, but nonetheless, I felt like this was a pivotal moment, and it needed to be dealt with quietly.

"A few years, darling. You didn't share what was happening with you, and I didn't share what was happening here. Are you angry?" With her necklace done up, she turned to look at me.

"No, I'm not angry at all. There is nothing I want more than for you to be happy after all these years. I often wondered why there wasn't anyone in your life, but I didn't want to pry, and I had my own troubles to sort through." I wiped a tear from her eye.

She grabbed a tissue from her dresser and dabbed her tears.

"No crying. We will ruin our mascara. Well, isn't this something? We're both heading out on dates."

We walked to the door of her room with our arms linked. "Dear, can you do me a favor?"

"Anything, Mom, you know that."

"Don't come home early." She reached for the doorknob, unlinked our arms, and walked out to the sitting room. I stood in her room with my mouth open.

"Jessica, Rob is here," she called down the hall, and I shook myself out of the state of shock I was in and went to the sitting room.

When I stepped into the room, I noticed Mr. Radliff had his arm around Mom's waist, and I couldn't help but smile.

Rob walked over and gave me a kiss on the cheek. "You look fantastic. Did you forget that we're just going to the cabin?" he whispered in my ear, and I gave him a slap. There was no denying I wanted this man. His voice alone made me flustered. "We better get going. Where's your bag?"

"It's at the door." I pointed, and Rob turned to grab it.

"Have a lovely weekend, dear." Mom hugged me. "Remember what I told you."

"I will. You have a good weekend too." I smiled at her and gave a quick wink. We backed away from each other, and she walked back to Mr. Radliff's waiting arms. "It was nice to see you again, sir."

"You too, Jessica. I hope to see you more often." He looked at my mom with adoration.

Rob and I walked out the door to his truck. He opened the back door and tossed my bag in, then opened the front door for me. He didn't let me get in, but backed me up so I was pressed against the seat, and he leaned down and kissed me with more passion than I had ever experienced. His hand locked on the back of my head, keeping me from breaking the kiss until he was ready.

"That's what I wanted to do when you came out of the room looking so beautiful." He motioned to the house with his head. "But there were too many eyes."

"The eyes haven't gone away though. They just moved." I saw the curtains move as Mom and her date scrambled away from the window.

Rob let out a husky laugh and met my lips again. "Let's go, or I won't make it to the cabin."

I let out the breath I had been holding while Rob was walking to his side of the truck. My palms were sweaty, so I rubbed them on my skirt. I didn't remember being this nervous before with Rob. He had been my first, and now I felt like I was about to give him my virginity all over again.

"Ready?" He looked at me, and I thought I saw concern in his eyes. I nodded and smiled at him while he put the truck in drive.

A few minutes into the drive, he said, "I stopped and got groceries before I picked you up. Mom and Dad were at the cabin earlier this week, so it's got some supplies already." He reached for the hand I held clenched in my lap. He curled his fingers curled around it, and I held on for dear life. It settled my nerves to feel him. He'd always been the one who could calm me and jump-start my heart at the same time.

"So, Mr. Radliff? How long has that been going on?"

It was the icebreaker I needed. His question shook me back to reality and made me stop thinking about what would happen hours from now. "Apparently a few years." I looked over at him with my eyebrows raised.

"Well, they sure have kept it quiet. I haven't heard a word about them." Rob let go of my hand and rested his on my inner thigh. He used to drive me crazy doing that. It still drove me to the edge, having his warm hand so close to my center.

"I'm glad for her. When I was gone, I worried about her being alone. It makes me feel better that for the last few years, at least, she has had a companion. But I just wish she had told me. I would have found somewhere else to stay." I looked out the window and didn't say anything else, so Rob let the subject drop.

We arrived at the cabin, and it looked almost exactly the same as it had all those years ago. Rob took my bag inside while I looked around; the sunset quickly descending to darkness. There was a firepit already set up just to the left of the cabin.

"Let's sit by the fire for a while. I got a fire going in the fireplace to warm up the cabin, and I have food in the crockpot for later, but it's too beautiful to stay inside right now."

I smiled and walked toward him. When we'd dated before, he was always taking us for drives to the river or for picnics or hikes or trail rides. I sat on a log while he started the fire, the smell of smoke and cedar filling my nose and bringing peace like I hadn't known for years.

"What did your mom tell you that you weren't supposed to forget?" Rob asked a while later, when we'd both been staring at the fire and holding hands.

I giggled and looked over at him. "She asked me not to come home early." I grinned at him, and Rob burst out laughing.

"Go, Daphney," he said through his laughter. When we both composed ourselves, he looked over at me. "She doesn't have to worry about you coming home early. You will be lucky to be back before Monday morning." He ran his hand up my thigh and moved it all the way up my body to my neck. Running his rough thumb along my collarbone, he spoke again, "You, darlin', have all my attention this weekend."

CHAPTER 9

"What do you feel like doing before supper?" The question was innocent, but it felt a little leading. I couldn't help but smile.

"Pretty sure we should probably take a walk. We have been cooped up in the truck for a few hours, and I need to stretch my legs." He moved closer to me, and I could feel my pulse increase. If being close to him felt this way, what would happen later?

I had always enjoyed walking amongst the trees. The benefit of Manhattan was Central Park. It always made me feel a little closer to home when I was deep in the park, where I could find a little solitude.

Usually, I was alone. Jeremy never wanted to wander with me. He said that wasn't what the park was for. He was a runner, and people meandering along irritated him. Come to think of it, everything I did irritated him.

Why was I thinking about Jeremy? He was gone, and right now Rob was here. The complete opposite of the man I had been married to. I wondered what my therapist would say about this. Our virtual appointment next week was sure to be a barn burner.

The walk was enjoyable, and just being able to spend time in the woods with Rob brought back fond memories of spending time here with his family before everything went sideways.

When we made it back to the cabin, Rob built a fire in the outdoor firepit, and we sat as close as we could to each other on the bench, trying to combat the chill that was forming around us as the sun was disappearing behind the clouds.

Rob held my hand and gently stroked it. I could feel the sensation from his thumb run down to my core.

He snaked a strong, work-worn hand up the back of my neck and wrapped my hair around his fingers. Rob claimed my lips again, but this time he felt possessive, as if claiming me as his. He gently repositioned me so I sat in his lap facing him, my legs instinctively wrapping around him.

Our hands explored each other. My light blouse was no barrier for Rob. He grasped my breast in his large hand and greedily kneaded it in his palm. Heat rose through me as I pressed myself down on Rob's lap.

Letting out a groan, he shifted, and before I knew it, I was laying under him. Rob slipped his hand down my side and grasped the hem of my skirt, sliding it up my thigh. His cool hand brushed across my bare mound, causing me to gasp.

He let out a chuckle. "You are full of surprises, aren't you? Or were you hoping our night would end this way?" I had surprised him by not wearing panties tonight. It made me feel powerful and confident when I really needed the boost.

"I'm not going to lie, I'd hoped we would find ourselves in this situation." Smirking slyly, I shifted my hips, so his hand covered me completely. His fingers moved like a pianist playing a soft romantic arrangement. I arched at his ministration and sighed loudly.

"I want you, Jessica. I need you."

Grasping his face in my hands, I brought his lips forcefully to me. I wanted him. Needed him. I shivered against the cold that had crept in around us. The wind whipped my hair about my head, and the once roaring fire was now reduced to embers. A distant rumble of thunder brought us back to the present. Rob leaned over, grabbed another log, and tossed it on the fire. Sparks flew as the wood popped from the heat of the flames, mimicking the sparks flaring between us under the dark night sky.

I sat back beside him, but he turned to face me once more, sliding his rough hand up my leg and making my breath hitch in my throat. Rob made quick work of the buttons down the front of my dress. I heard him inhale deeply as he pushed at each side. Slipping his hands behind my back, he made quick work of removing my dress and bra.

So much of her body was familiar. My fingers remembered where she longed to be touched. I slid my hand between her legs to find her slick and ready for me. Time had changed me. I wasn't the tentative lover that had learned along with her any longer. In the back of my mind, I worried that she wouldn't respond to me the way she used to.

"Jessica, I need you under me." Growling, I shifted and rolled her to the ground. The fire crackled and popped beside us as I worked my fingers inside her.

Jessica opened her eyes and looked at me. I felt as if she instinctively knew I had changed, and, staring into her hazel eyes, I saw an acknowledgment that she needed me.

"Rob," she panted as I brought her closer to climax. This wasn't how I wanted her to come. I popped open my belt buckle and unzipped my pants. There wasn't time to take them off, so I slid them down as far as I needed them to go.

"You sure you're ready, baby?"

"Yes," she whispered as she spread her legs to make room for me.

After one quick, forceful thrust, she moaned my name into the dark night.

The rain fell, hitting my bare ass, and the temperature dropped. There was no way I would stop what was happening at that moment, but I shielded her as best I could from the storm, cocooning her with my body.

Lightning illuminated everything around us, and for that split second, Jessica and I locked eyes. She met my thrusts with a force of her own. Urging me on. There was no tender lovemaking. This was a primal need to be as close to one another as we could physically get.

"Jess, I have to…"

She cut me off with a cry of ecstasy that echoed through the wilderness as she bit my shoulder. It was her cry mixed with the spasms that engulfed me that sent me over the edge. I groaned and collapsed on her. As I finished, a pack of coyotes returned Jessica's call, and the hair on my neck stood on end. I wanted to revel in the moment, but the rain was picking up by the minute.

I rolled onto my side, bringing Jessica with me. With my forehead pressed to hers, I closed my eyes and sighed. There was nothing that would make me more content than this moment right here.

Jessica's hair was dripping wet and plastered across her face. I brushed the strands away from her eyes and mouth as her breaths slowed to normal. When her breathing evened out, I leaned in and kissed her lips again.

Another rumble of thunder made Jessica jump in my arms, making us both laugh. "I think it's time to head somewhere warm. Can you walk to the cabin?"

Jessica was still wrapped around me. "I think so."

I stood and helped her up. She took a step toward me and kissed me, her hands combing through my wet hair and raking down my back while I pulled up my pants. This was not getting us inside, so I picked her up and flipped her over my shoulder, slapped her on the ass, and ran up the porch stairs. The uncontrolled laughter coming from Jessica made me grin. She returned the swat I gave her, and it made my heart light and full of joy to have her laughing and playful and back in my arms.

CHAPTER 10

The fire Rob started was still burning inside the cabin. We both huddled around the fireplace to get warm after our outdoor escapades. I was chilled to the bone but had never felt so warm and cozy on the inside. It didn't matter that I was standing here in front of Rob, completely naked. He had just made love to me and, although I'd spent years trying to get over him, he still owned me completely.

Rob moved quickly when he saw me shivering. Grabbing a blanket from the back of the overstuffed sofa, he wrapped it around my shoulders.

"This should help," he whispered as he kissed the back of my neck. "We should think about eating something too." When he turned me to face him, I knew he was talking about food, but I was in a saucy mood.

"Oh, I'm already thinking about it." I took a step closer to him. I could feel a flush creeping from my chest up my neck. It had been a long time since I had been this forward, and I was starting to second-guess myself.

"Don't worry, baby, there will be plenty of time for that, but I haven't forgotten how you get when you're hungry. I don't want to see that bear this weekend." He reached up and put his hand on the back of my neck and pulled me aggressively toward him. Our lips crashed into each other, causing unbridled and pent-up passion to explode between us.

When we pulled away, the flames from the fire were reflected in Rob's eyes, the heat making them the darkest brown I'd ever seen. The rain outside had cleansed us both, had washed away all our past troubles and made way for each other again.

"I'm going to get supper started. Why don't you go put comfy clothes on?" He rested his arms on my shoulders and clasped his hands behind my head.

"Sounds like a good plan." I leaned in and kissed him again. This time wasn't wildly passionate, it was tender and sweet. Ducking under his arm, I walked toward the bedroom and dropped the blanket as I went. I turned and gave him a wink as I carried on down the hall.

Rob was laughing as I closed the door. "You are going to be the death of me, lady."

Dressed in the warmest, coziest clothes I brought, I walked back out to the kitchen. Rob had stopped at a takeout place on the way here, so he had everything ready on the table.

"I remembered how much you liked barbeque, so I thought it would be the easiest thing to bring up here."

"That was the smell in the truck. I couldn't place it." I leaned over my plate and took in the wonderful smoky, mouthwatering roast beef. The mashed potatoes, gravy, and bun looked delicious.

"Sit. I'll pour a glass of wine." Rob turned back to the counter and grabbed a bottle and two glasses.

Supper didn't disappoint. I was so full I almost had to roll off my chair. Taking my wine, I grabbed the blanket and settled onto the overstuffed couch.

"So… earlier, that was different from what I remember." I ran my finger around the rim of my wineglass, staring into the dark red liquid.

He laughed, "I may have changed the way I do some things." Resting his arm on the back of the sofa, he played with my hair. "I forgot how much I loved your hair. I used to look at every woman who had anything close to your color, hoping it was you, that you'd changed your mind and come home." His voice was quiet and his eyes glossed over as he focused on the hair in his hands.

He snapped out of his daze before I could form a response.

"Old memories aren't what I want to talk about this weekend. All I want to think about is you. And our future." Rob set his glass on the table in front of us, reached for mine, and set it beside his. I slid over so I was sitting in the crook of his arm and relaxed back into him.

"You know the one thing I never forgot?" He made a quiet "hmm," in my ear. "The feel of just sitting with you. Your arm around me, making me feel small and protected. No matter what I did, it was what I longed for." Rob tightened his arm around me and pulled me closer to him.

"I missed holding you. I missed so many things, but my arms always felt empty."

We spent the rest of the night in each other's arms. I wasn't sure it was possible to make up for the eight years apart in one night, but we were certainly going to try.

Morning dawned, and I rolled over into a solid mass. Rob laughed as he wrapped his arms around me. "How did you sleep darlin'?"

His groggy, husky voice melted me. I scooted as close to him as I could. "The best I've had in a very long time. How about you?"

Rob pressed himself against my core. "How do you think?"

I couldn't help but laugh as I moved my hand down his chest to wrap around his erection.

When we woke a while later, we were still tangled together.

"What do you have planned for the weekend? An entire weekend in this room? Or are we going on adventures?" I ran my fingers lightly down his chest.

A rumble grew from deep inside him as I continued exploring his upper body with my hands. "I thought we could hike down to the falls, then come back here. I'm sure we'll be ready for a little rest by then." He placed his hand over mine before I could move it farther than his stomach. "But right now, we need to make breakfast. So get out of bed." He kissed the top of my head and slapped me on the ass before he rolled out of bed and sauntered to the washroom.

I got dressed quickly but grabbed one of his hoodies that was way too roomy for me, but it was cozy.

The living room was chilly, so I walked over to the fireplace and put new logs in the firebox. I crumpled up the newsprint and grabbed matches. When I struck the match against the side of the box, the flame came to life in my hands. Ironically, it felt like what my soul had done walking into this weekend. The warmth from the match was noticeable immediately.

I knelt down to light the paper, watching as the flame ignited it and took hold of the dry bark. It only took a moment to feel the warmth return to the main part of the cabin.

When I stood, I turned into the comfort of a sturdy pair of arms. "You didn't have to build the fire. I would have done it."

"Oh, big, strong man has to build the fire, and weak, frail woman needs to make breakfast? Is that how it's going to be?" I knew that wasn't what he meant at all. He had been raised by one of the strongest women I knew. Sandra wouldn't have lasted living with Brian all these years if she wasn't a force to be reckoned with. And I couldn't help but tease him a little.

"Oh, Jess, no, that's not what I meant at all." The color drained from his face, and I could see him searching his brain for something to make it better. I rose up on my tiptoes and planted a wet, messy kiss on his lips. "Let's make breakfast."

"I think I already have my breakfast." Rob said as he pulled me tighter to him.

"Nice try, cowboy. If we're hiking, I need to eat." I spun out of his arms and was met with a swat on my backside.

"Well, let's get breakfast ready then." Rob followed me to the kitchen.

I never dreamed that having someone to cook with would bring me this much joy. Jeremy used to expect to walk in the door to supper on the table. It didn't matter how crazy my day had been, I always had a meal ready for him. A whirlwind dating life hid all his narcissistic tendencies.

"Where did you go just now?" Rob took my hand as we sat at the table.

I closed my eyes and shook my head. "Nowhere important. The only place I want to be is here. It's the only place I've wanted to be for as long as I can remember."

There was no way you could miss the smile that spread across his face.

"So let's get this hike going." I broke the moment, but we had gotten into serious territory, and I needed to distract myself with something light and fun.

The weekend had gone by too fast. Reality set in while we were packing, bringing down my lighthearted mood. I would have been content to hide out here with Rob for the rest of my life. We were in a great place, getting to know each other again, and focusing on one another with no outside problems facing us.

I looked over at the man I had spent the last forty-eight hours with and couldn't believe he was mine again. Don't jump the gun, Jessica. I kept repeating over and over in my head. It was too easy to imagine us living the life we'd wanted and planned for so many years ago.

He hadn't lost the ruggedly handsome features that had

originally drawn me to him. His features were stronger, work worn, and they made him hot-as-hell. His charm knew no bounds, and he could easily bend me to whatever he desired.

Suddenly, he grasped my hand and took me back into the cabin. Stopping briefly to kick the door closed, he turned and ravished my neck.

I was thankful for the stretchy dress I had worn today because Rob had it off me in seconds. He ripped open his shirt and removed it with ease. My bra was the next thing to join the ever-growing pile of clothing on the floor. Backing me up until we reached the counter, he grabbed me by the ass and set me on it.

With a sly grin, he dropped to his knees and placed my legs over his shoulders, looking up at me. "I'm really enjoying this no panties thing you have going on this weekend. Please tell me you'll keep it up when we get home."

He didn't wait for an answer. He leaned in and ran his tongue over me. Losing myself in the moment, I grabbed his head and held him close, letting my head fall back and enjoying the attention he was giving me.

"Rob, as much as I'm enjoying this, I want you." I hoped he heard my breathless plea. He chuckled against me and stood. It seemed like it only took seconds for him to drop his jeans and pull me off the edge of the counter and onto him. I wrapped my arms and legs around Rob before he pinned me against the wall, and we crested the edge of ecstasy together.

ROB HERDED ME OUT THE DOOR AN HOUR LATER THAN WE planned, but the hour was one I wouldn't forget any time soon. Sitting silently in the truck, we held hands. It had been the perfect weekend to reconnect with each other without the scrutiny of extra eyes.

"I want you to meet Addison. I mean really meet her." As our drive took us closer to my house, I could feel Rob's hand shaking as he held mine. I knew he'd wanted to talk about something most of the drive home, but I wasn't sure what it was. He was quieter, more distant. All of a sudden, he pulled over to the side of the road and to look at me. "Jess, I have never had Addison meet a woman before. I never wanted her to get hurt. But I've also never been with a woman I wanted her to meet."

He looked so vulnerable. The only other time I had seen him like this was when he'd asked me to stay with him. I crushed his heart then, and I wasn't going to do that again.

"Rob, I'd love to officially meet Addison."

His eyes softened, and his hunched shoulders seemed to rise. I hadn't realized how much weight he carried over this. His smile seemed to light up the dark truck. We kissed, and he pulled back onto the road.

CHAPTER 11

*S*itting down with a therapist regularly had been my reality since my infertility diagnosis. Tasha was a great resource who I had been put in contact with by my doctor's office. She saw me through all the tests, failed IVF attempts, ectopic pregnancy, and the realization that being a biological mother wasn't in the cards for me.

Our appointments had moved from weekly to twice a month since I'd accepted my fate and learned to live again. She moved to Atlanta shortly after my divorce but was adamant that she keep me as a client, so here I was, in front of my computer, waiting for her to connect to our Zipp.Chat.

She knew snippets about Rob but not the big things. When I was trying to make my marriage work, I intentionally steered clear of topics that included him.

Her smiling, professional face popped up on my screen, and I smiled back. She looked like the typical therapist. With her hair pulled back into a bun that rested at the base of her head, glasses perched on the end of her nose, she waited for me to spill my guts.

"Jessica, so good to see you. How has the move back home

been?" I saw her lower her head and figured she was ready to write.

"It's been interesting. The wedding I was hired to plan went better than I could have ever dreamed. I have gotten quite a bit of business inquiries from it, which has been fantastic. I ran into my ex-boyfriend. We went out a few times and then went to his cabin together this weekend." I took a breath, thinking about what else had been going on while she waited patiently for me to continue. "Moving in with my mother has been a bit of a culture shock. She's dating. In fact, she has been for a few years and never told me. I'm happy for her. She deserves to have love, and I think she held back because of me." Finally stopping my monologue, I waited to see what she would pick up on.

I had no doubt in my mind what part of that she was going to want to discuss first, and I was prepared. Or so I thought.

"Well, sounds like you have settled into life pretty well, Jessica. I want to go back to the ex-boyfriend. Tell me how that came about."

"He's the brother of the groom who's wedding I planned. We dated years ago, just before I left for New York. We have been spending time together. Not much else to tell."

Tasha blinked, her eyes wide on the screen. "Wow, a lot has happened in the two weeks since our last session. What happened when you were reacquainted with your ex? How did you feel?"

I sat staring at the screen, my finger itching to hit the end call button, but I knew she would be relentless trying to get a hold of me if I disconnected now.

"How did I feel? I was nervous. It's been a while since I've been with anyone, and it's been a very long time since I've been with Rob. It was better than I remembered. He's changed in the best way. He's a dad, which was a possibility I had never thought of before I came home. I just hoped he was happy." My voice trailed off.

"Did you two part amicably all those years ago?"

"No."

I didn't want to talk about that night. If I talked about it, I would have to face my fear of Rob finding out about me taking his father's money.

"Jessica, if you shut down, we can't get through what is really going on."

"No, we didn't part on good terms. We fought about me leaving, and I never talked to him again until the day of his brother's wedding. His father paid me to leave, and I didn't even blink when he handed me the money. All I could see was the solution I needed to chase my dreams."

Her silence felt like a huge weight on my chest. How could she not be judging me? It was a cowardly thing to do, and I lived with it every day.

"What are you afraid will happen when Rob does find out?"

"I'm afraid he will be the one to leave this time. If he walked away from me now, it would be too much to handle."

"So, what's your plan?"

"I'm going to tell him and hope he understands my thought process at that time in my life. If he can't, then I guess I'll know I need to move on and stop living in the past."

Hearing myself say that was shocking. It wasn't something I had consciously thought about before. I never wanted to live without Rob, but if he chose to walk away this time, I'd need to accept that and move on.

"That's a very big thing to accept, Jessica. Something I don't think you had accepted before now, am I right?"

My silence was her answer. I didn't need to say it out loud.

"Jessica, I think this session was one of the better ones we've had. You've definitely had a breakthrough that I think will serve you well."

Her words didn't ease my mind about what his response may be, but they made me realize I would be all right if things didn't go the way I hoped.

"How are you going to deal with Rob's father?"

This I knew. I had it planned. Maybe not the day or the time, but I'd had eight years to think and practice what I'd say to him when push came to shove. Just as I was ready to dive into that plan, her timer went off, signaling that our session was over.

"All right, Jess, our time is up for this week. Do you think we need to go back to once a week? It seems like there is a lot happening in Texas, and I wonder if there are things we need to focus on with Rob having a child."

"I won't deny that it hurt when I found out he had a child with someone else, but I'm happy he has a child, given my situation."

It wasn't a lie. I was happy he had Addison, and if I let my heart go there, I would be happy to have the opportunity to be in her life.

"Let's leave our appointments the way they are, and I will call if I need more."

"Yes, that works. I will talk to you in two weeks. Well done, Jessica." She smiled at me, and I waved goodbye.

I felt good after this session. A little more accepting of my decision all those years ago, and more willing to have the hard discussions with Rob.

CHAPTER 12

There was no reason to be so nervous. I'd had made sure the house was ready for tonight, and supper was on the stove. Everything was clean, and Addison was in her room getting ready.

"Daddy, what are you doing now?" Addison asked as she walked out of her room. She had changed into a purple dress and had put her hair up in a ponytail.

"You look beautiful, Squish." I stopped cooking supper, leaned against the counter, and watched her twirl in her dress.

"Thank you. You look nice too." She walked over to me, pulled on my arm to bring me closer, and kissed my cheek. When Samantha had walked out on Addison and me, I worried about being a girl dad, but looking at her tonight, I had to pat myself on the back, because I thought the two of us were doing a damn good job.

A knock on the door made my pulse race, and I felt like I was a teenager on my first date. I opened the door to find Jessica's smiling face. She looked gorgeous in her tight jeans and low-cut V-neck purple shirt. "Hi." I smiled, stepped out toward her, and kissed her gently. I had missed her for the last few days. I hadn't seen her since we returned from the cabin because the ranch had needed more of my time. Suddenly, I heard a giggle behind me.

Jessica smiled at me, and I shook my head.

"Jessica, I would like to officially introduce you to Addison."

Addison pushed me aside, walked up to Jessica, and held her hand out. With a quick glance at me and a smile, Jessica knelt down and shook Addison's hand.

"It's very nice to see you again, Addison. I have this for you. Your dad told me you loved horses, so when I saw it, I thought of you." Jessica handed Addison the most beautiful glass horse figurine. Addison's smile seemed bigger than her face. She turned, handed it to me, and flung her arms around Jessica's neck.

I stood staring at the woman I had never stopped loving as she hugged my daughter like she had known her forever. "Addison, why don't we let Jessica come into the house?"

Addison let Jessica go, took her hand, and led her into the house.

"What can I do to help with supper?" she asked as I walked to the kitchen to check on the food simmering on the stove.

"Nothing. I think it's pretty much ready."

"Jessica, would you like to see my room?" Addison walked into the kitchen. She was absolutely adorable when she turned on the charm. She tilted her head, and her eyes pleaded with Jessica.

"I would love to. Let's go."

Addison held out her hand, and Jessica didn't even hesitate before taking it. The two girls who held my heart wandered down the hallway. I could hear Jessica ooh and aww at the things Addison was showing her. It made my heart soar.

I couldn't hear what they were talking about, but I could hear that Addison's voice was filled with excitement and laughter, and Jessica's was encouraging and inquisitive. There hadn't ever been a time I wanted to spy on Addison but I wished I was a fly on the wall to hear their conversation right now.

"You are one lucky girl to have a room like that," Jessica exclaimed as they walked back to the dining room.

"It's my favorite place in the house, you know." Addison was so serious, as if she had given the subject a lot of thought.

"You know what? I think that's very special. When I was growing up, my room was my secret place." Jessica leaned into Addison and lowered her voice as if to tell her a secret. "If my mom couldn't find me in the house, she knew she could always find me in my room. I was usually curled up on the window seat reading a book."

"I'm sorry to interrupt, ladies, but supper is ready." I held out my arms for each of them to take, and we walked over to the table together. Addison sat in her spot, and I pushed her chair in, then I went around and did the same for Jessica. Taking my seat at the head of the table, I began to serve supper.

"This is way better than a fancy restaurant." Jessica looked at Addison and smiled before looking up at me and winking.

"What was your favorite book when you were my age?"

"Addison, not with your mouth full, please. We may work in the barns, but you definitely were not raised in one."

She frantically finished her mouthful of food and asked her question again.

"Well, I think when I was your age, I really liked Anne of Green Gables. Do you have that one?"

Addison shook her head.

"I know I have more than one copy in my room. I will bring one with me the next time I come over."

Addison beamed. A love of reading was something she and Jessica shared, and it was clear that they were already developing a bond .

Jessica looked over at me to make sure it was okay. My

smile probably omitted the need for the nod, but I gave her one anyway.

When supper was finished, the kitchen looked like a disaster. "Addie, let's clean the kitchen and let your dad put his feet up. He cooked, so we clean up." Addison's face didn't look too excited, but Jessica ushered her to the other room.

"Will you tell me what Anne of Green Gables is about while we do all the work?" She rolled her eyes as she talked, and Jessica laughed.

"Yes, I can do that. Let's get to work. The sooner we start, the sooner we'll be done." Jessica stood and grabbed the plates. "Anne of Green Gables is about a girl who didn't have a mom or dad and went to live with a family in the country. She had red hair but wanted it to be brown."

I looked over at Addison, finding her riveted by Jessica's explanation of the book.

"Anne dyed her hair one day, hoping it would turn black, but it turned an awful green."

"Green, yuck. I'm never, ever dying my hair." Addison looked at Jessica.

Jess reached for Addison's hair and ran it through her fingers. "You don't need to worry about dying your hair, kiddo. It's beautiful just the way it is." She looked around the kitchen, and her eyes widened comically. "Why are there so many dishes, Addie?"

My daughter did her famous shrug and leaned toward Jessica. "We have a dishwasher. Let's use that," Addison whispered as they walked over to stand in front of it.

"Good idea," I heard Jess whisper back.

I didn't go too far. I didn't want to miss out on listening to them chatter on about books. Sitting at the island in the kitchen, I pointed out where things went. Their conversation was easy, almost natural. Jessica was born to be a mom. That was easy to see.

"Addison, you make a wonderful cleanup partner. Thank you for your help." Jessica wrapped Addison up in a hug.

"I had fun." She shrugged before letting out a giggle. "Wow, did I just say that?"

"Let's hope your dad didn't hear so you won't get stuck doing it all the time," Jessica said.

I pretended to look off in the distance, oblivious to what was being said.

"Let's go play a game. Dad, you think Jessica knows how to play Monopoly Jr.?" Her little whisper always managed to melt my heart every time.

"She probably knows. But if she doesn't, we can crush her." Addison and I laughed, and I looked up at Jessica, who was looking at the two of us with her brow arched.

"You both better get your game faces on. I'm a Monopoly pro."

Addison giggled and ran to get the game from the hall closet.

"Jess, thank you for making this so easy," I whispered in her ear, putting my arm around her waist and pulling her close to me.

"Are you kidding? I'm having a great time." She kissed my cheek, and we waited for Addison to come back.

We laughed, we argued, and in the end, Addison ended up owning most of the board.

"Okay, Squish, time for bed. You have school tomorrow. Get your pajamas on and brush your teeth, please." Addison slid off the couch as if I had just asked her to do the worst thing in the world. If she could have moved slower, she would have. "Thank you." I looked over at Jessica, who was trying to hide her smile. "She's not usually this difficult at night." I ran my hands through my hair and let out a frustrated breath.

"It's fine, Rob. The novelty will eventually wear off. I'm guessing sooner rather than later." Jessica moved to sit beside me and rested her hand on my leg.

Addison came back when she was ready for bed. She climbed up onto Jessica's lap and asked, "Will you be here in the morning?" She had rested her head on Jessica's shoulder and was cuddled into her.

With a kiss on Addison's head, Jessica started talking to her quietly. "No, sweetheart, I won't be. I have to go home to my house, but how about I come back out in a few days, and you can take me out and show me your horses and all the cows?" Addison nodded and hugged Jessica. "Good night, little one."

Addison jumped off Jessica's knee and took my hand.

"I'll be back shortly," I told Jessica as Addison led me down the hall.

Jessica's smile was understanding, and it made me feel like none of this was an issue.

Watching Rob walk Addie to bed warmed my heart. I glanced back to the table and decided I would start the Monopoly cleanup. It would be one less thing for him to do after I left. By the time he came back, I had the game put away, the chairs pushed in, and was waiting at the island.

"Wow, thank you. You didn't have to do that," Rob said as he leaned against the counter.

I walked over to him and into his arms. There was nowhere else that made me feel as comfortable and safe.

"Thank you for being so amazing tonight. Addison hasn't met anyone I've dated before, so she was overly excited."

I turned in his hold and wrapped my arms around his neck. "Don't forget, I was her a long time ago. Granted, mom's dates were few and far between, but they were still a big deal. She is perfect, Rob. You have raised an amazing little girl."

He leaned down and kissed me. Taking my hand, he led

me to the couch and sat as close to me as he could. "I would love it if you stayed the night," Rob whispered in my ear.

I smiled. "Me too, but not on the first meeting. Let me build a relationship with Addie, let our relationship unfold with her around, and eventually, it will just naturally happen."

He sighed and nodded. "You know we could make out like we used to."

I turned to face Rob and wiggled my eyebrows. "I'm not going to turn down that offer."

He wrapped his arms around me, and I moved in and grazed his lips with mine. He let out a slow breath. I smiled and captured his mouth with my own. Rob's large hands slid up my back and tangled in my hair. He kept pressure on my head, kept our lips in a perfect dance.

His intoxicating kisses were making me crazy. The desire was thick around us, and I was lost in his embrace.

"Dad, I need some water." Addie's quiet voice came from over by the kitchen. My heart dropped from my chest, and I could feel the heat rising up to my face.

"Okay, Squish, let's get you back to bed."

"Night, Jessica." Her voice was soft, and it caused a wave of guilt to wash over me.

"Good night, Addie." I turned and waved as she rounded the corner toward her room.

I dropped my head into my hands and couldn't believe what had just happened.

Rob's strong hands gently crossed my shoulders from behind me. "Jess, it's okay. We weren't doing anything wrong."

I stood and turned to look at him. "I know we weren't, but that doesn't make it feel any better. This isn't what I wanted her to see." My shoulders slumped, and I closed my eyes. "Rob, you're a single dad, and your number one priority is your daughter. We can't let this happen again. No making out when she's in the house. I won't put her through walking in on us again."

Rob walked over to me and drew me into his arms. "You're right, baby, I am a single dad, but I'm also a red-blooded man who is incredibly attracted to you." Gently, he placed his hand under my chin and made me look up into his eyes. "I won't stop showing you affection. We are just going to have to be a little more stealthy."

I couldn't help but laugh at him. "That's such a guy thing to say." I wrapped my arms around him, and we just stood together in silence. I had to think of what was good for Addison and not just myself now. This was going to be a shift for me. I wasn't just dating Rob again, I'd also been invited into Addison's life, and I wasn't going to complicate things for her.

CHAPTER 13

It was a gorgeous, sunny Memorial Day. I was meeting Rob and Addie in town for the rodeo. The rodeo grounds weren't big, so I stood on the grandstand and watched for Rob's truck.

The big black Ford looked like half the other tricks in the area, but the stick trailer with the Lonestar brand all over it was not easy to miss.

Quickly, I walked down to the parking area to meet them. Addie ran to me, and I swung her as she jumped into my arms.

"Hey, lady, how are you? Excited to watch Dad later?"

"I'm good." Her giggles were contagious.

With Addison in my arms, I walked over to the trailer where Rob was unloading his horse.

"Hi, beautiful, ready for a little rodeo?"

"Ready to cheer you on, cowboy."

He leaned into me for a quick kiss. Hoots and hollers erupted around us.

Rob laughed, and I smiled even as I blushed. I was sure I was eight shades of red at this point.

"I'm not up for an hour. Why don't we go get something to eat?"

I set Addie down, and she walked between us, holding both our hands.

This felt right. Glancing over at Rob, I couldn't help but smile because my heart was full.

As we were waiting for our food at the concession stand, the loudspeaker crackled. "Rob Morton to the barrel racing staging area. Rob Morton to the staging area." The voice wasn't jovial and sounded a little panicked.

I looked at Rob, who shrugged, and we grabbed our food and headed that way.

We got to the back of the arena to find utter chaos. There were people everywhere, and the ambulance was just leaving with Kate's truck following close behind.

"Nate, what happened?" Rob questioned when we ran into the ranch foreman.

"Don't really know. Kate made her run, and she and Tyler were heading to eat when all hell broke loose."

Nate was shaken. He took off his hat and ran his hand through his hair.

"Tyler got trampled by a bull. Thankfully, the paramedics were close by, and got him stable on the board before they took off. Kate is following in her truck. I was able to unhook her trailer while they were loading Tyler up so it wouldn't slow her down."

"Okay, go find my parents and tell them what happened. I'll head to the hospital."

Rob was talking a mile a minute and turned to look at Addie, who had wrapped herself around me.

"Oh, Squish, I'm sure he'll be fine."

Rob dropped to his knees, and Addie let go of me, immediately clinging to him.

"Jess, will you take Addison home?"

"You don't even have to ask. Of course I will."

His face relaxed for a moment, and he took a deep breath.

"Okay, Jessica will take you home, and Ill see if Mrs. Renunal can come over."

I shook my head. "Rob, I'll stay until you get back. Doesn't matter how long it takes."

With Addie still clinging to him, he grabbed me by the waist, pulled me to him, and kissed me.

"Thank you."

I nodded. "All right, Addie, let's let your dad get going, and we can go finish watching the rodeo." I reached out, and the little girl swapped hips.

"Can we just go home?" Her voice sounded so little coming from where she had buried her head in my neck.

"Of course we can. Let's go." The three of us walked together until we reached my car.

"I'll be home as soon as I can." Rob kissed Addie on the cheek and gave me a quick peck on the lips.

"Don't rush, we'll be fine."

I watched him sprint off toward his truck.

The drive home was quiet. What happened to Tyler was a lot to process for a little girl, and I wasn't sure how to get her talking.

"Want to watch a movie?"

She nodded and looked like she was about to cry.

"Hey, you know you don't have to be tough, right? This has been a scary day. You don't have to hide your emotions from me."

Addie's chin began to quiver and her eyes filled with tears. She climbed up onto my lap and let herself cry. I lost track of how long we sat there together.

"Jessica, can we watch a movie now?"

"Of course we can. What do you want to watch?"

"Um, Frozen."

"All right, sounds perfect, but I think we need popcorn and sodas first."

I hopped off the couch and got our snacks ready.

"Miss Addie, you better be ready for the best movie day ever!" She seemed to have perked up after our crying session.

I carried bowls of popcorn, chips, and candy over to the living room. Addison brought over our sodas, and we settled in on the couch for our movie marathon.

"Jessica, I wonder what being the star of a movie would be like . Dressing up fancy and having everyone look at you and take your picture."

"Well, kiddo, I planned a few movie premiers when I lived in New York, and they were very exciting. Maybe we'll have to go to one someday."

We watched movie after movie, had a brief interruption for supper, and were back to picking a new one once we'd cleaned up. I hoped I made a good day for her even though it had started off scary.

"I think it's time for bed, missy."

Glancing at the clock, Addie groaned.

"Can't I stay up until Dad comes home?" The puppy dog eyes were going to be my downfall.

"Sure, but you have to lie down out here on the couch. I don't know when your dad will be home, okay?"

She nodded, ran to change into her pajamas, and rested her head on my lap.

In no time, her breathing changed, and she was asleep. I didn't have the heart to move her, so I grabbed the blanket off the back of the couch and waited for Rob.

It was late. I was sure Addie would be in bed and hoped Jessica had found a bed to sleep in. She hadn't been alone with my daughter before, but I trusted her implicitly. Quietly, I opened the door and closed it behind me. Shrugging off my jacket, I noticed the TV was still on. It was there that I found

Jessica wide awake with Addison asleep on her lap. The scene made my heart burst. I walked over to sit beside Jessica and gently brushed my hand across Addie's curls.

"She wouldn't let me put her to bed. She wanted to wait up for you."

"How about I put her to bed, and then I'll fill you in?" I gently picked Addie up and carried her to her room. Covering her up, I kissed her forehead. "Dream sweet dreams Addie girl." I pulled the door closed behind me, then headed to the kitchen. I grabbed two glasses of sun tea and walked back into the living room to update Jessica.

"Oh, thank you." Jessica smiled and took the glass I held out in front of her. Sitting down beside her, I took a sip of my tea and shifted so I was looking at her.

"Well, how is Tyler?"

"He has a lacerated spleen, a broken collarbone, multiple broken ribs, and a collapsed lung. He went into surgery for the spleen. Kate sent me home."

"I pray everything goes well tonight. I'm glad you came home." She leaned over and kissed me. Setting my glass on the coffee table and taking Jessica's from her hand and placing it beside mine, I wrapped my arms around her and pulled her close.

"Thank you for being here, and being willing to take Addison when we all ran off." I looked over at her and her eyes were glued to me. She was gorgeous, and I was falling in love all over again.

"There's nowhere else I would rather have been. Thank you for trusting me." Jessica leaned back in and kissed me again. "I better get going. I have a busy day tomorrow. But I will be available if you need me. I can pick Addie up from school if you need me to."

It was my turn to smile. "I will keep you updated as soon as I know more. Are you sure you have to go?"

"Yes, I do. We don't need to explain why I'm still here in

the morning to Addie. There will be a time for that, but right now with everything going on, she doesn't need this to." Standing, holding out her hand, she helped me off the couch. Walking hand in hand to the door, we said goodnight.

"Call when you get home?" She nodded, and I watched her get into her car and drive away. I stood on the porch and watched her lights until I couldn't see them anymore. The lights at my parent's home were being turned off one by one. I hoped Gavin had got into town and was staying with Kate. Turning back into the house, I grabbed the glasses from the coffee table and took them to the kitchen.

CHAPTER 14

As the last few months passed my relationship with Addie and Rob had morphed after Tyler's accident, which he was mostly recovered from. We settled into a comfortable routine with each other, and I spent most evenings with them at their house. Tonight, I was happily cooking away while Rob helped Addie with homework. It was one of those domestic moments of happiness that I had given up on having years ago. We'd settled into a happy routine, and—while my mind kept waiting for the other shoe to drop—I deliberately kept myself in the moment to soak up every drop of happiness with them.

"Rob, you need to come to Tyler's with us." Brian came barreling through the door. "Your brother has stepped in it again. I'll explain on the way over." I noticed Sandra standing at the bottom of the porch outside, looking like she was going to cry.

"Do you mind staying here with Addison? I'll be right back."

"I don't mind at all."

He kissed me on the side of the head and walked out the door behind his dad.

Brian didn't even acknowledge me when he barged through the door, which was fine with me. I watched the three of them leave the yard as Addison came to stand beside me. "Jessica, what's happening?" All I could do was smile and shrug when I glanced down at her.

"I don't know, kiddo. Guess we'll have to wait and see. Why don't we go see if there is a movie to watch?"

WHEN WE WALKED BACK TO MY HOUSE, EVERYONE WAS QUIET. Neither Mom nor Dad had much to say. Somehow, I knew Tyler's past would come back to haunt him, but not like this. That ex-girlfriend was a piece of work. Now it was my job to go clean up the mess. There was no part of me that was happy about this.

Addison and Jessica were sitting on the couch watching a movie, cuddled up together. It helped ease some of my frustration when I walked in the door. "Addison, go grab your stuffed animal, you're spending the night with Grandma and Grandpa." I kissed her head and went to pack a bag.

"Daddy, where are you going?" Addison walked into my room with her favorite teddy bear.

I picked her up and sat on the edge of the bed. She cuddled into me; she knew something was wrong.

"Squish, I have to go help Uncle Tyler in Montana. I'll have to be gone for a few days, but I need to leave right away. In the morning, Grandma will come back and get your clothes, okay?"

We walked back out to the kitchen, and I hugged her one more time before she left with Mom. Jessica stood against the sink, waiting for an explanation. I leaned up against the opposite counter and gave her half a smile.

"Montana?" She tilted her head slightly, wanting to hear

the explanation, her arms crossed in front of her, and a frown on her face.

I nodded and ran a hand down my face. "Yeah, some drama with Tyler and his ex."

She could probably see the stress on my face, the tension pinching my lips because she walked over into my open arms, and I engulfed her as she rested her head on my chest. We just stood together in silence for a moment.

"Drive me to the airport, and I will explain it all."

Jessica tilted her head up to look at me and nodded. We didn't move. I knew I needed to get going, but I wanted Jessica in my arms more than I wanted to go save my brother's ass. "I should pack." Slowly, I released my arms, and Jessica backed away from me. "It will only take me a few minutes." When I headed to my room, she walked back into the kitchen and put away the supper she was making.

"Ready?"

Jessica turned and walked to the door. "Is it wrong that I'm pouting just a little?" she asked as she slipped her shoes on.

Grabbing her arm as she walked out the door, I pulled her back to me and rested my hand on her cheek. "Nope, it isn't because I'm not really happy about it myself. I had much better plans for tonight that didn't include flying on an airplane." The way Jessica looked at me made my insides burn. I wanted her so badly I almost said screw Tyler, but I couldn't do that to Kate. She was far better than my idiot brother deserved, and she needed the truth.

I needed Jessica close so I could kiss her. Backing her up to the closed door, I pressed her against it. Our lips never lost their connection, our hips pressing into each other.

"Rob, we need to get going, or I won't let you leave," Jessica whispered as I kissed down the side of her neck and caressed her breast. My displeasure at the thought of leaving was growing. I kissed her lips greedily again. After making herself presentable, Jessica stepped out of the way and let me open the door.

I told Jessica everything I knew about what was going on with Tyler and why we were headed to Montana.

She sat behind the wheel with her mouth open. "Poor Kate. I'm sure she's devastated."

"She's packed some things and headed back to her ranch. I'm not sure how Tyler will get her back."

We pulled to a stop at the airport, and Jessica turned to look at me. "I'm going to miss you. In the last few months, we haven't really spent much time apart. It's going to be strange not seeing you." She looked down at her hands in her lap.

I grabbed her hand, bringing a smile to her face. "I'll be home as soon as I can. Will you pick me up?"

"You don't even have to ask. I'll be here waiting." She looked back up at me.

"I should go." I got out of the car and grabbed my bag from the back seat while Jessica walked around to my side of the car.

"Call when you land?" She wrapped her arms around my neck. I felt like I was in an old movie with the plane behind me waiting to take off and the woman in my arms begging me not to go.

"Absolutely. It's going to be late." I said, leaning down to kiss her passionately. I dropped my bag and gathered her into my arms.

"I'll be up until I hear from you." She took a step back and looked at the plane, then back to me. "Come home to me." Her eyes danced but were also sad.

I pulled her into my arms and kissed her again with everything I had in me. "You can count on it. You're stuck with me now." Bending down, I grabbed my bag and turned to walk to the plane.

A whistle rang out behind me. "You sure look good walking away."

Glancing back over my shoulder, I gave her a wink. I walked up the stairs quickly, then turned and waved before I went through the door. When I flopped down in my seat, I looked out the window and saw Jessica leaning against the car with her arms crossed, waiting for the aircraft to take off.

I wasn't one to jet around in private planes and make people bend to my will, so this flight was so far from normal for me. I hated taking all these people away from their families as much as I hated being taken away from mine tonight.

The engines roared to life, and we taxied down the runway. I waved at Jessica through the window, and before I could look back, the plane was in the air.

"Mr. Morton, we expect a clear flight to Montana. We should be there around twelve thirty. Your father called and arranged for a car to be a car waiting for you. Keys will be in the console." The flight attendant delivered her message and walked to the back of the plane.

After half an hour or so, the flight attendant, whose nametag read Sarah, came by again. "Sir, we have reached cruising altitude. You can move about the cabin if you like. Would you like anything to drink?"

I glanced at my watch. "Sure, can I get a rum and Coke, please?"

She nodded as she walked away, then returned quickly with my drink. I had a renewed frustration with my older brother as I took my first sip. I had lost count of the number of times I'd had to bail him out of one ridiculous situation or another, but that had been over ten years ago.

All those times, driving around to find lost vehicles, random pickups at strange women's houses, and far too many bar rescues because he was too hammered to drive.

But Tyler had changed. He'd grown up. The way he ran both ranches was nearly to perfection. He had Kate at home, and I knew he was totally in love with her. So this didn't seem like the brother I knew now.

Just the thought of what I could be doing to Jessica right now increased the anger I was feeling. I was ready for a fight, and I thought it would do me some good to take my frustration out on him once and for all.

My drink was gone before I had a moment to savor it. The ice clanked in the glass as I set it down on the small table across from me. "Mr. Morton, can I get you another one?" Sarah always seemed to be only inches away.

I nodded, knowing I shouldn't have another, but there were three hours left on this flight, and being stuck up here wasn't helping my mood.

Remembering I had grabbed a book off my nightstand, I reached for it and set it on my lap while I waited for my drink to arrive.

I had always been a reader and loved picking up a book after my work was done on the ranch most days. It made me think of something other than the same old, same old. Books in which the main character leaves his life and starts over were my usual go-to reads. I would never leave Addison, but I always dreamed of taking her and running away to Alaska. Having a different life than the one I was raised in and thinking of all the adventures we could go on together.

Maybe I should take Addison and Jessica on a vacation. We needed to make memories outside the ranch and have fun together when I wasn't worried about cattle, horses, or the ten hired men I had to organize daily.

I stared out into the black sky and was startled out of my daydream. "Mr. Morton, we will begin our descent into Bozeman Badlands Private Airport in roughly five minutes." The pilot's voice came across the intercom, and I packed up the book and waited.

Safely landed, I waited for the door to open and the stairs

to be moved to the plane. I shook the pilot's hand As I walked to the door. "Tony, another pleasant flight, thank you."

As Tony released my hand, he asked, "Will you be staying overnight?"

"Yes, we have to. It's too late now to make the flight home, and the airport back home will be closed. With short notice like this, they won't make an exception." I exited the cabin, and Tony followed.

"Say hello to your wife when you get home and thank her for letting us steal you away." I shook his hand again and walked to the waiting car.

On the ground in Montana, I felt the anger building again. I was hours away from my daughter and my girlfriend. This was not where I wanted to be.

Connecting my phone to the car, I called Jessica.

"Hello?" a sleepy voice answered my call.

"I thought you were going to stay awake until I called." I joked with Jessica.

"Really, I just dozed off. Okay, well, maybe like an hour ago." She giggled on the other end of the line, and the longing I felt made me ache.

"Well, I just wanted to call and tell you I got here safely. But I have to make a half hour drive now, and I'll be in and out of service. How about I call you in the morning?"

"You better call me in the morning, or I might just end up on the doorstep of that ranch tomorrow afternoon."

"Is that a threat or a promise?" I asked huskily.

"A promise, cowboy."

"Hmm, that's very tempting." There was a laugh from her end of the line.

"Good night, drive safe," she almost whispered.

"Night, baby, talk to you tomorrow."

The line went dead, and I was alone again but wishing she was with me.

CHAPTER 15

*D*uring the drive, I imagined all kinds of terrible things I was going to do to my brother. And even worse things if he was with that hussy. I pulled up in front of the house to find it lit up like it was the middle of the afternoon instead of one in the morning. I took a deep breath and walked up to the door, pounding out my anger on it. Tyler opened the door, and my fist immediately met his face.

Tyler and I hadn't had a good fight in years. It was time to let out the frustration I had with him for taking me away from my family. I had lost Jessica for eight years, and now that we were back together, every moment away from her was torture. Here Tyler was, with a wonderful woman at home who had given up her life to save her family, and he was messing around on her, squandering the good thing he didn't even realize he had.

Taking steps inside the house as Tyler stumbled backward, I clenched my fists, ready to throw one again. "How could you do this?" I swung, and Tyler stopped the blow with his arm.

He was invested now. He caught me in the stomach, and I doubled over. I ran toward him, pinning him against the wall, and took advantage of a cheap shot to the kidney. He groaned.

"Rob, what the hell?"

I caught him in the jaw before he said anymore.

That's the way I liked my brother best, not talking. He could drone on for hours. We traded punches. I unleashed some of my rage , and Tyler was fighting for an explanation.

Soon, we both sat on the floor, panting and staring at each other.

"What on earth are you doing here? And what did I do to deserve that for a hello?" Tyler rubbed his jaw where I'd hit him.

Once my senses returned, I remembered the woman he was with. "Where is she?" I jumped up from the floor and stormed through the house.

"She? Who are you talking about? Who do you think is here?"

I turned and glared at Tyler. "Lona posted pictures of the two of you all over social media. She was draped all over you at dinner tonight, sitting on your lap with her hands everywhere they shouldn't have been. And yes, Kate—your wife—has also seen them. She moved out."

Tyler seemed to lose all color in his face. "That bitch. I guess there are no photos of me removing her from my lap and telling her to leave me alone? You have to believe me. I'd never hurt Kate like that. I love her more than anything. Rob, she's the only one I want."

"How the hell did she take so many pictures on your lap, then? Tyler, this is the old you rearing his ugly, and I do mean ugly, head." I crossed my arms in front of me and waited for the answer. Tyler wasn't a good liar, and during all the years I bailed him out, I could always tell when he was lying before he even started talking.

"I don't know. One second, I was in the most heated nego- tiations we had been having all evening, and the next thing I knew, everyone was laughing and having a great time. The deal was done, and I relaxed.

"I was getting up to settle the tab just as Lona strutted over and sat down. I don't even remember her having a phone in her hand to take pictures with." Tyler plopped down on the couch and let his head fall into his hands.

"She flung her arm around me, said some incoherent words. I stood, and she fell to the floor while I walked away. I came home and have been trying to call Kate since." He stood and ran past me to his bedroom. He started throwing his stuff into his bags.

"Rob, you have to believe me. I pushed her off my lap the second she sat down." He was pleading with me, and that was not something the old Tyler would have done. He would have made a joke and brushed it off. This version of my brother was a loyal husband, who I knew wouldn't hurt Kate after everything she had scarified for her family.

I was missing my family just because some woman from Tyler's past was jealous? That wasn't right. There had to be something else going on here, but Tyler was innocent, that I was sure of after speaking to him in person. "I gotta get home, Rob. This is so bad."

He called Delaney, but she hung up on him. His ashen face was now almost transparent. Despite my irritation with having to fly all the way here, I felt bad for him. Tyler knew the good thing he had, and I truly believed he wouldn't mess that up. Although, I wasn't sorry he was going home with some bruises. Years of bailing him out meant he deserved them, even if he was innocent on this occasion.

After Tyler packed his bags and headed out to the airport to make his milk run home, I was exhausted. I wished I could leave with him, but I had other business to attend to while I was here. Tomorrow was going to be busy if I was going to get to the bottom of this mess, and I needed to make heads roll, but sleep didn't come easy. All I could think of was how in love with Jessica I was.

I flopped down on the couch as the realization hit that I was completely in love with this woman again. To be honest, I had never not been in love with her. This mess needed to be cleaned up fast so I could get home.

I felt a driving need to claim her, make her mine permanently, so she wouldn't ever leave me again.

With the Lona situation figured out, I had to deal with Mike. He had been feeding business information to Lona all this time and he had to be stopped. I had long thought of him as a friend, and the thought of him being involved in this was disappointing. I needed to know why Tyler had been set up like this, and I wanted to catch Mike off guard. But I didn't want him pleading his case. We couldn't risk this happening again.

The following morning, I sat down with Mike. "Mike, thanks for meeting with me. Tyler had to head home, and I'll be taking over his duties here. So, due to confidential information being leaked to a third party who wasn't in the need to know, and that woman showing up to an important business meeting, your services will no longer be needed here." I slid the termination papers across the desk.

Our business manager had been feeding Lona information and making promises. I felt vindicated handing him the severance package our lawyer had drawn up. There was no time to relish in the victory, though. I had to start the search for a new person to keep things running here. I was out of my element and getting growly about it. My phone rang, and I didn't look at the number before I answered.

"Hello," I barked into the phone.

"Well, I guess I don't have to ask how things are going." Her voice on the other end of the line was concerned.

"It's just been a long day, and unfortunately, it's not going to end any time soon. But enough about that, how are you?" It was easy to change my tone. All she had to do was talk, and I felt like a weight was lifting off my shoulders.

"I'm fine. It's been a busy day here, but more importantly, what can I do to cheer you up?" Her voice was soft. She was too good for me, and I knew it.

"Come up here?" As much as I was joking, I wanted her here beside me.

She laughed, and it dissolved some of the stress in my body. "I can't, Rob. I have a meeting with a client tomorrow, but I might know a way I could get you into a better mood."

I sat up and grinned. "Oh yeah, how?" I knew this woman better than I knew myself, yet she continued to surprise me. Was it any wonder I'd fallen in love with her again?

Her voice dipped lower as she began. "Are you comfortable? Where are you?"

"Well, I'm sitting in my office."

"Hmm, is the door locked?"

I couldn't help but laugh as I got up to lock the door. "It is now. Where are you?"

"Me? I'm standing in my room. I just got out of the shower."

"What are you wearing?"

"Just a towel, but—oh no—it just fell off. So, I guess that means I'm naked now."

"Jess, you are torturing me." I rested my head back on my chair and let out a slow breath. Picturing her naked made my breathing and pulse speed up. "Do you have any idea what I would do if I was there with you naked?"

"Well, you could always just tell me what you would do." Her voice was seductive and playful. "I'm just going to lie down on my bed."

CHAPTER 16

I stood anxiously waiting on the tarmac. Rob's plane was fifteen minutes late. The week had gone by slowly, and I was over waiting, so I paced around my car. The clear blue sky made it easy to spot the airplane as it started its descent.

As the plane taxied by, I spotted Rob through the window, and I felt settled for the first time in almost seven days.

He walked off the plane, shook hands with the pilot, and jogged over to where I stood. I launched myself into his arms as he dropped his bag and held me tightly. Our lips met, and I suddenly felt light, like a weight had been lifted off my shoulders. I was overflowing with a happiness I wanted to explain, but no words could describe how I felt.

"You don't know how much I missed you," Rob said as we hugged.

"Oh, I might have some idea. I had the same week without you, remember." I leaned in and kissed him again. "We should get going if you want to be home when Addie gets off the bus."

He let me down, and I tossed the keys at him. "You're driving, cowboy."

He tossed his bag in the back seat, and we headed home. Rob rested his hand on my thigh, and I basked in the comfortable and familiar feelings this gesture brought. "You know, I realized something while I was gone. I am completely in love with you." His hand gripped my thigh tighter, and I placed mine over it.

"Rob, I know we've said these words before, and I've definitely had the feelings almost since the first time I saw you again, but I am in love with you, with my entire being." This wasn't a great place to declare our love. We were in the middle of the interstate where we couldn't stop, couldn't spend time in each other's arms.

We drove in happy silence. It was always something we had been able to do. We could be quiet and content together. There wasn't the need for incessant talking and constant conversation.

"What would you think about spending the night?" Rob's voice was calm and calculated. I could tell he was holding back, not wanting to get his hopes up.

"There's a bag in the trunk for such an occasion." I glanced at him from the corner of my eye, and he looked like he was on cloud nine. I felt good about this. We had been seeing each other for a while, and had spent the appropriate with Addison, so I felt ready for the next phase of our relationship to start.

It was one thing not achieved during round one for us, but I wasn't going to let that happen again. After I sent a quick text to my mother, I wouldn't worry about anything but being here with Rob.

"How long until Addie is home?" I asked as we pulled into the driveway.

"Um, about an hour." Rob looked at his watch, then up to me and wiggled his eyebrows. "I think I can figure out something to do with most of that time."

"Is that all you think about?" I rolled my eyes and flung

open my car door before he could get his hands on me. When I realized I could get to the side stairs of the porch before him, I took off running.

I looked back, and I could see him trying to figure out the quickest way to head me off. He decided the front stairs would get him to the door before me, but as I dashed for the side door, I heard him let out a defeated growl.

When I got into the house, he was leaning against the kitchen island with a sly grin across his face. Slowing my pace, I walked closer to him and arched my brow. "Well, you won.. What do I owe you?"

Rob grabbed one of my belt loops and pulled me toward him forcefully. "Oh, I think I have a few ways to claim my winnings." His phone rang, and he held up his finger. "Hold that thought."

"Hello? Yeah, just a bit ago. Are you serious? Right now? Addison comes home in forty-five minutes, and I plan to be here. Fine, I'll be right over." He slammed his finger on the red button and threw his phone on the counter.

"I've been summoned. Can we put this on hold for later?"

"There's nothing I can say that will keep you from the person who summoned you. That's something I haven't forgotten." I stood on my tiptoes and kissed him as passionately I could. "Something to help you remember what's waiting back here."

"Like I could forget." We kissed again and he left.

The clock ticked by slowly, and I wasn't sure he would make it back in time for the bus. Footsteps bounded up the stairs, and the door crashed open. Rob wasn't one to show emotion, but I could always read the feelings on his face.

"That man has lost his mind." Rob's frown was deeper than I'd ever seen. I hadn't ever seen his face so red, and I swore I could almost see steam coming out of his ears.

"Dad knew." Rob was pacing, and I was lost.

"Knew about what?" I stepped out of the way because I was sure Rob was so mad he didn't even see me standing in his path.

"He knew Lona had been causing trouble in Montana before Tyler went there. She's been asking questions, looking through books, and calling investors on behalf of The Lonestar." His arms were outstretched, and his mouth open, waiting for me to say something.

"Was Tyler aware?" The words were almost a whisper. I couldn't believe his dad would let those things happen. It didn't surprise me at all Brian knew what was happening in Montana. I was a little shocked he would have willingly sent Tyler into a potentially bad situation, but I should never put anything past him. Look at me being a little hypocrite, I was keeping my own secret from Rob and judging Brian for keeping his. This was not the time to bring up my secret, that was for sure. Rob was already spitting tacks about his father, I didn't need to add to the drama.

"Apparently not. It's not a good time to talk to Tyler, but we have to do something. My father can't be the one to oversee things in Montana anymore. Goodness knows what he let that crazy bitch look into." Rob walked to the table, yanked out a chair, and sat down, looking very lost.

"Okay, so let's think about this. She had access from Mike and to all the files, obviously. You need to call the bank and make sure that the only people with access are Tyler, Gavin, and you. I would even suggest removing your dad from the account until you can follow trails she left." There was a pad of paper and a pen on the counter, so I started making notes.

There was a rumble outside, which signaled the bus coming into the yard. "We will finish this later." Rob stood, quickly kissed me and turned to go get Addie off the bus.

Wʜᴀᴛ ᴄᴏᴜʟᴅ ʜᴀᴠᴇ ʙᴇᴇɴ ᴀᴠᴏɪᴅᴇᴅ ɪɴ ᴛʜɪs ꜰᴀᴍɪʟʏ ᴡɪᴛʜ Jᴇssɪᴄᴀ around? That might be a question I would have for the rest of my life. And guilt I would carry for letting her go without a fight. I was willing to fight for this family but when she needed me to fight for her all those years ago I failed. That wasn't going to happen again.

The bus pulled to a stop, and I could see a little head bobbing along the aisle between the seats. Addison stopped at the top of the stairs, and her smile lit up her face when she saw me. I caught her as she launched herself into my arms.

"Dad, you're back. I've missed you so much." Her arms squeezed my neck tight.

"Oh, I've missed you too, Squish." My arms tightened around her as I turned and walked into the house.

Jessica smiled when she saw us together. I set her down, and she started asking questions.

"Do you have to go back to Montana? Uncle Tyler came home, and you didn't. Why?" She rattled on for what seemed like forever before I could get a word in. I didn't want her to worry about why I was gone and why Tyler came home. She was too young to know.

"Hey, Addie, why don't you tell your dad about your field trip yesterday?" Jessica changed the subject, guiding the conversation away from my time in Montana.

It felt good to be home with my girls. I was definitely a homebody, and they needed me. The evening flew by, and I was suddenly exhausted. When I glanced at the clock, I took a deep breath. "Addison, it's bedtime sweetie."

"Will you take me to bed, Dad?" Her voice was quiet and tired.

"You never have to ask. It's always yes." I stood and took her hand, and after a week away, I got to put my daughter to bed. All felt right in the world again.

"Jessica, will you be here in the morning this time?" Her

tired eyes could barely stay open, so I scooped her up and waited for Jessica's response.

"Yes, Addie, I will be. Is that okay?"

"Good, see you in the morning." Addison wrapped her arms around my neck. I smiled at Jess and turned to take Addison to her room.

When I came back to the living room, Jessica had the mess from supper cleaned up and the lights turned down, and she was relaxing on the couch.

"You have no idea how nice it is to know you don't have to make that drive tonight. I can hold you in my arms and wake up with you in them too." I sat down beside her and brought Jessica close to me.

"I'm not complaining about not making that drive tonight. Also, I think waking up in your arms will be almost like heaven. It's been a long week without you." Jessica cuddled into me and sighed contently.

"Think we should call it a night?" I whispered in her ear.

"Sounds like a good idea to me." We both stood, and I lead Jessica down the hall to my room.

"Oh, I forgot to grab my bag, it must still be in the car." I never let go of her hand and kept walking. When we entered the room, her bag was sitting on the end of the bed next to mine.

"I wouldn't make you carry it in." Casually, I reached around her and closed the door. I had Jessica in my arms the moment it clicked shut.

"Lock the door," she whispered as she turned and walked away from me. She glanced back at me as she grabbed her bag and walked into the bathroom, smiling slyly as she did.

Waiting for her to return from the bathroom was agony. I had waited for a week to hold her, and it felt like she was taking longer than usual to get ready for bed. I sat on the edge of the bed, feeling anxious. Would sitting here make it seem like I was bored? Maybe I should relax back on the bed.

I moved to the head of the bed quickly, adjusting my pillow and reclining back. Did this make me look like a little too eager? When had this become so difficult? It wasn't like Jessica and I hadn't slept together before tonight. In an effort not to seem too enthusiastic, I sat up, ready to change positions again.

The door of the bathroom opened as I was half in and half out of the bed. Jessica came to a halt and looked at me, confused. "What are you doing?"

She stood before me wearing a black silky robe, her gorgeous legs exposed due to the short length of the hem. I followed those legs up to her torso and onto her breasts, which the robe hugged perfectly . Her perky nipples created perfect tents under the black fabric, and the neck gaped just enough so I could see the curve of her cleavage. She was driving me crazy, and I was sure she knew it.

I got to my feet and walked over to her. "Okay, look, I was trying not to look too eager, or too bored, while I was waiting for you. Then my brain went into overtime, and I didn't know what to do."

The smile that crossed her face turned in to a full out laugh. She moved toward me and placed her hand on my chest as she leaned in to kiss me. "It would never cross my mind to think of you as either of those things. But I'm eager, so you should get out of those clothes."

She wouldn't have to ask me twice. I ripped open my shirt and tossed it aside as Jessica reached out to and undo my belt buckle and pop open the button on my jeans. I grabbed her in my arms and moved us both toward the bed.

The tie on her robe fell away with one quick pull. Pushing it off her shoulders revealed her goddess-like naked body. "You weren't lying; you are eager."

"For you, I am." Her hands slid down my sides and paused on my hips before she slid my pants down and over my ass.

I stepped out of my pants as I laid her down on the bed. "I dreamed about this moment all week," I whispered as I let my hands move all over her body.

CHAPTER 17

*D*uring the month after Rob returned from Montana, I spent as much time with him and Addison as possible. I was falling in love with Rob all over again and being around Addison was a balm for my soul. Sometimes I caught myself thinking of us as a family. In these moments, nothing mattered but the three of us.

After dinner one night, Rob and I sat on the porch swing listening to the cicadas. It was peaceful and was everything I'd ever wanted. But I couldn't keep secrets from him anymore. They were eating me up inside, even more than the mess in New York had. I had to talk to him, tell him the truth. So many truths.

"Rob, there's something you should know." My voice was shaking, and my breathing increased as my heart raced. There wasn't an easy way to tell him this, and stalling now wouldn't help.

Rob shifted on the porch swing so he was facing me. His face changed from content to worried. His brows were furrowed, and he took my hand in his. "You know you can tell me anything. There are no secrets between us."

If he only knew that wasn't true, but one revelation tonight would be enough. I took a deep breath and looked at him. "Remember when we talked about our future all those years ago and that we wanted to fill our home with kids?" I picked up the pillow from beside me and hugged it.

His face lit up, and his eyes danced. "Baby, are you pregnant?" He took my face in his hands and kissed me passionately. Rob wrapped his arms around me, hugging me so tight I couldn't move or breathe. "We're going to fill this house with love and laughter. I can't wait to have a dozen kids with you. How are you feeling? Have you been sick?"

Suddenly realizing he was crushing me, he let me go and took my hand. His face changed from elation to concern, and my heart dropped into the depths of my stomach.

"Rob, I can't have kids." I thought I was okay with my diagnosis since I'd had five years to come to terms with it, but a tear rolled down my cheek and landed on my hand. Rob moved away from me on the swing, and his face told me everything I needed to know. He was looking at me like half a woman. Slowly, he reached up and brushed the tear away with his thumb, then put his arm around me. I couldn't bring myself to look back up at him.

"It's the one thing I'm supposed to do as a woman, but my body has betrayed me."

"Jess, I want you to see a specialist. It doesn't matter what it will cost." Rob's eye pleaded with me.

Shaking my head, I let my eyes fall to the ground. "I've looked into every option. I had an ectopic pregnancy, and I had to have surgery to remove one fallopian tube and an ovary. The other ovary never produced good quality eggs, but we still tried IVF for years... and nothing." I couldn't even look at him, but I could almost hear the wheels turning in his head as he sorted through options.

"You can't give up, Jessica. There must be something we can do. Try new treatments." His voice cracked as I shook my head again.

"I won't put myself through the soul-crushing defeat that every negative test brought. The agony of loss after every miscarriage took every ounce of hope I had. It's not something I want you to experience. It's taken a lot of therapy sessions to keep me from letting myself slip back into those feelings. In fact, I still see a therapist about it."

When I found the courage to look at him, Rob's mouth gaped and his eyes were wide. He shook his head and gave me a sympathetic smile, but I could see the sadness creep into his almost black eyes. He was trying not to, but he never could hide what showed in his eyes.

The silence was awkward, and I finally broke it, my words soft and cracked. "Please say something."

"I… um… wow, that's not at all what I thought you were going to say. Obviously."

"I should go."

"No, Jess, please stay."

"Honestly, Rob, you have some thinking to do. I've had five years to come to terms with this, and you've had five minutes. We'll talk tomorrow."

There was no way I could sit there and wait for him to say something. I kissed his cheek, stood, walked to my car, and left. He hadn't moved from the porch. It looked like he was frozen in place. That's what hurt the most. He hadn't moved.. He didn't stop me from leaving. I told him he needed to think, but I hadn't expected him to let me walk away.

The drive home felt like it took forever, and when I made it home, I quietly walked in the front door. Many times, I knew living with my mom wasn't the best idea, but tonight, I was glad I wasn't walking into an empty house.

"Jessica, you're home early." Mom looked down at her watch. There was concern written across her face.

"I told him, Mom."

"You told him what?" She was trying to figure out which one of my secrets I'd finally spilled.

"That I can't have kids."

She dashed over to me, pulling me to the couch, and wrapped me in her arms. "Oh, my girl. What did he say?"

"Nothing. He just stared at me and let me leave. I left him sitting on the porch swing," I said, putting my head down on her shoulder and letting the tears fall.

"I can't believe it. I really thought he would be different. Jeremy said it didn't matter, that we could adopt as many kids as I wanted, but in the end, I wasn't enough of a woman for him. Now it looks like it's happening again."

"Honey, there was more than that wrong with Jeremy. Don't forget he was sleeping around before the ink was dry on your marriage license. The baby thing was just his way out." Her voice was flat. The same way it was every time we talked about Jeremy.

"You never liked him."

"I never liked him." She shook her head and arched her brow. "I didn't hide it when you were together, and I'm not going to hide it now."

"Oh, Mom, I should have listened."

"Yes, you should have, but that's water now. You set fire to that bridge, and it's time to build a new one." She kissed my head and smoothed out my hair before she set her cheek down on my head.

"I would give Rob a few days. He's a good man, and I don't really think this will scare him off."

Through my sobs I whispered, "I hope you're right."

We spent a quiet night watching TV and eating ice cream. It was my mom's sure-fire way to get over heartbreak. It had worked when I'd broken up with my seventh-grade boyfriend, when my date for prom never showed up, and when I came home after the first time I caught Jeremy cheating.

Two days passed, and I hadn't received so much as a text from Rob.

"Okay, that's it. No more pouting about. I need help, and

you're all I've got. Let's head out back to the garden and pick raspberries because we have jam to make." Mom walked into the living room and pulled the blanket off my legs, startling me enough that I slid off the couch and onto the floor. "The farmers' market is starting a week early this year, and with you here, I'll be ready in time."

She handed me a basket, and we walked out to the raspberry patch. This is what I'd missed while in New York. Some of my best memories involved spending time in the garden with her. When we couldn't talk to each other, we came out here and worked. Or if we needed a break from the world, we would come out to hide in the tomato vines, and she would tell stories about growing up with her sisters.

While we were in the berry patch, I heard the phone in the kitchen ring and looked up at Mom. "Let it go to the answering machine." She waved it off.

"Mom, it's voicemail now." I laughed, and she shook her head.

"Same thing. Less chatter, more picking, and quit eating more than you put in your basket." Her hands were on her hips, and she was trying to look mad.

I burst out laughing. "Yes, ma'am."

The downside to working in silence was that it gave me far too much time to think about the past.

I thought back to the night we were on the hill where Rob's house now sat. We'd sat in awkward silence after I told him I'd be leaving for Manhattan in two days. Rob wasn't happy that my move to New York City was happening so soon. Part of me wondered if he'd hoped he could talk me out of going.

"Why do you have to go now? Can't you wait for a few weeks? It's so busy on the ranch right now." He let go of my hand and moved away from me.

"Rob, please understand. This opportunity won't come up again. It's not every day that the premier event planner in

Manhattan offers a nobody a job." I dropped my head in my hands. He didn't understand, and I knew he never would. As supportive as he had been until now, it didn't surprise me that this was happening. It was a typical Rob response to disappointment. He ran away every time.

I looked over at him, and he was staring off into space. "Rob, are you going to say anything else?"

"What do you want me to say? You're going to do whatever you want, and there's nothing I can do to keep you here. Your mind was made up the second you sent the application, with no regard for my feelings." He stood and turned his back to me. "You only ever think of yourself."

I felt like I had been launched off the earth as I jumped up, ready to battle with him. "Are you listening to yourself? You knew this was my dream. I have never been shy about telling you what I want out of life, and I thought you wanted those things too." I walked around to face him. "So all the talk about getting away from your dad and this ranch was what? Were you lying to me? Getting my hopes up that you would actually come with me?"

Rob started to walk away, and I hated when he did that. "No, Robert Morton. You don't get to walk away from this." I ran and stood in front of him. "You don't get to walk away from me."

"Me? You won't let me walk away from you? That's rich, Jess." A disgruntled smirk crossed his face. "That's exactly what you're doing to me. You're the one walking away from me." He shoved his hands in his pockets and stood there, waiting for me to say something.

"Rob, I want you to come with me. It doesn't have to be tomorrow, just as long as you come." The tears began to fall down my face. I hated crying, and I hated crying in front of him even more. "Rob, please say you will." My voice had lost all strength. I whispered my hope.

"I can't."

Those two words broke me. The look on his face shattered my soul, and watching him walk away nearly killed me. I stood without moving for what seemed like an eternity. Somehow, I made it to my car and drove home.

She didn't even have to ask. Mom always knew when something was wrong. I walked into her outstretched arms and she let me cry. "Are you going to tell me what happened, or am I going to put the pieces together?" Guiding me to the couch, she pushed me down gently and sat beside me.

I wiped my face and took a few shaky breaths before I started. "I told him about the job offer, and that I took it. Then I said I had to leave tomorrow, and he changed. He said I was selfish for leaving." My head dropped over onto my mom's shoulder. "It's over. He isn't coming with me, and I'm going to New York alone and single." My tears started again, and we sat together in silence.

Hours later, a knock at the door made me move off the couch. I wiped my face and knew it would do little to help how I looked. Silently hoping Rob would be standing on the other side of the door, I opened it.

"Mr. Morton," I said, surprised by the identity of my visitor. Rob's dad stood before me, looking very serious. Rob favored him and could almost have passed as his twin in side-by-side pictures from his youth. "Please come in." I stepped out of the way, and he walked into the house.

"I won't take much of your time, Jessica. You're probably wondering why I'm here. I want to give you this," he said as he handed me an envelope. I turned it over and opened it. I'd expected a letter from Rob, hoping to work things out or an explanation of his thoughts. What I found was a check for $40,000. My mouth dropped open, and I looked up at him.

"Sir, what is this for?" I looked back down at the paper and felt my eyes bugging out of my head.

"It's for New York. Rob told me you were leaving. This money has some strings attached. If you want the money, you agree to them, am I understood?" I nodded and waited for him to continue. He took a step closer to me and spoke softly. His voice was low, almost a whisper. "You leave and leave my son alone. No contact, no rekindling a relationship. You forget you ever had a relationship with him. Move on, Miss Walshay."

I could feel tears welling in my eyes, and my chin quivered. "Why?"

"I need my son. There's no way I would let him run after you. Do you agree to the terms?" His voice was filled with hate.

All I could do was nod. He turned to go and closed the door behind him. My tears fell on the envelope as I turned and looked into my mother's concerned eyes.

$\mathcal{A}$n hour later, with the berries picked, we were in the kitchen. I was standing at the sink washing and sorting while Mom was stirring the jam. There was a knock on the door, and Mom looked up. "You get it, dear. I don't want to stop stirring."

I nodded, wiped my hands on my apron, and walked to the front door.

"Rob?" I said, surprised to see him standing at the door. The dark circles under his eyes were an indication that he hadn't slept well. He still made my heart skip a beat after all these years.

"Hey. Got a minute?"

"I'm helping Mom with her jam for the farmers' market." I stood in the doorway with my arms crossed.

Mom peeked around the corner. "No, you aren't. Get out of here and talk to that boy. Hi, Rob."

"I'll have her back soon, Mrs. Walshay," Rob called into the house.

"She's under foot. I don't need her back anytime soon."

I rolled my eyes, and Rob let out a chuckle.

"Again, I need to move," I reminded myself, but I took off

my apron and tossed it at Mom before slipping my shoes on. I wasn't sure how much more heartache I could take, but for Rob, who tended to run instead of facing problems, being here and wanting to talk was a big step, so I was going to try.

"Want to go for a drive? That way we have privacy."

Jessica nodded, but her face told a different story. Her eyes were full of pain, her brows creased, and her lips pursed. She grabbed her coat and bag and walked ahead of me to the truck, barely sparing me a glance.

I drove until we were out of town and sitting at Old Bluff Lookout. Nobody came here anymore since the river had been dammed up. Apparently, looking out over a dry riverbed at weeds wasn't romantic.

"Jess, I want to tell you how sorry I am about the other day. The way I handled it, or rather didn't express my thoughts, was terrible." My words sounded lame to me, and I hoped they sounded better to Jessica.

I gripped the steering wheel and turned to look at her. She stared out the windshield, refusing to acknowledge me. I'd screwed up so badly.

"What I should have said was it doesn't matter. Of course, in a perfect world, I want kids with you. I want our daughter to have your straw gold hair and your bright smile, but it doesn't matter as long as I have you."

A tear rolled down her cheek. "I've heard those words before, and I still ended up alone. If you don't mean them, or if you think you'll change your mind, please tell me now. I can't go through being told it doesn't matter again only to find out it does."

"What did he do to you?"

Jessica turned her head toward me. "What did he do? He started fooling around on me two months after our wedding.

Then he decided children would help our relationship. When we ended up not pregnant month after month, I went through fertility testing and found out it would be almost impossible for me to get pregnant without medical intervention." She closed her eyes. I was sure she was thinking back to that time, and watching the emotions play out on her face was heartbreaking. "We tried so many IVF rounds I lost count, and those didn't work. I suffered miscarriage after miscarriage and an ectopic pregnancy through it all. He said we could adopt all the kids we wanted, and he'd be happy. Three months later, he came to me and told me his mistress was pregnant."

I balled up my fists and slammed them on the steering wheel as the anger built in me, making her jump. I breathed heavily and waited for her to continue.

"He said biological children were the one thing he wanted in this world. Since I couldn't give him that, he wanted a divorce so he could build a real family."

I opened my fists and gripped the steering wheel so tight my knuckles were turning white. I imagined it was his neck, that I was squeezing the life right out of that weasel. I had never wanted to hurt a man more than I did right now.

"I'm not him. Despite my behavior over the last couple days, which made it seem like I am. Jess, look at me, please."

She turned toward me, and the look on her face made my heart break. As much as I knew I hadn't handled the news well, I would never have hurt her like he did. Seeing her cry made me tear up. I reached out and brushed her tears away. Resting my palm on her cheek, I took a deep breath to calm my nerves and slow my thoughts.

She had laid herself bare, and it was time for me to do the same.

"I've been thinking about the future. Jessica, I only want you. Our life together will be whatever we make it, regardless of how or if we add more kids to it." It was a lie. I had always wanted more kids, but I wanted her more. There were other ways to bring kids into our home, but right now wasn't the time to get into that discussion.

Her eyes changed from pained to hopeful before her face relaxed.

"Are you sure? I don't want you to regret this." She had turned to look out the side window. I held her heart in my hands, and I knew that the next thing I said would have the power to build up or further destroy Jessica's confidence.

"My only regret is that I didn't tell you this two days ago. Can you ever forgive me?" I felt a cold sweat break out on my forehead while my hands shook as they rested on the seat between us, and I tapped my toe inside my boot.

"You're forgiven," she whispered as she put her hand on mine and scooted over to the middle seat.

ROB AND I HAD SETTLED INTO AN OLD-MARRIED-COUPLE routine. Well, a married couple that lived in separate homes. Addie and I had grown increasingly comfortable around each other, and there was a nice flow to our lives over the next few weeks.

There was still the issue of the money Brian had given me, and that hung around my neck like a noose, casting a shadow over our domestic bliss. The only person I could think of that might have some answers about what I should do about Brian and the money I had taken to leave was Kate. She knew what he was capable of, and I hoped she would listen.

I'd texted Kate beforehand to be sure she was home and that we would be alone. I knocked on the door and waited for Kate to answer.

"Jessica, if that's you, come on in," Kate called from inside the house.

I hesitantly opened the door and poked my head in. "You sure?"

"I'm in the kitchen."

I closed the door behind me and followed the sound of her voice.

"Sorry, I'm making burgers." She turned and showed me her meat-covered hands and made a face. "I'm almost done. Have a seat."

Her smile could ease the most worried of minds. It was genuine, and her eyes smiled as much as her mouth. I hadn't been close to Kate when we were kids. She was a few years older, and other than going to the same school, I didn't know her well when we were growing up.

"I'm so happy you called." Kate washed and dried her hands before grabbing the pot of coffee and mugs. She poured two cups and set one in front of me, then sat down across the table. "It looks like you've got something on your mind. You never look this worried."

After the situation in Montana several months before, Tyler was able to explain the misunderstanding and setup he'd been involved in with Lona. Now, they were blissfully happy, and Kate was almost halfway through her pregnancy. She had the most perfect baby bump and looked absolutely gorgeous. Kate rested her hands on the round belly in front of her as I sat staring at it. Once again, my heart sank, knowing that would be a feeling I would never experience. There was a small pang in my heart, knowing I wouldn't hold my own babies. I would never know the thrill of feeling the first movements of a little one.

Shaking myself out of my pity party, I looked up. There wasn't any great way to transition into this conversation, so I just started talking. "Kate, I have a secret, and I think I'm going to burst if I don't tell someone. I know I should tell Rob, and don't worry, I will, but I need a practice run first."

"Jessica, are you pregnant?" Kate's eyes lit up like Rob's had. I needed to start blurting out my problems so people might quit asking me if I'm having a baby. I spilled that secret to Kate and watched her eyes change from elation to sadness as the realization hit her that I would never know the feelings she was experiencing right now. She looked at me with pity, even though she tried to hide it. I was used to it.

I looked down into the black liquid, took a deep breath, and continued, "When Rob and I broke things off all those years ago, Brian paid me to leave. But I had to agree to stay away and to keep from contacting Rob."

Kate choked on her coffee.

"He what?" she croaked out, trying to clear her throat.

"I wanted to try life in New York. I didn't have the money to go, but then Brian stepped in." The shame I felt made it impossible to make eye contact, so I picked up my coffee cup and took a sip.

"So, what's the big secret?"

"Rob doesn't know, and a caveat to receiving the money was that he couldn't know. We fought the evening before Brian showed up at the house, and I left the next day. We never talked again. Until your wedding."

"Okay, why did he want you gone?" Her jaw was clenched and her eyes narrowed.

"I wasn't good enough. I grew up on the 'wrong side of the tracks' with a single mother, and definitely didn't run in the right circles." I picked up my cup but never took a sip of my coffee, and knew I needed to tell Kate the entire story. "Rob wanted to come with me. To get me settled in and help me get started with a new life. He didn't like the idea of me going alone. I always knew he would want to come home, but we had planned a life there for a while."

Kate was riveted as I spoke. She hadn't taken her eyes off me and was hunched over the table to get closer.

"But then I got this amazing job and needed to leave faster than Rob was ready for. He said he wasn't coming with me at all, and we had this huge fight. Then later that night, Brian came to see me. He told me there was no way he would let Rob go with me, and he handed me an envelope. I will never forget what he said, 'Here's $40,000. You'll be set for months while you get settled at your job. Leave tomorrow morning and never breathe a word of this to Rob.'

"I couldn't even protest before he turned and left because I was so stunned. So, I packed everything I could fit in my car, and was gone. A few months later, I confided in my mom, and she told me to come clean then. But it was easier to stay gone and avoid him. Then I met Jeremy, and life seemed to get easier again."

"It was better to make you disappear than let Rob be in love?" Kate flopped back in her chair and crossed her arms. "Brian is something else. Always conniving, trying to get something out of people, so this doesn't surprise me. Unfortunately, I can believe he wanted to ruin Rob's chance to be happy." Kate's cheery disposition was gone. I knew she had her issues with Brian, and that's why I knew I could confide in her.

"I'm not sure it had anything to do with Rob being happy or not. It had everything to do with the thought of Rob leaving the ranch. Kate, I'm sorry to dump this on you, but I had nobody else to talk to. My mom doesn't want to hear any more about it." Letting my head fall into my hands, I groaned. "I never thought this would come back to bite me. Oh, Kate, what am I going to do?"

She stood, walked to the sink, then turned before speaking. "You're going to go tell Rob everything. Trust me, hiding Brian's antics isn't going to help at all. So many of the issues we had could have been avoided if I had just told Tyler his father was going to continue trying to ruin my family." Kate came back to the table and sat next to me.

"Jess, just tell him. It's won't be easy, and I'm sure things may be rocky, but if you really want this relationship to work, you have to," Kate said and rested her hand on mine.

Just tell him. The words were so simple, but they sent fear into my heart. I thought back to our dates, our nights, and Addison. How could I possibly lose her? She had become my world, and I didn't want to hurt her. I looked out the window and knew, with this one secret, I could end up alone. Without my second chance at love and a life with Rob. There would be no coming back from this. He would accept me or he would leave.

CHAPTER 19

With Addie staying over at Tyler and Kate's, Jessica and I had a rare night alone. I appreciated the time together without little eyes and ears close by. Addison was my world, but sometimes I longed to be alone with Jessica. Kate noticed that today and took advantage of the way Addie adored her. Jessica and I decided to take a walk down to the river. The sun was just beginning to dip below the horizon, and it shone across the water. I looked over at Jessica and got lost in the beauty that sat by my side.

"Rob, why are you staring at me?"

"I stare because every time I look at you, I can't believe you're here sitting next to me. I know we haven't been back together long…"

I looked into the blazing fire before us. My heart raced and my hands shook. "And I know you're still trying to sort out your past, but I don't want this moment to slip away again. I was a fool to let you go all those years ago. I should have followed you and fought for us."

Tears slid down her face as we both remembered that night. Time had a funny way of keeping things at bay until they needed to be out in the open again.

I leaned over toward Jessica, placed my rough, permanently tan hand at the base of her neck, and gently pulled her to me. Our lips met, and time seemed to stop.

Breaking the kiss, she whispered, "I thought I wanted more than this, Rob. I wanted to see things. Spend time in a place where there were no dark night skies. I wanted to ride the subway, walk in Times Square… see everything I couldn't see here." Her voice trailed off. "Can I tell you a secret that's been eating at me all these years?"

I wrapped my arm around her and brought her into my embrace.

"You can tell me anything."

"It wasn't worth it. Giving up the life I left, the life we should have had. I was so wrong. And—and , Rob, your father paid me to leave and never see you again. I didn't want to agree, but I didn't feel like I had a choice."

I could feel my brows furrow and my jaw clench. My stomach dropped as I processed what she had just said. This couldn't be real.

"This has to be a mistake. He wouldn't…" My voice trailed off because I, in fact, knew he would. There was no doubt in my mind. Somehow, I knew in the back of my mind her leaving wasn't all her idea. Jessica had dreamed of going, but she didn't have the funds to leave. Then, suddenly, she was gone, and I was alone.

"Rob, please say something." Her hands were shaking, and I could tell she was on the verge of tears.

As much anger as I had inside me, I knew she would have been intimidated, and he would have made it worth her while to go. I couldn't blame her for it. He made her loftiest dreams come true.

Gently, I put my hand under Jessica's chin and lifted her head so she had to look at me. "Want to know something? I would have never stopped you. Visiting a place where there were no dark skies, I could do. Live there? Not my thing. I don't need to see everything, but—God—that porch light would have been on every night waiting for you to come back and tell me everything you saw."

A tear rolled down her cheek as she looked away. "I know you would have waited for me forever, but it wasn't fair to you," she whispered as she avoided looking at me. "There wasn't a day that went by when I didn't regret the decision to take your dad's money. I cried every night for months and picked up the phone to call you every single day, but I was so sure you would hate me."

My heart broke because there wasn't a night that passed that I didn't want to talk to her, hear her voice. Hell, just hearing that she was alive and well would have been enough.

I smiled at Jessica when she finally looked up at me. "I could never hate you. I picked up my phone so many times, hoping your number would be the same, but I never had the courage to call."

Shifting on the river bank, I pulled her close to me. "You were chasing a dream, and once I accepted that, I knew it was where you were supposed to be. We would read newspaper articles over the years about your triumphs and fantastic events. I was so proud every time."

"You followed my career?" Her face filled with shock and love.

"Of course I did. It was a way to feel like I was keeping you close. As far as my dad goes, I will deal with him." I looked down at my hands.

"I have the money to pay him back. Every time I planned an event, I would put money aside to one day pay him back. I carry the check around in my wallet, waiting for the day I can give it back to him." She looked down river, avoiding eye contact with me again.

"See, that's why you're a better person than most. Anyone who was paid to leave wouldn't carry around the payback money waiting for the right time to give it back."

I took a deep breath, rubbing my hand over her knuckles. If this was the night for baring our souls, I needed to tell her my secret too, and it wouldn't be easy. But I couldn't stand to see the guilt that had been wreaking havoc on her sweet soul for years.

Her confession caused feelings of guilt to wash over me like waves, and I had to tell her the truth. "It's my turn for a confession now."

"I'm afraid I'm the one who caused him to come see you. I asked my dad for the money. My plan backfired a little, I guess, but I did know he was going to sneak off and give you the money."

I took her hands in mine, but she immediately pulled them away like she had touched a hot stove.

"You asked him to pay me to leave?" Her voice barely registered above a whisper. She stood quickly and backed away from me, turning to head back to the house where her car was.

"Jessica, please don't leave. We need to talk about this. It's not what you're thinking." I caught up to Jessica before she'd made it too far. I grabbed for her arm and turned her toward me.

"I'd decided I needed to go with you. After our fight, I went to him for the money. I told him I was going with you." I cupped her chin while she searched my face for more explanation.

"My dad lost his mind when I told him I wanted to leave. He told me the future of this ranch would end without me here, but I didn't care. My heart wasn't here, it's always been with you."

Tears flowed down her face. The revelations tonight had brought out a lot of emotions for us to come to terms with. I knew we would be fine, but I had to face the reality that I couldn't spend my life without her.

"Rob, I need to go." Her words were whispered, and she didn't look at me.

"No, you don't. I'm sorry, Jess, but I won't let you leave like this. We have to stop running. Our life together can't be based on running away and meeting back up when time has passed and the dust has settled. Please stay." I rested my hands on her shoulders, keeping her where she stood.

She slipped from my hold and turned away from me again, but I caught her and wrapped my arms around her, keeping her with me. My heart was breaking seeing her like this. Jessica's breathing became shallow and quick, and I could feel her heart beat like it was going to pound right out of her chest. She pushed out of my arms and put some space between us.

"Rob, no matter who I try to blame, it boils down to me. I'm the problem. I'm the one who left, and I'm the one who walked away. Good lord, I didn't even question it when your father handed over the money."

All these years, I thought I was the reason she left, but in reality, she took money and hightailed it out of town. I was shocked she'd even take his money.

"Rob, you must have feelings about this."

I looked at her in the setting sun, and I could feel the anger boiling in me. "You want me to say something? Fine. Do I blame you for leaving? No, I don't. But you did crush the life out of me. Yes, I get it, you were chasing your dreams, but you did that without me. Going alone. It killed me, Jess."

"Why didn't you come to me that night if you knew your dad was up to something?" Jessica had found her voice.

"Because I never imagined you could be so easily bought." She stumbled backward. I knew it was a low blow, but she wanted to know, and I was angry.

Tears flowed down my face. I backed away from her, and suddenly, I could see she wasn't prepared for my honesty.

"I was trying to get the money together for us to go

together. I didn't want you to leave me alone. Life without you wasn't anything I wanted to live." There was the truth of the matter, I had finally told her.

"You never said anything."

"Why do you think I was working so hard? Did you think I liked spending every waking moment away from you? That was the only way I could make your dreams come true. You left me." Words were flowing out of me, and I couldn't stop them.

"You left us, Jessica." I was upset and needed to be. Up until now, we had been living behind rose-colored glasses, pretending we were okay, but we weren't. We were both angry, and I still had to deal with my father, but the one thing I wanted above anything else was to be with Jessica, even after these revelations.

"I can't live in the past, and I want you, Jessica. I always have. It's going to take some time to work through these feelings, but baby, I can't live without you again."

I walked back toward her. I was long past hiding my emotions from her, and I let myself cry as she sobbed into my chest. It was the first time we had really mourned the life my father had taken away from us.

"I have to go," she whispered and walked away.

"Jess, please text when you get home." My words felt like they were spoken into the air and taken away on the breeze. She didn't acknowledge me at all.

CHAPTER 20

There was no way I could process this. For all these years, I thought I left for him, and now I found out I left because of him. If he hadn't asked his dad for the money, none of this would have happened. Rob had wanted to go with me, and he tried everything he could to make it happen. But he never told me. And I hadn't told him that his dad paid me to leave either.

Once again, lack of communication was eating away at our relationship. It hadn't only ruined the relationship the first time, but it was about to ruin our second chance.

I didn't remember the drive home, which scared me just a little. When I walked in the door, Mom was sitting on the couch waiting with two mugs of hot cocoa and a bowl of popcorn.

"You know." I kicked the door closed with my foot, dropped my purse and my coat, and flopped onto the gaudy floral couch my mom refused to get rid of because 'there's nothing wrong with it.'

"I never thought this would happen. There was always a chance things could go bad, but mom, this is beyond bad."

There appeared to be no end to my tears. I thought I'd cried them all on the drive home, but they kept falling.

"Well, girlie, I don't know what to tell you. I always thought this would go badly, and unfortunately, I'm right. But that doesn't mean I want to see you hurting." She leaned forward, grabbed the mugs, and handed one to me.

"Mom, he was working to have the money to come with me. He had gone to Brian to ask for the money when I told him I was leaving early. Rob didn't even know anything about it." I wailed the last part, and I felt slightly overdramatic, but it seemed warranted.

"Have some hot cocoa before it's cold." Mom did her best to calm me down, and she knew cocoa would comfort me. She patted my head, which was resting on her shoulder. She reached for the remote and pushed play.

Although I often complained about moving back to my childhood home, this was one reason I was happy to be living with my mom. She always knew just how to deal with a broken heart.

Dirty Dancing was over. My tears had quit falling about the time Johnny and Baby danced at the Shelldrake, and I felt exhausted.

"Mom, thanks for tonight." I wrapped my arms around her.

"Oh, it feels like old times, dear." I let her go and stared at her. "We had quite a few of these nights, Jessica. Don't even try to pretend it's not true, it seems like they happened at least once a month." She stood, grabbed the mugs, and headed to the kitchen.

I followed behind her with the popcorn. "Okay, who do you think was the worst breakup?"

She turned and leaned against the counter. "David Booth. You thought you were going to marry him. Senior year, two weeks before graduation, you were devastated. I thought we would never get you through the graduation ceremony without puffy eyes and a runny nose."

Mom's smile made me think back to that time. He was supposed to be my forever. Oh, how wrong I had been. I had always fallen for guys easily. They were usually the bad boy and always left me in tears.

All that changed when I met Rob. He made me ditch the bad boys and rethink who I had been spending time with. He was a hardworking, loyal, and a wonderful man. He hadn't changed; he was still that same man.

"Jessica, go to bed. Sleep on all your thoughts, and hopefully they will be clear in the morning. Oh, and no dreaming about David Booth. He turned out to be useless. Good night, girlie." She hugged me and walked down the hall to her room.

I walked around, turning the lights off, and stopped in the hallway to look at my parents' wedding photo. The way my mom looked at my dad in this photo was what I'd always longed for.

They were so young, had their whole lives ahead of them, and never got to have the life they dreamed about. I blew a kiss to my dad and went up to my room.

Taking my phone out of my back pocket, I saw four texts from Rob. I felt a pang of guilt for not letting him know I was home. It buzzed in my hand with another text from him.

Rob: I'm hoping since I haven't gotten a call from your mom, that means you got home okay.

Rob: Good night Jess, I love you.

Me: I love you too.

Laying down on my bed, I let my head fall back onto the pillow and stared at the ceiling.

I wished my phone would ring. His voice was what I needed, but I wasn't going to be the one to make the call.

Morning dawned, and it was not the wake-up I had planned. I woke to the sound of mom laughing and talking to someone I expected was Mr. Radliff. I was sure I ruined their evening coming home early last night. Waking up with Rob would have been much preferred. I rolled over and tried to go back to sleep. That was the only thing I planned to do today; sleep. And maybe have a pity party when I woke up.

CHAPTER 21

Two days had passed, and I hadn't heard from Jessica. I managed to play my normal role for Addison, and it was easy to get through in the mornings before she left for school. But inside, I was dying.

It had been easier to face losing Jessica last time because I was alone and only had myself to worry about. Every time Addison asked about Jessica, I came up with some reason she wouldn't be around.

I sat at the table with a cup of coffee, staring off into space. Addison would be home in three hours, and I needed to get myself back to normal.

"Hey, Boss, I need some help with a heifer."

Suddenly, I felt someone put a hand on my shoulder.

"Earth to Rob." Gables raised his voice and brought me back to the moment.

"Hi, what's up?" I stood and turned to face him.

"I need some help with a heifer. Going to need to be cut open to deliver this one, I expect." He walked out the door and waited for me to follow.

We walked to the barn, and I checked out the heifer. The

calf she was trying to deliver was far too big. "I'll call the vet. Let's move her into the maternity pen while we wait."

Gables and I rarely had to talk while we were working, things just got done, and we were good at our jobs.

"Vet's busy on another call. We'll have to do what can." I slammed my fist down on the wall, frustrated that we would have to do this without the vet's expertise. There was little to do now except try to keep the heifer and her calf alive.

We were quiet while we worked and talked in hushed tones, hoping to keep the heifer settled.

"What are you guys doing in here?" I turned to see my father walk in.

There was no way I wanted to deal with him. I had managed to avoid him for an entire day, and I hoped it would last a few more, but of course, I wasn't that lucky.

"Rob, just get in there and get the chains on."

"Oh, sure, why didn't we think of that, Gables?" I couldn't hide the derision on my face.

"Don't you ever speak to me like that, boy. I'll forget more about cattle than you'll ever know." He moved closer to me, pointing his finger in my face. At this closer proximity, I could smell the booze on his breath.

"Dad, get out of here. You've been drinking. Get out before you get somebody hurt." I tried to direct him out of the pen.

"Hey, get your hands off me. You think you know every-thing, don't you? Everything but how to keep a woman, right Nate?" he laughed condescendingly.

"Get out of this barn." I pointed at the door.

"Or what? What are you going to do, Robbie?" Hearing the name that only my mother called me coming from him was almost enough to make me hit him. I knew he was mocking me.

"Get out, old man. You don't belong here."

"I'm your boss. You don't tell me what to do." My father was inches away from my face.

I grabbed the collar of his jacket and started pushing him back while he continued to yell.

"Hey, you two. I don't know if you remember what we're trying to do here, but you aren't helping. Both of you, get out of this barn right now." Nate Gables rarely raised his voice and hadn't with me in many years.

Gables shooed us out of the barn, and I couldn't help the anger that was building inside me.

"You are absolutely useless around this place, Dad. And not just around here. You're also a useless father." Words flowed out of my mouth. I knew better than to say them, even if they were true, but I couldn't stop them.

"What are you talking about, boy? I'm far from a useless father. I've done for you boys, and this is the thanks I get?"

"Dad, come on. You forced Tyler into a marriage that only worked because Kate is one of the most phenomenal and determined women I have ever met. And Gavin can't even be around you for more than a few hours."

"And what about you, Rob What do you hate me for?" He leaned up against the fence, looking smug, like nothing I said had even fazed him.

"I'm not getting into this, Dad. Nate needs help." I turned to go back into the barn.

"That's right, you have nothing to hate me for. I saved you from Jessica and all the drama she would have brought to the table wanting to work in the big city. Then I bailed you out of a hasty marriage to Samantha. That could have cost us a lot more, son. We got off lucky." He looked proud of himself, and all I wanted to do was wipe that look off his face.

"You saved me? How on earth did you even twist that in your mind so you could even think you saved me? You ruined my life." My fists were balled up as I took a few steps closer to him.

"You went behind my back and sent Jessica away. She left thinking I hated her and wanted nothing to do with her ever again. And Samantha was only in the picture because you sent Jessica away." I couldn't look at him anymore. There was one thing I had never done, and that was hit my father, and as much as I wanted to, I wouldn't start now.

"Always so dramatic. You really need to work on that. Is that why Jessica left in such a hurry two nights ago? She couldn't handle the drama? You probably aren't man enough for her."

I saw red and swung. My fist hit his jaw, making his eyes grow big. He took a few choppy steps backward and fell to the ground. I looked at the man who raised me laying in a heap, and I didn't feel a thing.

This would become a ten-round boxing match if I didn't leave now. I turned to go and left him groaning on the ground. Looking in the barn window ,I saw that, somehow, Nate had delivered the calf. It looked like the momma was doing her job, so there was nothing more for me to do here.

I couldn't go another day without talking to Jessica. It was clear I would have to go to her.

I walked to the main house and found my mom in her office. "Hey, could you meet the bus? I need to go to town."

"Honey, of course I can. Go talk to Jessica, I'm sure you will work it out." She stood and walked over to me and gave me a hug. "I also saw you hit your father. We're going to have to talk about this later. Lord knows your father isn't the easiest man to deal with, but you can't leave it like this. Trust me."

She spoke from experience. She hadn't talked to her mother for the last fifteen years of her life. The disagreement that had torn them apart was the reason we had stayed in Montana all these years.

"We'll worry about your father later. Go." She pushed me out her office door and closed it behind me.

I walked away from her office smiling. She ran this family.

Regardless of what it looked like, my mother was the one that who this family work. She was the glue that held us together.

"You. Get over here."

Of course, I couldn't get out of this place without running into my father again. I let out an audible sigh and turned to face him.

"Your position here is precarious at best, boy. I would be careful about your next move." He walked closer to me, waving his finger in my face. "Rob, you're on a very short leash around here, so I suggest you get back out there and get to work."

"That's not going to happen. I'm heading to town." There was no way I would stay here and listen to this. I turned on my heel and headed toward the door.

"I didn't say you could leave. Get back here." His voice raised more than I had heard since we were kids. That tone still made my blood run cold, even as a grown man.

"Brian, go sleep it off. You're making an ass out of yourself. He's a grown man, and without him, you would run this place into the ground. You have no idea how to handle the day-to-day around here. Rob, go to town." Mom stood in the doorway of her office with her arms crossed and a look of disgust on her face as she glared at my father.

I left the house and sprinted to the truck. I had to go get the woman who would set me straight like that when I was being a jerk.

The drive to town felt like it took forever. I pulled up in front of Daphney Walshay's house and found Jessica's car in the driveway. Taking a deep breath, I stepped out of the truck, walked to the door, and knocked.

Daphney opened the door, her face changing from a smile to a frown.

"Hello, Rob." Her voice was monotone, and her expression was flat.

"Hi, Mrs. Walshay. I'd like to speak to Jessica, please,

ma'am." I was standing here feeling like I was a twelve-year-old boy waiting for permission to talk to a girl.

"She's not here. She left this morning."

I could feel my face fall, and I took a few steps back, looking crushed, I'm sure. Why did life always repeat itself? Here I was finding out the woman I loved had left me behind again.

Mrs. Walshay must have seen my thoughts written all over my face, because she said, "No, Rob, she's coming back. Kate invited Jessica to go with her to Dallas for the day. She called her early this morning. I'm sorry for making you think she was gone." Her face softened, and she even smiled a little.

"Could you tell her I was here?" My voice was quieter than I had ever heard it.

"I will, yes. Rob, I know you love my daughter. If you didn't, you wouldn't be here now looking like you didn't sleep last night." Daphney came out onto the porch and ushered me to a chair near the railing.

"Well, that's because I didn't sleep. I've been worried about Jess, worried about us, and now when I get home, I get to deal with the fact that I hit my father." I let my head fall back and looked at the ceiling of the porch.

"It's about time one of you boys hit that man. My money has always on Tyler, but I'm happy it was you."

My head shot up, and I looked over at Daphney. She stared off across the street with a sly grin on her face. She leaned over and patted my leg. "It's going to be okay, son. Jessica will be back in your arms before you know it."

I nodded and smiled at her. "I better head back. Thank you for talking to me." Standing, I headed to my truck and got in. Daphney was still standing on the porch as I put the truck in reverse, so I gave her a wave and pulled out of the driveway.

CHAPTER 22

Kate and I spent the better part of the day in Dallas and pulled into my driveway very late that evening. Shopping with her had been a wonderful distraction from my thoughts of Rob.

Mom had left the light on but was long in bed, so I quickly changed and brushed my teeth before I climbed into my bed. Sleep came easily because I was so tired.

I walked into the kitchen the next morning to find my mom was already up with the coffee ready. "Well, good morning. What time did you get in last night?" She poured a cup and handed it to me.

"I think it was midnight. We got carried away shopping." I sat down at the table and waited for more questions.

"Rob came to see you yesterday."

My head shot up, and I felt my eyes bug out of my head.

"What did he want?"

"He came to apologize for what he said. Girlie, he loves you. A man doesn't punch out his father if he isn't in love." She took a sip of her coffee and was quiet.

"Mom, I'm going to see Brian Morton today. I can't avoid

this anymore." I sat at the kitchen table, spinning my coffee cup by the handle.

"Well, girlie, it's about time. Do you know what you're going to tell him?" she asked as she sat down across the table from me.

I shook my head and shrugged. "I don't know, Mom. This conversation is overdue. I used to sit in my apartment imagining the things I wanted to say. Over the years, the anger has decreased, as have the strength of my words. Not that I wanted to have the anger dissipate, but I had to let it go, or I wouldn't have been able to move on. Moving on maybe wasn't what I thought it would be."

I needed to repay Brian now that Rob knew what his father had done and said. Finally knowing that Rob had wanted to come with me only reinforced that.

"You aren't going to get to the ranch sitting here, Jessica." My mother's eyes bored a hole into my soul. I made a face at her and stood to go. "Honey, it will all be fine, just speak your piece."

A weak smile crossed my face, and I headed out to do what had been too long coming.

My hands shook as I knocked on the door to Brian's office. My heart was racing, and my head was telling me to turn around and leave. I could just mail the check with a letter, and I wouldn't have to face him. I could move to a new town and start over again. Could I walk away from Rob again? And now Addie? The answer in my heart was a resounding no. I loved them both, and I needed them. I took a deep breath to calm my nerves and crazy thoughts and waited for a response.

"Come in," his voice, gravelly and loud, called from the other side of the closed door. Reaching for the knob, I took a deep breath and opened it.

I had met with celebrities and Manhattan socialites and hadn't broken a sweat, but Brian Morton terrified me. "Mr. Morton, I would appreciate a few moments of your time if you're free." I closed the door behind me and hoped it would make him realize I had no intention of going anywhere.

He scanned his desk calendar and nodded. "Sit, please." Moving to the chair in front of his desk, I perched on the edge of the seat and waited for him to say something.

"What can I do for you, Miss Walshay?"

Digging through my bag, I found the envelope I was looking for and held it in my hands. "Eight years ago, you showed up at my home, much like I've arrived here today. Unexpected and full of things to say without being interrupted." I saw his brow arch and, if I wasn't mistaken, the corners of his mouth slightly turned up. He nodded, and I continued.

"Thanks to that night, I'm in complete control of my life. These last six months have been a change I wasn't expecting, but the reports of my life being ruined were far from the truth. Eight years ago, you gave me $40,000 to start my life and business in New York City." I couldn't help but smile as I thought back to those early days exploring the city and making new friends, but I always thought of the tears at night when I was without my best friend.

"Those years were some of the hardest, but some of the best I have ever had. The hard parts of them were because I didn't have Rob beside me. That was your fault, and now I know it was completely avoidable if you had been less selfish." My voice was powerful, my back straight, and my posture set to intimidate.

I stared at Brian, and he looked down at his hands. "I have recently learned that Rob was the one who suggested giving me that money, and he wanted to go with me to help get my dreams off the ground. He didn't want to get rid of me like you led me to believe. I can't worry about that anymore. We have to figure out if we can move past the lie you perpetuated to ruin our lives or not."

"Am I free to say anything yet?" he asked quietly and folded his hands in front of him on his desk. Part of me wanted to grant him the ability to speak, but I was worried I would end up losing my nerve.

"No, I am going to finish what I came here to say." Leaning forward, I slid the envelope across his desk. "In that envelope, you will find the initial money you invested as well as the appropriate interest as determined by my bank." His face fell in shock, and I smiled in satisfaction. He stared at the envelope and then looked back up at me. "Thank you for your time, Mr. Morton. I will let you get back to your work."

I stood and turned toward the door. He didn't need to say anything. If I could get out of the office without giving him the chance to speak, I knew I could hold the upper hand. I walked out the door, closing it behind me without turning around. Shoulders back and head high, I walked out of the Morton house. When I got into my car, I let out the breath I had been holding and let myself slump into the seat.

After holding onto this secret for over eight years, I could finally let go of this guilt. The mill stone around my neck was suddenly missing. I felt like I needed to shout at the top of my lungs that I was finally free of Brian Morton.

A KNOCK ON THE WINDOW SHOOK ME BACK TO THE MOMENT, and I looked up into the face of my love. Things were still tense between us since we hadn't talked for a few days, but I smiled and opened the door so I could out. We had brought up a lot of past hurts in the last few days, but I still wanted to feel his arms around me, so I hugged him.

"What brings you out here this early?" he huskily asked as he held me tightly to him. "I was kind of surprised to see your car in front of the house." Backing away, he reached up and brushed a stray piece of hair away from my face.

"I had some business to discuss with your father."

He nodded, and I didn't need to say more. Rob knew

exactly what I'd had to do. "Are we okay?" His voice was hesitant and quiet.

I couldn't look at him, so the ground seemed to be the best option. Fear flowed through me because I didn't want to let him go again. It wasn't just him, either. Addison was giving me the opportunity to know what it was like to have a child around, and I was beginning to love her like she was my own.

Rob moved his hand and placed it under my chin, bringing my head up so I was looking at him. "We can't dwell on our past. It is what it is, and for us to have a future, we have to accept it and move on. There will be no forgetting it, but I think we're going to be stronger because of it." He looked deeply into my eyes, and what I saw in his was truth and love.

We wrapped our arms around each other and just held on for a few moments. I was afraid to let go and afraid not to.

"Come to the house, let's have breakfast."

I nodded into his chest, finally releasing my hold. He directed me to the passenger seat, and he drove the short distance to his house. We walked hand in hand to the front door.

CHAPTER 23

"*D*o you want to sit on the porch?" he asked. His voice was soft and filled with concern.

I glanced over to the main house and shook my head. Right now, I wanted to forget that Rob lived on the Morton compound and I needed to avoid thoughts about his dad.

We walked into the house, and I looked around. This was supposed to be my life. I was the one who created the initial conflict by wanting to leave, wanting to spread my wings. I moved toward the couch and sat on the armrest so I faced Rob.

"It's perfect, Rob. I never really looked, but you built this house for me. Everything I wanted is here. It's like when I mentioned something, you wrote it down."

Rob took the few steps toward me and placed his hands on my shoulders. "I started building the week you left. I was hoping that when you came home to see your mom, I could bring you out here. I dreamed you would look around this place and see the love I had for you."

He took a shaky breath. "I didn't know how to tell you

then, so I built your dream home, but I will spend the rest of this life telling you how much I love you."

Tears streamed down my face as I looked up at him, and as much as I loved New York, I would have been so much happier here with the love of my life.

"I'm sorry I left. If anyone ever asks me what my greatest regret in life is, I will have to say leaving you." I dropped my head when his strong arms encircled me, and he held me while he let me cry.

"Jess, you left to live the dream you had at the time. Life evolves, and it's easy to look back and say it was wrong or right, but it was right in that moment."

He helped me stand, and we walked around to sit on the couch. I cuddled into the crook of his arm and just listened to him breathe. It was a balm for my soul. Every day we spent together repaired my shattered heart.

I was lost in thought when the door swung open and an ear-piercing scream came from the doorway.

"Jessica, you're here!" Addison ran to me and threw her arms around my neck. "Daddy said he didn't know when you would be here next."

Hugging her tightly, I looked up at Rob and smiled. He winked and cleared his throat.

"What am I? Chopped liver?"

"Dad." She giggled and ran over to hug Rob.

Our evening was full of laughter and stolen glances between homework questions and complaints about math.

"I'm so glad you're here, Jessica. Dad's been grumpy, and I think it's because you were busy," she whispered before running off to bed.

"I'll be right back." Rob grazed his hand across my back, and it sent shivers down my spine and sparks to my core.

He wasn't gone more than ten minutes, but I had lit a fire and cuddled under a blanket.

"You look comfy," he whispered in my ear as he leaned over the back of the couch.

"I hope you don't mind." I looked at him as he sat down.

He leaned over and kissed me. It was the first time we'd kissed since our fight. There was no denying we had chemistry. It was the one thing that could always solve an argument or put the other in a good mood. Rob was a good kisser, and he knew just when I needed to be loved on.

Out of nowhere, the tears started falling again. I wasn't even sure what had caused them this time.

"Hey, baby, what's with the crying?" His voice mimicked his furrowed brows and sad eyes.

I just shrugged. "No idea, it's been a really rough few days." I rested my head on his shoulder as he sighed.

"I know. But it's over now. We're going to come out of this stronger than we ever have been. I think my father finally understands that he ruined most of my life. And I realized that, no matter what, you and I belong together."

His arms tightened around me, and he held me as I cried the last tears I had for our past. It was time to look toward the future. A future with Rob and Addison, and whatever life dealt us, we would face together as a family.

"Let's go to bed. I want to hold you, and I don't feel close enough to you right here," Rob whispered into my hair.

We stood and walked hand in hand to his room. Rob threw back the covers, stripped down to his boxers, and climbed in. I slipped in to the bathroom to change. Tonight had laid me bare already, and I wasn't prepared for the vulnerability I would feel if I changed in front of him.

The slinky green lace nightgown sat on top of my bag, taunting me because this evening hadn't ended the way I had envisioned.

Once I had the nightgown on, I took one last glimpse in the mirror, and I was horrified at my puffy eyes and my red, drippy nose. It wasn't going to get any better, so I opened the door and walked back into Rob's room.

His eyes scanned me from head to toe, and I heard him let out an audible sigh. For the first time in what felt like hours, I cracked a smile.

"Come here." As he pushed the blankets back, his words were quiet and filled with concern.

I crawled in beside him and snuggled into his waiting arms. "It seems a little early to be going to bed."

A low rumble came from his chest. "Oh, I didn't bring you in here to sleep, baby."

I propped myself up on my elbow and looked at him. "Well, what did you have in mind then?"

He rolled over onto his side to face me. Ever so slowly, he traced the curve of my breast that peeked out over my night-gown. "We always had a great time making up after a fight."

Goosebumps broke out along the path he was making. I sighed, let my head fall to the pillow, and gazed at the man before me.

"Is that an invitation?" he asked as he trailed kisses down my neck.

"You don't need an invitation. You're always welcome."

Rob flung the blankets off the bed and made quick work of straddling me. It was then that I realized he had already planned this out. He wasn't wearing boxers anymore, and he was quite ready for the evening that awaited us.

"Wow, aren't you the overachiever." I said as I looked him over hungrily.

He laughed. "I had planned this all for a few nights ago and got shut down, so I'm more be ready.

Rob slowly slipped his hand under the hem of the night-gown and over the top of my leg, letting it rest on my inner thigh.

The sensation of his hand so close to my centre sent thrills through me. It didn't matter how many times we had been together, his touch always sent me over the edge.

"I want you, Jess." His whisper was full of need and passion.

"What are you waiting for then?" I slowly moved my legs apart as well as I could with him positioned over me.

No further words were spoken, Rob settled himself between my legs and entered me in one swift movement. Our bodies were so familiar with one another, so we easily moved in rhythm together.

In this moment, we had finally spoken the truth to each other, and from here on out, we could move forward.

CHAPTER 24

The ring was burning a hole in my pocket as I drove home. I had made a quick trip to the bank to my safe-deposit box, where I had kept the ring I'd bought for Jessica all those years ago. I hadn't been able to get rid of it. It hurt to think of pawning it, and even though I had thought of driving to the Brazos River and tossing it in to let float down to the Gulf of Mexico on more than one occasion, I never did it. In this moment, I was very glad I had kept it.

The stress of the day was getting to me, and I was feeling anxious. Addison knew what the plan was, and I'd told Mom, which meant Dad knew. I knew there would be a conversation coming, and I welcomed it, but I hoped it would wait for another day.

Pulling up in front of the house, I mentally went over the to-do list in my head. There was a knock on my window and my stomach dropped when I saw my father looking less than thrilled. I sighed and opened the door of the truck and got out.

"Dad, what do you need?" I tried to make my voice lighter than I felt.

We wandered over to the corral fence and I stared off into

the pasture. "I hear you're going to ask Jessica to marry you. You really think another marriage is what you need?" He crossed his arms and leaned against the fence. "I hope you've seen Merrit about drawing up a prenup. This place has too much to lose if Jessica runs off again."

I could feel my blood start to boil, and I was ready to take him on today. "Well, you know, Dad, it would have only been one marriage if you hadn't 'helped' me." My hands were clenched into fists, and I had to turn away from him or I was going to hit him.

"Dad, you have no right to give me advice when it comes to Jessica, and I'm marrying her whether or not you approve. I'm in love with Jessica; I have been since the day I first saw her. The years apart haven't changed that, and I'd have to say that being in love with Jessica is part of the reason my marriage with Samantha fell apart."

I had never been honest with my father about my marriage to Samantha. Many could argue over the years that I drove her to look elsewhere. Any time I saw a news article about Jessica, I would shut down for days. It wasn't fair to her at all.

"Rob, you didn't make that woman sleep around. I had her figured out from day one." He turned and crossed his arms over the top rail.

"So you interfered with my future with Jessica, but you didn't open your mouth about Samantha? Boy, that makes sense, dad." I said sarcastically. I couldn't stay here. He was aggravating me, and I needed to get my head back into the task at hand.

I knew walking away from him was rude, but it was all I could do at that moment. There were things I had to get done, and keeping our conversation going wasn't one of them.

A quick glance at the list in my hands reminded me I needed to get the candles out and supper in the oven. I'd picked up her favorite Italian food from the place in town, hoping to make this night memorable.

The clock ticked exceedingly slowly. No matter how many times I checked my watch, it felt like the hands weren't moving. I paced my house waiting for Jessica to get here. Never in my life had I been this nervous.

The purr of her engine stopping at the house broke me out of the trance I was in, and I made myself look occupied in the kitchen when she came in.

"It smells wonderful in here. What are you up to?" Jessica walked over to me and wrapped her arms around my waist. I swiftly placed my arm around her shoulders and pulled her to me for a kiss.

"Just making tonight special."

"Rob, every moment we spend together is special. You don't have to keep impressing me." She moved a hand to my chest and gently rested it there.

"Well, isn't that sweet? At some point you're going to get annoyed with me." I kissed the top of her head.

"Oh, don't worry, I know." She spun out of my arms and walked over to the island to pour the wine I'd opened. "But really, Rob, why did you go to all this work? What's so special about today? You've been busy on the ranch, turning out bulls and moving cows, so how did you manage to get away today?"

"Listen, that's for me to know and you to find out. Take the glasses to the table, and I'll bring the plates." I snuck past her to set the warm plates on the table and pulled out her chair.

"Thank you." Jessica set the glasses down and took her seat.

We ate the chicken Parmesan like she'd eaten on our first date in silence. I didn't really taste the food. I was too nervous about the next item on the menu.

"Rob, that was wonderful. Almost better than being in the restaurant." She leaned over the table and kissed me.

"Jess, you and I have been through a lot to get to this point. I have lived with you and without you. Our years together when we were young were the best years I knew, but the years we were apart almost killed me." She sat back in her chair, and I watched a slight smile cross her face. I could sense that she knew where this was going, but I wanted to stick to my plan.

"Jessica, I don't want to live without you any longer." I slipped off my chair and knelt on one knee in front of her. "Jessica Walshay, will you do me the honor of finally becoming my wife and spending the rest of your life with me?"

Her eyes welled with tears, and the smile on her face grew. "Yes," Jessica whispered. I took her hand and slipped the ring on her finger.

CHAPTER 25

 e moved on from dealing with Brian over the next few weeks. He was still very cool toward me, but I didn't care anymore. He had no power over me.

As I was working on plans for an upcoming event, Rob came flying into my office. Turning in my chair, I looked up at this man standing in front of me. He looked like he was in a panic, which made me start to worry. My heart began to race, and my mind went through a million different scenarios.

"Jess, I need you to plan a surprise party for Addison. Her birthday is in a week. Do you think you can come up with something?"

"A week? You and your family like to make me work hard, don't you?" Standing, I moved toward the door and closed it. I leaned against the door and arched my brow. "It's going to cost you, Mr. Morton." Rob walked over to me and slid his hands over my hips, pulling me toward him.

"I can think of payment." He moved his head to nibble on my neck, and I slid my hands to his ass and grabbed his wallet. His head shot up, and I couldn't hold back my laughter. "You are mean, so mean." Rob moved away from me, and I laughed more as I handed back his wallet.

"Okay, but seriously, I don't want payment unless it's later, after our date." Moving toward Rob, I wrapped my arms around his waist and looked up at him. "What are you thinking, or do I get to plan it all myself?"

He frowned and leaned down to kiss me. "You aren't going to get away with this little bait and switch, just so you know. Do whatever you think Addison will like."

I spent the week making calls and plans to make this the best party Addison had ever had. Why not use the contacts and resources I had to spoil her?

Saturday rolled around, and Rob took her into Hammond for lunch while all of her friends showed up at the appointed time. I texted Rob when everyone arrived, and then it was time for the waiting game. The door to the barn creaked open, and when the lights went on, ten little girls jumped out from behind well-placed bales and yelled, "Surprise!"

Addison's hands flew to her mouth, and she screamed. The girls all gathered around her and hugged her. I had transformed the barn into a movie theater with a red carpet walkway leading into the theater. I had rented a gigantic screen and a real movie projector. The popcorn maker was popping away in the corner and the photographer on the red carpet was snapping photos nonstop. I couldn't wait to send the pictures to the girls and make Addison a photo book.

Supper was a success. They had hot dogs, nachos, and more popcorn than I had ever seen eaten in my life, and now it was time for the cake. I managed to pull some strings and had it made by the best baker in Dallas. The cake was made to look like movie reels with every frame on the film made up of pictures of Addie, her family, and her friends. It was perfect.

I turned the lights of the barn down, and Rob flicked on the projector. All the girls squealed then quieted down.

I had made a huge seating area out of hay bales covered in fleece blankets, and I'd arranged things so they all had spots for their soda and popcorn.

Rob came up and wrapped his arms around me. "Thank you for today. She's going to remember this forever." He made me smile and cuddle back into him. "What time did you ask the parents to pick up their kids? I don't want to be out here too late. You deserve a thank you for this."

I smiled. "They should be here in a few hours. We have to clean up though, because I have to have the film equipment back in the morning."

"Well, it shouldn't take long to clean up." Rob gently brushed the hair away from my neck with his fingers, sending goosebumps over my skin before he nibbled on my ear.

The movie ended and Rob turned the lights back on as parents started showing up to pick up their daughters. All the girls were talking a mile a minute as they left the barn. Addison waved until all the cars disappeared down the drive.

Addie flung her arms around me and hugged me tighter than she ever had before. "Jessica, I know you did all this, because let's face it, my other parties weren't this epic. My friends are going to be talking about this forever. Thank you."

"You're welcome, sweetheart. I was happy to do it for you." I looked up at Rob and smiled. "Addie, you should thank your dad too. He's the one who came up with the idea."

"Dad, you're the best. It's been the greatest day ever." She launched herself into Rob's arms, and he swung her around in circles.

"Love you, kiddo. Happy Birthday, baby. But now you need to go get ready for bed." Addie ran out of the barn, leaving Rob and me alone.

"What can I help you with? Why don't we start with the screen." He walked over to it and started to lower it and get it put away.

I boxed up the projector and film and hummed one of the songs from the movie. "Why don't you take these to the car? I'll get the cake and put it away in the fridge. I can clean up the rest of it tomorrow."

Rob nodded and went to work hauling the things out to my car. When I came out of the house, Rob was standing beside my car, waiting. His arms were crossed, and he looked sexy in the moonlight. "Come on, it's late. I'm not letting you drive home." Hitting the button on the key fob, he locked the doors and took my hand and led me to his house.

When we walked in the door, Addie was bouncing from the kitchen to the living room. Rob tried to keep a stern face, but I saw his lips trying not to tip up in a grin. "Well, Missy, do you think you can sleep after all that sugar and excitement?" Addison's giggle was heartwarming and made me feel so happy. Rob's question went unanswered as she twirled around the room.

"I'm going to say no." I shook my head and smiled at Rob.

"This is your fault. You get to stay up until she crashes." He turned and walked down the hallway, closing the door behind him. Rolling my eyes, I turned to look at Addison.

"Okay, you." I pointed to the wild child making laps around the couch. She froze and looked at me. "We're going to get you settled in bed, then we'll read a few books and go to sleep." She smiled and ran to her room.

I turned right instead of left, grabbing the doorknob, and peeking in to find Rob relaxing on the bed watching TV. He was the sexiest man alive, and it felt like I'd been the one doing laps around the couch as fast as my heart was beating.

I winked at him, catching his twinkling eyes. "Twenty minutes. I'll be back. You better be ready." He laughed, and I closed the door and went to Addie's room.

"Are you ready for a story?" I walked over and sat on the end of her bed. She nodded, and I covered her up and lay down beside her. She handed me the book she was reading, and I had to smile. It was Anne of Green Gables, and she was about halfway through.

Flipping open the book to her bookmark, I said, "Addie, I am so impressed with how well you read. I was eleven when I read this for the first time." Taking a deep breath, I began where she'd left off.

After about ten minutes, Addie's breathing changed to quiet, deep breaths. A peaceful, soft look had crossed her face, and I gently kissed her forehead. Sneaking off the bed and out of her room, I pulled the door closed without a sound.

Rob had turned the lights off except for the one in the hall that lead to Rob's room. Quietly, I opened his door and found he wasn't on the bed. I heard the shower turn off, and I sat on the end of the bed waiting for Rob to come out of the bathroom. Wrapped only in a towel, he smiled as he grabbed the tucked in part and let it fall to the floor.

He slowly walked over to me and kissed me while laying me back on the bed. "One of us is entirely overdressed for the plans I have right now," he whispered in my ear while popping open the button of my jeans and untucking my shirt.

CHAPTER 26

With the sun shining through the window, I woke up feeling warm wrapped in Rob's arms. I looked at the clock and decided I needed to get up. Sneaking out of his embrace, I grabbed some clothes and got ready for the day.

The coffee running through the pot smelled divine. I stood in front of it, anxiously waiting for it to be done. Large hands wrapped around my waist, and I was pulled back into a solid, warm body. "My arms were empty when I woke up," he whispered in my ear sensually, and it sent flutters through me.

"I wanted to get breakfast started before you got up." I turned in his arms while his hands trailed to rest on my butt.

"I've decided I don't enjoy waking up alone. I also don't like going to bed alone. So I had a thought this morning before I got out of bed." He backed me up until I was pinned between him and the counter. "Move in here. It would solve the issue of living with your mom. You're kind of cramping her style." Rob looked so serious when he talked about my mom. It made me giggle.

"Yeah, Jess, are you moving in?" Addison walked into the kitchen and immediately started bouncing.

Rob was waiting for an answer, and Addie had wrapped her arms around me as well.

"This is a big decision, you two. One that shouldn't be made before we've had breakfast." I tried to blow off the questions. Every part of me wanted to shout yes from the rooftops, but there was more than just moving in. There was the balance in this home that, when I was here periodically, was fine. Being here full time would cause a disruption I wasn't sure Addie, or Rob for that matter, would be ready for.

"Maybe we should discuss this more," I said quietly as I looked at Rob. He looked like I had crushed his hopes and dreams.

"You're right, but I want you to know I need you here. With Addison and me." He dropped his head, and our lips met. "We will talk more when I get home tonight." Rob reached up and grabbed two mugs and poured us coffee, handing me a steaming cup as we moved to the table.

I couldn't help but think about moving in. It would mean mornings like this. Sitting here having coffee with Rob, waiting for Addie to wake up. I couldn't help smiling thinking of it.

"What's that smile for?" Rob asked as he brought his coffee to his mouth.

"I just got to thinking about what it would be like to be here every day. Coffee in the morning together, not having to make the thirty-minute drive back to my mom's at the end of the day." My coffee was calling my name, so before I told him I would move in, I took a sip and a second to think about my words. Addie ran out of the kitchen to get dressed.

"So, is that a yes?" His eyes grew wide and his smile grew.

"No, it's still a wait to talk later, but I'm thinking it will be a yes." I smiled from behind my coffee mug and waited for his reaction.

It didn't seem possible for his smile to grow any more, but

as I watched it, I couldn't help but grin at the scene in front of me. "What are you up to today?"

He sighed and looked at his watch. "Well, have cows to check and move. It's probably going to take all day. Addison's going to be ticked. She has to come with me. It'll be a boring day for her."

"Why don't I stay here? She can come with me to return the party stuff, and then we can have a girls' day."

Addie walked back into the room, clearly overhearing our conversation. "Please, Dad. I don't want to ride all day." She wrapped her arm around his shoulder and gave him the biggest puppy dog eyes.

"I can't battle both of you, so it looks like you girls win." Rob hugged Addie and smiled at me. He mouthed "thank you," and the look he gave me made my heart sing.

AFTER A TRIP TO TOWN AND A FEW PHONE CALLS, WE GIRLS were having a party. Kate, Delaney, Naomi—who had been dating Gavin for months and felt like a wonderful addition to the family—and Sandra all showed up, and we ate leftovers and finished the cake from Addie's party. It was so nice to spend time with these women without our men hanging around. The dynamic was different, and we had a blast. Laughter rang out constantly.

"I haven't had this much fun in ages," Sandra said as she walked to the table to refill her wineglass. "Naomi, what's happening with Gavin? He really should be around more. That boy needs to give his head a shake." We looked at each other, and Kate hid Sandra's wineglass. "Sorry, I just don't understand. He's got a brilliant girl and a place of his own here, but he's being stubborn." She reached for her glass, but it was gone. The frown that crossed her face was priceless.

"We see each other as much as our schedules allow. He's

here all next week overseeing the build for a log home. It's going to be so nice to have him to come home to every night."

"Speaking of every night. Jessica, your car has been here in the mornings more often. Things are going well, I take it." Sandra turned the twenty questions toward me. I could feel my face turn red.

"Daddy and I asked Jessica to move in. She said we need to talk about it." All eyes in the room shifted from Addison to me, waiting for an answer. All I could do was smile.

"Addie, why don't you run and get your jammies on?" I tried to keep my voice light and not perturbed. She ran to her room, unaware of the onslaught of questions she had instigated.

"Move in?" Kate whispered.

"You didn't say yes immediately?" Naomi questioned, looking sad.

I could tell Sandra wanted to ask questions, but she was giving me the time to explain.

"Okay, look, it's been Rob and Addie alone for five years. She doesn't remember what it's like having someone else live here. There has been little to no sharing Rob with anyone else." I didn't want to say too much because I knew she would be back in a few moments.

"It's just something Rob and I need to talk through." The excuse sounded lame even to me. Their faces were showing me I didn't have a great argument.

"Grandma, can you put me to bed? I'm tired." Addie came back to the living room, and she looked like she would collapse any second. The day had finally caught up to her. She made her rounds and said good night to us before she walked hand in hand with Sandra down the hall.

Standing, I picked up glasses and plates. The conversation came to a screeching halt, but I knew it would start again when Sandra returned. Kate and Naomi helped me, and we were ready to sit back down when Rob's mom returned.

Glasses topped off, it only took one sip for Sandra to ask her question. "Do you want to move in?"

It felt wrong having this conversation with her present, but I'd always known how close this family was, and I didn't expect that to change. I bit the corner of my lip, scanned the anxious faces of the three women, and nodded. "Yes, I want to move in." It was something I had thought of all day and never let myself speak aloud.

The women squealed, and all three were grinning. All I could do was shake my head.

"Rob wants you to move in, and Addie brought it up, so that sounds like another yes. What's holding you back?" Kate was the rational one, and now she was making me realize I was being overly cautious. I needed to make this move.

Our evening was ending, and Kate and Delaney had just left. Naomi had headed back to town since she worked an early shift tomorrow, but at least she wouldn't have the hang-over Sandra was going to have to deal with.

With the house cleaned up from any of the evidence from girls' night, I changed into my pajamas and waited for my cowboy to come home.

I hardly recognized Rob when he walked through the door. He was covered in dirt and who knows what else from a long day of working cattle. Before I could grumble about the amount of dust he was tracking through the house, he pulled a bouquet of sunflowers out from behind his back.

"They aren't two dozen long-stemmed roses, but I hope you like them." He leaned down, and we kissed, then he handed the flowers to me.

"Babe, they're beautiful, and far more stunning than any roses in my mind. Thank you." I turned and looked through the cupboards until I found something to put them in. A plastic pitcher wasn't the most esthetically pleasing vase, but it worked.

"I want to move in if the offer still stands," I said

nervously. My back was to Rob as I kept arranging the flowers. When I turned, I didn't need a verbal answer. His grin spoke his truth.

"When can we move your stuff in?" He walked up and stood beside me.

"I should break the news to my mom, and then we can make a plan."

"Break the news to your mom, Jess. You're cramping her style. She wants you out so Hank can stay over." Rob folded his arms over his chest and waited for me to answer.

"She's never said anything. If it was a problem, she would have told me." I said as I turned to look at him.

"Jess, if you'd gone home tonight, or last night, you would have found Hank's car in the driveway." He took a step closer to me. "It's time for her to move on, and it's time for us to take that next step."

He was right. She needed her life back, and I had to get mine started.

CHAPTER 27

The past few weeks had been tense, liberating, and unexpected. Rob and I were working through the truths we had just spoken to each other. We tried to keep things light when Addison was around. She accepted me into her life, and Rob and I didn't want to cause any unnecessary drama.

Now that I was settling in, I wanted to spend some one-on-one time with Addison. She was relentlessly after Rob to take her out for a long ride, so I offered to take her. The excitement on her face warmed my heart, and the appreciation that crossed Rob's sent butterflies through me.

We saddled up, packed our lunch, and headed out for the day. After lunch, the clouds changed instantly, turning from puffy white marshmallows to gray, ominous walls closing in around us. "Addie, get on JP and ride for the trapper's cabin. I'll be right beside you." I saw the trust in her eyes change to fear. "Addie, I believe in you. You're a skilled rider." She was scared, but I saw her nod.

I threw my leg over Shadow, and Addie settled in on her horse. "Go," I yelled over the wind. She kicked the horse into action. JP was a sound horse and knew what he needed to do.

Taking off across the pasture, the horses ran at breakneck speed. They didn't want to be out there any more than we did. I looked over at Addie. She was holding on to the saddle horn with a death grip. I smiled at her, and she turned her frown into a small smile.

The trapper's shack appeared out of nowhere, and I'd never been more relieved to see a building in all my life. I reached over to grab JP's reins and pulled them back as I pulled on my own. The horses slowed, and I hopped off before Shadow had even come to a stop.. "Get in the cabin." I hollered to Addie as she flopped off her horse. I watched her run in and quickly stripped the horses of their saddles, blankets, and halters. They were going to have to outrun this storm, and they needed to be as unencumbered as possible. I tossed everything in the cabin, ran back out, and slapped both horses on the hind ends, watching them take off toward home. As I watched them leave, it felt like I was saying goodbye to the last hope I had of getting us back home. But I knew we couldn't outride this thing, and it was safer to hunker down here.

The sky had changed from gray to an evil green. A shelf cloud was forming, and it felt like if I reached out, I could touch it. The air smelled different. A sweet aroma of freshly cut grass and wildflowers filled the air, and it was thick and heavy. Suddenly, it got eerily quiet, and all the hair on the back of my neck stood up. This storm was turning out to look a lot like the one thing I had hoped it wasn't. A tornado. Taking one last look at the sky, I darted into the cabin.

I gathered Addie in my arms as she had started to shake. I wasn't sure if it was the fact that we were soaking wet or because she was scared, but if I had to guess, I would say it was both. Scanning the cabin, I didn't see much here that would protect us. The pipes under the sink were my first thought. I opened the cupboard doors and tossed out all the supplies that were housed there. It was going to be a tight fit.

"Addie, undo your belt. When I get in there, we're going to attach it to mine." She scrambled to undo the buckle and waited. I grabbed a few blankets and the harness from my horse. I threaded it through my belt loops and crawled under the sink. Addie crawled in on top of me. I looped her belt through mine and did her buckle back up.

"Jessica, your hands are shaking," Addie observed and whispered.

"I'm just cold, kiddo." I tried to make my voice as light as I could, but I didn't think she believed me.

Grabbing the blankets, I tucked them all around us as best as I could and pulled the door shut. We now sat in the pitch-dark and waited. I could feel Addie's shoulders move and hear the soft sniffles she tried to hide. "It's okay to cry, Addie Girl." She turned her head and buried her face in my shirt. I wrapped my arms around her and held on as tight as I could. Tears streamed down my face as I watched my life flash before my eyes like pictures. The wind outside picked up and howled, as if calling me to battle it for our lives. I scooted closer to the pipe and wrapped my arms around it while using my body to shield Addie.

I could hear shingles lifting off the roof and what I imagined were larger parts of the roof under the shingles as well. The walls were shaking, and I suddenly imagined I knew what laundry felt like in the washing machine. I heard wood splintering, and I could see daylight around the cupboard doors. I knew this was it. We would be okay or we wouldn't. Whispering prayers to keep Addie calm, I suddenly felt a calm wash over me. I felt a hand on my shoulder. It seemed familiar. The smell of Old Spice original came from out of nowhere. "Dad," I whispered.

The cabin cracked and the wall that had protected us on one side was gone. The rain was pelting us, so I pulled the blanket up around Addie's head to protect her from flying debris. Out of nowhere, something grazed my head, and something warm trickled down from my hairline. Without needing to open my eyes or touch it, I knew it was blood. It smelled metallic, like raw ground beef. I hated the smell of iron, and here it was, trickling down from my head.

As quick as the storm had started, it was over. The weight that had been resting on me lifted, and the smell of my father's aftershave dissipated with the breeze. I opened my eyes and wiped the blood from my face. The only things left of the cabin were the sink and the pipe I had attached us to. I kissed Addie's head and prayed, thanking the Almighty for keeping us safe. "Thanks, Dad," I whispered into the atmosphere. I could still feel where his hand had rested on my shoulder. I touched that spot, hoping to hold on to him for just a little while longer. It was a touch I missed, and one I never wanted to go away.

I fumbled to unhook the harness from the pipe. The missing wall on one side made it much easier to get out of the cupboard than it was to get in. My legs had gone numb, so I sat with them stretched out in front of me for a few moments.

"Jessica, how did you know to do that?" Addie asked, in awe. I tried to come up with a brilliant answer, like they had taught me in school or my dad showed me what to do, but I only had the truth.

"Saw it in a movie." I shrugged, then winced, now acutely aware of my head throbbing from the gash on my forehead. I ripped off a piece of the blanket and folded it up. Taking out my pocket knife, I cringed as I sliced through the reins to secure the piece of fabric covering the cut. It was a long way back to the house, and I didn't know what time it was, so I took Addie's hand and started walking.

CHAPTER 28

I didn't have time to get from the main house to my home before the storm hit. I prayed that Addison and Jessica had taken shelter in the basement. Bounding up the stairs, I barreled through the door yelling for my girls. The house was quiet. I ran to the basement, but it was empty. I grabbed my phone and dialed Kate.

"Rob, is everything okay at your place?"

"No," croaked out of my mouth. "Jessica and Addie went riding out to the lake."

"Tyler, we need to get to Rob's. Now!" I heard her yell at him. "We'll be there in two minutes." The line went dead, and now all I could to do was wait and worry.

Tyler must have called my parents because I saw them fly out the side door and run toward me. My dad got to me first, and I collapsed in his arms. He set me down on the step, and my mom hugged me. "They're going to be fine, Rob. I just know it. Jessica will have done everything she could to keep them safe." I nodded, but couldn't find the words to reply. I prayed they were fine, but worried they wouldn't be.

Tyler came to a screeching halt in front of my house, and he and Kate jumped out and ran toward me. Everyone was talking a mile a minute. We were trying to make plans, but with everyone talking over each other, nothing was getting done.

"Enough!" Kate screamed, and the talking stopped. "Here's what will happen. Tyler, Rob, Brian, and I will take two trucks out to the lake. We'll stay a few hundred yards apart and drive straight out. From there, we can take paths around the lake." Kate was firm and in control as she finished. "Okay, now we need to get going."

"Are you sure we shouldn't go on horses?" I questioned her.

"Rob, if either one is hurt, we need to get them back the easiest and quickest way possible." I appreciated that she said hurt and nothing more. My tears flowed, and she gathered me up in her arms. "They're fine, Rob. I know it. There isn't time for this. I'm sorry it seems harsh, but get yourself together, and let's go. The sooner we find the girls, the easier everyone will breathe."

I nodded, wiped my tears with the sleeve of my shirt like I was a child, and took a deep breath. "Let's go." I sounded far more sure than I felt.

As we drove out of the yard, two horses came running into the pasture. I slammed on my brakes. "Dad, that's JP and Shadow. Where are their saddles?"

"Jessica took them off. Gave them a better chance of making it back safe. She's a smart one, son. I have even more faith that they're okay now. She would never have let them go if they weren't somewhere they would get through the storm." Dad patted my leg. "Let's get going. The horses will be fine. Some of the men will see to that." I stepped on the gas, and we headed toward the lake.

We crested a hill and saw the devastation where the trapper's cabin had once stood. There was debris scattered for a mile. I stopped and looked over at Tyler. He shrugged, and we kept driving.

It wasn't the wreckage that caught my attention. My eyes zeroed in on the two most important people in my life. Addison's pale pink shirt stood out in the sunlight as she ran toward my truck. I floored the truck the last hundred yards and threw it into park the second I came to a stop. Dad lurched forward in his seat but refrained from saying anything. I flew out the door and ran to my daughter, scooping her up. She had started to run when she saw the trucks. I scanned her quickly for any bumps, bruises, or scrapes, but she was unscathed. I looked around for Jessica, finding her slumped down on her knees. I could see her face glistening in the sun. Running to her as quickly as I could with the death grip Addison had on me, I noticed a bandage on her head soaked with blood.

"Addie, you have to let me go for a second. I need to check on Jessica." Addie climbed down and ran over to Kate, who scooped her up and held on to her tightly. I knelt down beside Jessica. "How was your ride?" She looked up at me and collapsed into my arms.

"I've had better," she mumbled into my shirt.

I chuckled. "I bet you have. Let me look at that head." I peeled off the makeshift bandage and saw a gash about four inches long and deep enough I thought I was looking at her skull. "Jess, I need to get you to a hospital. That's going to need stitches, and they're going to want to check you for a concussion."

Jessica waved her hand. "It's fine, just get me home, and I can look after it."

"Jessica, it's bad. You need to go." My father had come over and looked at her head. "If you won't believe Rob, you're going to believe me. Four years as an army medic taught me a few things." He never spoke of his time in the service, but every so often, his training was put to use. Jessica looked up at him and nodded. I gently lifted her off the ground and walked back to the truck. Dad opened the back door, and I set her down on the seat.

"Addie, why don't you come with us and a doctor can check you out too." She nodded, climbed in, and cuddled up beside Jessica. Jessica placed her arm around my daughter and held her close. I had so many questions, but they could wait until I knew they were fine. Tyler and Kate stayed out at the cabin to do a little cleanup and make sure it was safe for the cows. I waved at my brother, who had wrapped his arm around Kate and pulled her to him.

"I'm going to need my purse, Rob. My insurance card is in there." I looked at her in the rear-view mirror and smiled. I drove into the yard, finding Mom standing on the porch waiting. She must have called Daphney because she stood next to her. Both women ran down the stairs toward the truck as I pulled to a stop and hopped out.

"Rob, where's my girl?" Daphney looked terrified to hear my answer.

"She's in the truck. She has a nasty gash on her forehead that needs to be looked at, but as far as I know, that's all," I said.

She nodded and ran to open Jessica's door. "My baby, you're okay. I was so worried about you." Tears flowed down Daphney's face as she gathered her daughter in her arms.

"Mom, it was Dad. He was there. I felt his hand on my shoulder, smelled his aftershave, and he protected us." I barely heard her whisper it out. A tear slid down my cheek and I sent a silent thank you to a man I had never met.

"Oh, darlin', I know he was there. I felt him this afternoon as well. That's how I knew you would come home." Both women were crying now.

"I don't want to break up this moment, but Jessica, we really need to get you looked at." I said, putting my hand on the truck door.

She nodded, and Daphney backed away from the truck while Dad hopped back in after a few words with mom.

"You don't need to come if there are things to do here, Dad."

He turned to look at Addison, who had fallen asleep, and Jessica, who was staring out the window. "Right now, this is where I'm needed, son. Now drive." I looked at the man who had ruled with an iron fist and saw how he had changed when the girls showed up and challenged him around this place.

The drive to the hospital felt like it took hours. I hoped it wasn't busy. Dad had called ahead, and they would be waiting for us. Pulling into the empty ambulance bay, I turned to see Jessica asleep.

"No, no, no. Jessica, come on, you have to wake up." Flinging my seatbelt off, I jumped out and ran around to her side. I opened the door and patted her face, but she didn't stir. "Dad, she's asleep," I said as he came to stand beside me.

"Move, son," his voice was kind but commanding. I stepped aside and watched him give Jessica a quick sternal rub. She flinched, and I heard Dad breathe a sigh of relief.

Within moments, medical personnel surrounded the truck. Dad was talking to them about the events that happened. Addie had woken up and was sitting on my hip with her head tucked into my neck, trying not to watch what was happening.

"Well, I hear you're a pretty brave girl. Why don't you and your dad come with me and we'll get you checked over?"

"Naomi!" Addie said excitedly and wrapped her little arms around her neck.

"I think you're just fine, but let's go anyway. I may even have a treat for you." The girls giggled, and I turned back to look at Jessica. Never in my life had I ever felt so torn.

"I will stay with Jessica," Dad said from behind me. "Go with Addison. She needs you more." He patted my shoulder. I never imagined trusting my dad with someone I cared so much for, but he was different today. In fact, he had been different since our fight. He was paying attention on the ranch and checking in with me more about daily business.

The way he took over making sure Jessica was okay in the pasture was unlike anything I'd ever seen from him before. She was going to be fine while he was on watch, so I followed Naomi and Addie into the hospital.

CHAPTER 29

*S*itting in a stark, cold white room with utility boxes of supplies on the walls and papers all over the countertops, I clung to Addison's hand. It felt so tiny in mine. Her long nimble fingers curled around mine. She wanted to take piano lessons, and I'd told her no because we didn't have a piano. Truth be told, I just didn't want the added noise. But after the fear I felt today, I decided I would go buy her a piano tomorrow. The thought of almost losing her scared me. My life would be nothing without her and her noise.

The massive door creaked as it opened, and Naomi walked through with a doctor following close behind. "Rob, this is Dr. Klein. He's going to check Addie over to make sure everything is fine." I stood and shook his hand as he motioned me over to the door.

"Mr. Morton, I assure you if there is anything underlying with Addison, we'll find it, but Naomi's assessment was very complete, and I, as of right now, agree that your daughter came through this tornado experience with no injuries." Closing my eyes and breathing a sigh of relief, I smiled at him. I glanced back at the stretcher to see that Addie had woken up and was playing thumb wars with Naomi.

"Naomi is really quite good with your daughter. It's like they know each other well." Dr. Klein smiled, and I felt like he was doing some visual assessment.

"Well, Naomi is dating my younger brother, so we're used to having her around."

"Oh, you're Gavin's brother?"

I smirked when I saw the doctor's face change when he realized I who I was.

"I guess we should get this examination completed." He jumped into action, and the next hour and a half was a blur. Lab techs came and went. The doctor ran in and out, checking on results. Countless nurses came through Addison's room to see the miracle girl who survived a tornado without a scratch. She was eating up the attention.

I stepped out into the hall for a moment while the ER staff surrounded Addison. Scanning the hallway for my father and glimpsing him, I maneuvered around the hall, trying to stay out of people's way.

Dad was standing in the hallway leaning against the doorframe of Jessica's room. His face was pained, and he looked terrified when he saw me.

"Dad, what's happening?" My voice frantic.

"She slipped into a coma, son. Whatever made that gash on her head caused her brain to bleed. The doctor has called in specialists, and they're on their way." I stumbled backward and plunked down onto the chair behind me. It was like someone had let the air out of me. Dad took the chair next to me.

"He doesn't know how she was able to walk to meet the trucks. Rob, she shouldn't have been able to. I called Daphney, and your mother is bringing her here." I had never seen my father upset like this, but his eyes were glistening and his demeanor was soft. He wasn't his usual tough self. The elation I'd felt that Addie was okay dissipated with every word my father spoke.

"How's Addie?" he asked.

I looked at him and shook myself out of what felt like an underwater world. "She's going to be fine. Holding court in the exam room. Everyone wants to meet her." I smiled, thinking about how excited she was going to be about being the most popular patient in the emergency department.

"You go to Jessica. I'll take a shift sitting with our princess." He patted me on the back as he walked past. I'm not sure how I got to Jessica's room, but I stood at the door and watched the team buzz around like worker bees on the wildflowers she loved so much. I needed to pick some for her, so when she woke up she would see them.

"Mr. Morton, I'm Dr. Sondars. I spoke to Miss Walshay's mother, and she has given me permission to update you on her condition. The gash on her head has been closed up. She has had a brain bleed, Mr. Morton, but I suspect your father informed you of that. We'll do another MRI in a few hours to assess its current state. As of right now, Miss Walshay is in stable but critical condition. We will move her to the ICU shortly. It's a miracle she's done as well as she has. That's a good sign. Can I answer any questions for you?"

I shook my head. I couldn't think straight enough to form words, much less ask questions. He nodded and went back to Jessica's side.

"Rob, what can I do?" Turning to look at Naomi, I couldn't keep it together anymore. I felt wetness drip down my face. First one drop, then two, then I lost count. Naomi pulled me into a curtained off area and wrapped her arms around me. "She's going to be fine, Rob. I know it. There's so much for her to fight for. She fought to keep Addie safe. She fought to get back to you, and she will fight to stay here for your future together. There are also the epic Morton girls' nights she has to be around for. Pretty sure it's mostly that she's fighting for." Naomi let go of me, and I let out a laugh, wiped my face, and took a strengthening breath.

"Thanks, I needed that. We need to stop seeing you here. You have to come around more often."

Naomi giggled. "Well, if Gavin was around more, I'm sure you would get tired of me."

"How are things going?" I quizzed.

She just shrugged. "Good, but I'm tired of FaceTime and phone calls." She slapped her hand over her mouth, and her eyes were as big as saucers.

"I won't say anything, but if you need anything, please ask us."

She nodded and turned to go back to Addie's room. I made a mental note to slap my baby brother upside the head for toying with her. He needed to decide where this relationship was going.

"Mr. Morton, we're getting ready to move, Miss Walshay. She will be in room four. I can take you to the waiting room, but it will be about an hour before you can see her," the nurse informed me. She didn't look old enough to have a four-year degree under her belt.

"Thank you. I know where the waiting room is," I said.

She nodded and turned back to the nursing station. I quickly dialed Daphney's phone and told her what I knew.

CHAPTER 30

I sat in the waiting room alone. It hadn't seemed like that long ago since I'd been here with Kate after Tyler had been injured at the rodeo. I had tossed Jessica into the deep end that night with Addison. It made me smile thinking of them together.

"Rob, is there any change?" Daphney came flying through the door of the waiting room. I stood, and she grabbed me in a hug.

"No, I haven't heard anything." I motioned for Daphney to sit.

"Rob, dear, I'm going to get your father and Addie and go home," Mom said as she hugged me.

It was agony just sitting here waiting. Jumping every time someone walked out of the closed doors. Wondering what was going on behind them. It felt like hours had gone by when the doctor came out and walked toward us. Daphney grabbed hold of my hand when she saw him, and her knuckles turned white from the tight grip she had on me.

"Mrs. Walshay, I'm Dr. Kurts. I'm happy to tell you Jessica is in stable condition. She has not woken up yet, but that's to be expected with the type of trauma she suffered.. We will do another MRI in the morning to monitor the brain bleed. Her vital signs are all stable, and she's continuing to breathe on her own, which is a good sign. She is settled, so if you both would like to go in, I can allow that."

Daphney, who still had a firm grip on my hand, jumped off the chair, and in turn, I stood, and we followed the doctor into the ICU.

I stopped at her door and let Daphney go in first. I wanted her to have a moment alone with Jessica. Saying a brief prayer and taking a deep breath, I walked to the other side of her bed. Bruises that I hadn't noticed before were starting to show. Her beautiful face was adorned with angry purple marks. The wound on her head was bandaged, and I noticed a few on her arms as well. How had I missed all these injuries? Stumbling backward, I plopped down into the chair behind me.

The sudden motion startled Daphney. "Rob, are you okay? Do you need me to call someone?" Her eyes glistened with tears.

"No, I'm fine. She looks worse lying here than she did in the truck." My voice trailed off. I didn't want to scare Daphney any more than she already was. Scooting the chair closer to the bed, I rested Jessica's hand in mine and waited.

Night crept in, and the darkness outside seemed to surround everything. It only made the already somber mood worse as the hours ticked by. My head was filled with thoughts of Addie. I hoped was asleep peacefully. I'm sure my parents, Tyler, and Kate had spoiled her. Longing to hold her in my arms, I wasn't sure I could wait for morning to do so.

"You're thinking about Addie, aren't you?" Daphney asked.

Looking over at her, I smiled. "Yeah, I hope she's sleeping soundly. Mom texted me and said she would sleep in their room tonight just in case she needed them." Letting go of Jessica's hand, I stood and walked over to the window and stared out into the black abyss dotted with sparse yard lights.

"Why don't you head home? It doesn't look like things are changing here. Be there when Addie wakes up. She needs you more than Jessica does right now." Daphney walked up behind me and rested her hand on my shoulder. It was easy to see why Jessica was the way she was. Daphney was a soft soul. She thought about everyone else before herself. She had taught Jessica how to make people feel like they were the only person in the world when she was speaking to them.

I shook my head. I couldn't think of leaving her now. She was so vulnerable lying in this bed. My heart was screaming that I needed to protect her, but my head knew there was nothing I could do.

"I will head home in the morning before Addie gets on the bus."

DAPHNEY SMILED AND SAT DOWN AT JESSICA'S BEDSIDE. HER phone buzzed, and she looked at the number.

"Rob, I need to go take this. It's one of the truckers who used to work for my husband. They've been taking turns checking in on Jess and me over the years and filling in when Jessica needed a father figure. I'm sure word's gotten out that there was an accident. They seem to know everything." Her voice trailed off, and I could see her eyes glisten with unshed tears.

She stood and left the room quietly.

The night passed by slowly, and I watched the sun peek its head over the horizon. When we were keeping new calves safe from predators, first light was a relief, a time to breathe, but I was afraid the day would be just like the night.

"Rob, go to Addison. I'm not asking, I'm telling you to go." Daphney's voice was firm, and I knew there was no arguing with her.

I walked over to Jessica's bedside, kissed her cheek, and squeezed her hand. "I'll be back in a few hours, beautiful."

Daphney hugged me, and as I left, I looked back at the woman who held my heart.

The drive home was a blur, and when I pulled into my driveway, I turned the truck off and sat there. The lights were off; there was nobody inside waiting for me. It felt empty. The sun was up and felt hot already. I walked over to the horse paddock and leaned on the fence to watch the horses quietly graze. Addie's horse wandered overlooking for a treat. "I'm sorry, pal, I got nothing today." He nudged me, and I wrapped my arms around his neck and cried. It felt like a weight had lifted off my shoulders.

The tension of the previous day poured out of me and onto that horse's neck. When I had cried all my tears, I patted JP's neck. "Thanks for getting her to safety."

He gave me a chuff that almost seemed like an acknowledgment and wandered off. I walked back to the house and lay down on the couch, not able to bring myself to go to my bed. Life wasn't right. Both my girls were in beds elsewhere, and I needed them home.

A while later, when I knew Addison would be awake, I walked through the door of my parents' home and heard familiar laughter. Addie was happy. I stood at the doorway of the kitchen and watched her interact with Mom. They made me smile when they were together. She looked like she was totally fine. Like nothing had happened the day before. "Squish."

Addie turned and looked toward me. Her big eyes grew to what seemed like her entire face. She jumped off the counter and ran into my arms. "Daddy, I missed you! But I got to sleep in grandma's room. Dad, grandpa snores." She rolled her eyes a little, making Mom chuckle.

"Are you telling stories about me, miss thing?" Dad walked in behind me and placed his hand on my shoulder before asking, "How's Jessica, son?"

"No change. Stable, but the doctor is still concerned about why she hasn't woken up yet."

Dad nodded and patted my shoulder, then walked over to my mom and kissed her cheek.

"Daddy, when can I see Jessica?" Addie had climbed up into my lap at the table. She rested her head on my shoulder and sighed.

"I don't know, sweetie. When I go back to the hospital, I'll text Grandma and let you know how she is." Her little head nodded against me.

After a week of trips back and forth to the hospital, there was still no change. I wondered how long this could go on. The doctors couldn't give us any indication of what would happen.

When I arrived at the hospital for what felt like the thousandth time, Daphney and I swapped places, and I took over our vigil. Resting my head on the back of the chair, I closed my eyes. It had been a long, sleepless week.

"Rob." I heard a whisper and thought it was in my dreams again, but suddenly, there was a tap on my knee.

My eyes flew open, and I was staring into the sea-green eyes of the woman I loved. "Hi," was all I could say. I had spent so many days thinking of what I would say when she finally woke up, and that's all my brain could come up with.

"Hi. How long have I been out? Looks like a few days by that beard you've got going on." She scrunched up her face. Scruff at the end of the day was okay, but the beard was a no-go for her. Her face was still battered, but her bruises were healing. Those green eyes I loved were finally open, but they still showed exhaustion. For someone who looked the way she did and had been in a coma for a week, her voice was surprisingly strong.

"Babe, you've been asleep for a week."

CHAPTER 31

I thought I heard Rob say I had been asleep for a week, but it was hard for me to process. I'd heard everything going on around me but felt like I was trapped, unable to interact, and now I knew why. Hearing my mom cry, listening to Rob read his book aloud, and hearing the medical staff talk in soft tones and whispers all made sense now.

"What's going through your head? I see the wheels turning." Rob was struggling to keep his face relaxed. He had never been good at hiding his feelings, and right now I could see the concern creep in.

"Just trying to process that I've lost a week," I said, and then a terrifying thought hit me. "Rob, what about Addie?" I tried to sit up, but he jumped off the chair and put his hands on my shoulders.

"Honey, she's fine. Totally fine. Begging to come see you, wondering when you'll be home." His eyes danced, and he smiled when he talked about her. "Jessica, you kept her safe. I'll never be able to show you how grateful I am to you."

"I thought I heard two voices in here," Doctor Kurts said as she stood at the door. "Rob, I hate to ask you to step out, but we're going to need to assess Jessica now that she's awake, but I'll give you both a minute before we start." She stepped back out of the room, closing the door behind her.

"While they give you the once over, I'll call your mom. I'm sure she'll be up here before you're done with the doctor." His grin was catching. I couldn't help smile back at him.

"Call Addie too. I want to see her as soon as I get out of here."

Rob nodded in acknowledgement as he stood to go.

"Hey cowboy, you don't get to leave that easy. I have a week of kissing to catch up on." I grinned, and he walked toward the bed. Our lips met gently, as if he was afraid I would break. "You definitely need to shave," I whispered when we parted.

"I promise."

At that moment, the door banged open, and the nurse came in.

"See you soon," he said as he began backing away.

I nodded and watched him walk out of my room.

There was a flurry of activity in my room as the nurses got things ready for me to move out of ICU. Finally, I was settled in a quiet room of my own. There were no machines beeping steadily here, and I could doze off.

I wasn't sure how long I napped, but I woke to whispers from beside my bed. Mom and Rob were in deep conversation about where I should go when I was discharged. It may have been sneaky, but I kept my eyes closed and listened to them.

"Rob, I don't know. Are you sure you can make her take it easy?" Mom sounded concerned, and there was a hesitancy in her voice.

"Daphney, it will be fine. I can take a few days off to get her settled in. You can come out and stay." Rob was always thinking ten steps ahead of everyone else, always thinking of others before himself. The protector, the fighter of those he loved, and underneath all that tough exterior, he had the soul of a man who loved deep and wanted to make others feel like they were the most important person ever.

I heard a pat on his leg and knew mom struggled for words. A sniffle and the pull of a tissue out of the box lead to my mother blowing her nose. "Thank you, son. I might take you up on that, but I'll give you a few days."

Rob's hand was resting on the bed beside me, so I took a hold of it and squeezed it. I didn't need to break their moment, but I wanted him to know I appreciated him. The squeeze I received back acknowledged that he understood.

"It's about time you woke up. I was getting worried," he said. From the sound of his voice, he was likely still looking at the TV mounted on the wall, so I opened one eye and gave him an appreciative once over before he could catch me.

"Girlie, you gave us a scare." Mom moved around to the other side of the bed and kissed my head gently.

"I'm sorry, mom. It won't happen again."

"No, it won't," she said, giving me a soft smile.

Rob finally caught me appraising him and said, "Addison is driving me crazy wanting to see you, so I'm going to go get her. I'll be back soon." He leaned down and kissed me. He seemed a little shy kissing me in front of mom.

"See you soon," I whispered before he turned to go.

I HAD ARRANGED FOR MOM TO MEET ME AT THE HOSPITAL IN half an hour so she could take Addison home. A seven-year-old could only sit in a confined space, trying to be quiet for so long.

We got out of the truck, and she grabbed my hand. As happy as she was to be here, I think she was a little scared. "It's okay, Squish, just hold my hand. Jessica can't wait to see you."

I knocked on the door and opened it. The way Jessica's eyes lit up when she turned and saw Addison made my heart soar. There was no denying she loved my daughter. Addison ran and jumped onto the bed before I could stop her.

"Addison, you can't…"

Jessica cut me off. "Rob, it's fine. She can't hurt anything." Jessica's arms enveloped Addison, and her eyes glistened with tears.

"Let me look at you." Jessica scanned Addison for bumps, bruises, and injuries. Her tears flowed freely now, and they hugged each other again. "I'm so very glad you're okay, Addie."

"Please don't leave me again, Momma." Her words were quiet, but I was sure I'd heard her correctly.

My eyes flew up to Jessica, who was looking at me like a deer in headlights. Neither of us knew what to say. Jessica started crying again, and I sat down on the chair beside the girls. Jess stuck out her hand and pulled me into their embrace.

"I'm not going anywhere, baby. I'll always be here for you." It felt like she had said it as much to me as Addison.

We stayed sitting together until Mom and Dad showed up to get Addison. "Oh Jessica, you had us worried, my dear." My mom gently hugged her when she came into the room.

"You are an amazing woman, Jessica. Our family will always be in your debt." My dad stood at the end of Jessica's bed. He was sincere, and if I wasn't mistaken, his eyes held unshed tears.

"Addison, we better get going. You have to feed JP before supper." Mom could sense that I wanted Jessica alone.

"Bye," Addison whispered in Jessica's ear.

"See you soon, sweetie. Give JP an extra apple from me. He deserves it."

Addison giggled, hopped off the bed, and took my mom's hand.

"Sandy, I just need to talk to Rob and Jessica for a second." Dad fumbled through his words.

"Yes, you do," was all Mom said before she and Addison left the room. She quietly pulled the door shut behind her.

Dad dug into his coat pocket and pulled out an envelope. "Just over a week ago, you brought me this check and put me in my place. Somewhere I'm being put frequently nowadays. It's also someplace I should have been put a long time ago." He fidgeted with the envelope and shook his head. Walking over to the head of Jessica's bed, he stood looking at her and handed the check to her.

"I won't accept this. You've made a success out of yourself, and I have no doubt it would have happened regardless of me stepping in. I find it admirable that after all these years, you did this." He held up the envelope and continued, "The love you two have is stronger than anything thrown at you, and I see that now. I regret not seeing it eight years ago."

Jessica took the check and handed it to me. "Brian, I don't think I can ever forget the eight years I lost with Rob, but I don't regret that those years gave him Addison." She looked up at my dad and took my hand. "You two need to fix whatever is broken between you. That isn't something I need to know about, but please don't let this be the catalyst that ruins your relationship."

I looked from her to my dad and nodded. We had so much to work through, but I genuinely wanted to repair our relationship.

"I better get going before your mother calls. I'm glad you're on the mend, Jessica," he said, giving her hand an awkward pat. It was clear he was uncomfortable but was trying. "I'll talk to you later, son."

I nodded, stood, and shook his hand. "I'll call you when I'm on my way home." I followed him to the door and closed it after he left.

Jessica and I had so much to talk about, and this moment probably wasn't the time, but when I turned and looked at her, I knew we needed to have the conversation right now.

Jessica looked down at her hands as I turned the chair to sit directly in front of her.

CHAPTER 32

There was no way I could have imagined how stressful being on this side of a wedding would be. I had planned hundreds of high-profile weddings, and here I was the day before my own, feeling like the world was falling down around me. The sun shone through the window, and I immediately started going over the lists in my head. Rehearsal at six, and supper at seven. Rob would send Addie home with Brian and Sandra. The wedding party had decided to go out for a few hours. Rob had arranged it, and as much as I wanted to control the timeline, I knew I should let Rob oversee some of the plans.

"Stop, everything will be perfect," Rob mumbled beside me as he yawned. "You woke me up with your worrying." He reached his arm across me and pulled me to him.

"Good morning to you too," I quipped as he laughed.

"What can I say? You turn me on. And you've had me cut off for a week." His hand slid up to my breast, and he pinched teasingly.

I slapped at his hand, which only encouraged him more.

My alarm went off, and I removed Rob's arm from me and got out of bed.

"Jess, babe, come back to bed. Please." He was so cute when he begged.

"Nope, sorry, I have things to do." Leaning over the bed, I kissed him.

"Are you sure you can't stay? I'm quite enjoying this view." He caught me and pulled on the neck of my shirt, arching his brow and making an "mmm" sound.

I stood and walked to the bathroom as he pretended to cry. "Drama queen," I called over my shoulder as I closed the bathroom door.

His laugh broke through my tension. In thirty-two hours, I would finally be the wife of the man I always dreamed about. Butterflies floated through my stomach, and I couldn't help but grin.

My day flew by, and I found myself staring at our reception space. We were using the barn on the Morton property where Tyler and Kate had gotten married, but I'd transformed it by taking massive white fabric panels and draping them from the rafters and tying them at the posts all along both sides of the barn. Tall white rose arrangements would sit on each table with dark green foliage to set the roses off. The florist would bring them in tomorrow.

I confirmed with the caterer the times he would be arriving. As soon as I hung up, my phone rang again. "Hello?"

"Jess, are you on your way?" Rob sounded concerned.

"I'm out at the ranch. What's the problem?" My heart started to race.

"Have you looked at the time?"

I glanced at my watch and panicked. "Oh no. Rob, I'm sorry, I got carried away here and didn't watch the time. I'll be there in twenty minutes." I took off at a sprint to my car.

"Hey, don't be crazy. Just take it easy. We have plenty of

time. That's why I called now and not thirty minutes from now."

"I love you. Bye." Speeding out of the Morton's property, I couldn't believe I'd been so careless. How does a wedding planner show up late for her own rehearsal?

I PULLED INTO THE CHURCH PARKING LOT AND LOOKED IN THE visor mirror. I fluffed my hair, wiped the black marks from my mascara off my eyes, and reapplied my lipstick. Just as I finished, there was a knock on my window, and I turned to see Rob. He had his hands on his hips, a clenched jaw, and he was frowning. I wondered what is problem was. I wasn't that late, and he'd already known I was running behind.

I SMILED AS I OPENED MY CAR DOOR AND STEPPED OUT. "I'M SO sorry I'm late…"

"I don't care that you're late. You made it here in seventeen minutes. Jess, it should have taken you twenty-five minutes at best." He turned and walked away.

I couldn't believe my heavy foot would be the cause of his anger. "Are you serious? You've made that drive in less time than I did. And you were proud of it." I ran to catch up to him but didn't anticipate him stopping, so I ran square into his back. I bounced off his back and couldn't help but laugh.

Rob turned then, and it was clear he was trying to be mad, but the corners of his mouth turned up, and his eyes danced. "I just want you to be safe. I could never live without you again," he whispered as he wrapped me in his arms.

"It won't happen again," I said as I returned his hug.

He made me feel safe, and when I was wrapped in his embrace, nothing else mattered. Even this wedding. At the end of the day tomorrow, we would be husband and wife. It didn't matter how we got there or what amazing flowers were on the tables. It just mattered that he would be mine.

"Let's get this over with. Then we can have some fun." Rob kissed the top of my head, and we walked into the church hand in hand.

TO SAY REHEARSAL WAS A NIGHTMARE WOULD HAVE BEEN AN understatement. Jessica was trying to direct people when she was supposed to be focusing on herself. I checked my watch and saw that we had ten minutes before we needed to be at the diner for supper.

I put my fingers to my lips and whistled before shouting, "Look, people, it's not that difficult. Let's do this one last time, and if you mess up, you're out. We can find someone to fill your outfit."

The crowd froze. Their faces were priceless. They all looked at each other and then to Jessica.

I chuckled. "Well, not everyone can be replaced." I pointed at Jessica. "You have to be up here with me."

I watched her stress melt away. Her eyes shone again, her frown disappeared, and her shoulders relaxed.

"You heard the man. Let's get going." She turned on her heel, and the bridal party followed close behind.

One by one, everyone filed in properly and seriously. The doors opened, and Jessica stood there with her mother, and as I looked at her, all I could envision was what she would look like tomorrow.

With rehearsal complete, we all made our way to the diner, and as we sat in the small restaurant, the chatter was almost deafening. When Jessica and I were making plans for this weekend, there had been only one place we wanted for our rehearsal supper. This diner was where I'd first seen her, where we had our first date, and where we rekindled our romance on our second first date. It wasn't hard to reserve the entire place for the evening. I made sure it was worth it for Nancy, so she didn't lose out on her day's profit.

I stood, and everyone looked at me and quieted down.

"Now I'm not one for speeches, but I have a few things I want to say." Reaching down, I took Jessica's hand, and she stood beside me. "Too many years ago to count, I walked into this diner and saw the most beautiful woman in the world. I knew right then that she was going to be mine. What I never dreamt of was that we would take the roundabout way to get to where we are. But I'm so glad we finally made it. Jessica, seeing you walk back onto the ranch made my heart stop."

I looked over at Jessica, seeing tears in her eyes and a shy smile on her face, and continued, "I didn't think I'd get a second chance at happiness with you, but every day we're together, you make me the happiest man in the world."

"I'm lucky too, Dad," Addison said as she hopped up on her chair. She hung on to my dad's shoulder to steady herself. "Jessica, can I call you mom after tomorrow?" Jessica let go of my hand and walked over to where Addison stood and wrapped her up in her arms.

"You can call me whatever you want, sweetheart."

I didn't think I'd ever been so happy. Addie hadn't called Jess "Mom" since the day at the hospital weeks ago. But seeing both my girls hug, the love shining in their faces mirroring my own, I knew all was going to be well with the world as long as we were together.

CHAPTER 33

*J*stood on the porch drinking my coffee. It was early, and I wanted Addison to sleep as long as she could today. The morning was tranquil, and if the day stayed like this, it would be perfect. I noticed Jessica's car over at the barn. She had been adamant that we didn't see each other before the wedding, so she had stayed at her mom's last night, so I wasn't sure why she was here so early. My critical-thinking side said to stay here and drink my coffee, but my love-for-Jessica side said to go see check on her. Before I could make the decision, I was walking down my stairs and over to the barn.

She was sitting in the car, so I slid into the seat beside her. "Quit biting your lip, there's no need to be nervous."

Her eyes were as big as saucers. "We aren't supposed to see each other before the wedding," she said. Her voice was quiet, and it felt like she didn't want the superstitious powers that be to know we were together.

"Jessica, we've overcome everything that should have torn us apart, and here we are, on the morning of our wedding, spending a quiet moment together. That's what today is about.

Us, together." I grabbed for her, wanting to show her I didn't care about any of the old-fashioned rules.

She turned to look at me with tears in her eyes. "How did I get so lucky to find you all over again?" she asked as she squeezed my hand and smiled.

I leaned over and pulled her toward me. Our lips met, our passion and hunger for each other igniting. "Your car is too small. I need to hold you," I whispered in her ear.

"Being in your arms usually leads to more than just holding. As much as I wouldn't mind, I think we should wait until tonight, when we're alone and not in plain sight of your parents." Her eyes danced, and her smile was mischievous.

I looked over her shoulder, and sure enough, there they were, standing on the deck outside their room. "I think I live too close to my family," I groaned as I rested my head on hers.

"Yeah, but I love your house, so we aren't moving. We'll just have to be sneaky from now on." Sliding her hand up my thigh, she arched her brow and grinned.

I clamped my hand on top of hers before she got to her destination. "Apparently, we have to wait for tonight," I joked, sticking my bottom lip out and pouting.

"Okay, stop pouting and get out of my car." She pointed to the door, laughing. "I have to get back to town, and I'm not allowed to speed anymore." Trying to frown, she broke into laughter.

We kissed again, and I finally got out of the car and headed back to my house.

I GAVE EVERYTHING THE LAST ONCE OVER AND WAS READY TO have this wedding behind me. I was definitely not meant to be the bride and wedding planner at the same time. Sometimes I missed my business in Manhattan, and right now was one of them. I'd had a team of people who could take over for me

there. Here, I was the only one who could make sure everything was running smoothly.

"Girlie, breathe. This all looks beautiful, and you're about
to marry the man of your dreams. Stop worrying. If there's
something out of place, nobody will know, and more importantly, nobody will care." My mom patted my arm as we stood
at the back of the church, waiting for the doors to open. Mom
was beaming; she looked beautiful in the peach dress she wore.
It had a flutter hem and flowed beautifully around her.

The music changed, and the doors to the sanctuary were
opened. All eyes turned to look at Mom and me. She took a
step, then I took a breath and followed. The guests stood as I
entered the room, and every one of them was looking at me,
but focusing on Rob at the end of the aisle made all my jitters
disappear. The walk seemed to take forever, but after a few
moments, I was finally standing beside the man I loved.

"Who gives this woman to this man?" the minister asked
in a loud, booming voice.

A voice from behind me spoke, "On behalf of the people
who worked for Martin Walshay and have had the distinct
honor of being her fill-in fathers when needed, and on behalf
of her mom." I turned to all the men who had worked for my
dad standing.

"We do," came a chorus of voices.

I looked at the men through tear-filled eyes and looked at
my mom, who whispered, "Surprise." She hugged me and
handed my hand to Rob. When she hugged him, I heard her
say, "Take care of my girl."

He nodded, and we turned to face the minister.

We said our I dos and recited our vows, then I turned to
Addie and knelt down to speak directly to her.

"Addison, you are an important part of this marriage also.
Maybe the most important part. I love you more than you will
ever know. You made my life complete when I didn't know it
wasn't. Please accept this ring as my promise to never leave

you, to love you for all my days, and to be there for all your good days and bad." I pulled a ring off the end of my pinkie finger and put it on her right hand, earning a beaming smile from the girl I could now call mine.

Standing back up, I turned and faced Rob again. My big cowboy was crying, and there was nothing he could do to hide it. I smiled up at him as he mouthed, "thank you".

Our exchanging of rings was done through the tears, our marriage certificate signed, and we turned to face our guests.

"What God has joined together, let nobody separate. By the power vested in me by the state of Texas, I now pronounce you husband and wife. Rob, kiss that bride of yours."

Rob took a half step toward me, wrapped his arms around me, and we sealed our marriage with a kiss that was too passionate for church. The crowd hooted, hollered, and cheered. We parted, and people crowded the front for pictures. I held out my hand for Addie to come stand with us, and we stood there together as a family for the first time.

THE RECEPTION SPACE IN THE BARN WAS PERFECT, AND I HAD been impressed that my new team pulled it off with no hiccups.

"All right, everyone, the moment you've been waiting for. Mr. and Mrs. Rob Morton," our DJ announced. He played music we'd chosen, and the crowd cheered as we walked in. We walked to our table and promptly gave the people what they wanted. A steamy kiss before we sat down.

It was hard to believe I was here in this moment. I glanced at Rob and smiled.

"What's that smile for?" he whispered as he placed his arm around me and pulled me closer.

"I was just making sure this was real. I dreamed of this so many times, but then when I'd wake up, I was always alone. But now my dreams have come true." My heart was full, and I leaned in to kiss him. Nobody was paying attention to us, and in this full barn, it felt like it was just the two of us.

We danced late into the night and stayed until our last guests left. When the night was over, the only remaining guests were Rob's family, my mom, and Mr. Radliff, who were sitting around laughing about something. I looked around and knew I had been gifted a wonderful life. I leaned into Rob, and he go the hint that I was ready to head out.

"Well, we have to make the drive to Hammond for the night, so I guess we should be going," Rob said as he stood and held his hand out to help me up from my chair.

"Wait, I want to get out of this thing before we leave. No need to drag it with us." I walked hand in hand with Rob back to the house. Addie followed close behind so she could get her suitcase to stay at Sandra and Brian's for the week we'd be gone.

"Addison, go get your stuff, and we'll meet you in the living room. I'm going to help Jessica." Rob told her.

She nodded and bounced off to her room.

When she was out of earshot, Rob whispered, "Mrs. Morton, let's get you out of that dress." He ushered me to our room at the end of the hall, then kicked the door closed and looked at me. "Turn around." His voice was full of lust, and I silently cursed the fact that we had an hour drive ahead of us. He unlaced the corset back and walked around to face me. My dress fell off me and fell into a puddle on the floor. Rob smiled and his eyes flowed down my body.

"Why are we driving to Hammond tonight? That's one hour of torture because I can't have my hands all over you." Rob had walked over and reached for me, so I walked into his waiting arms and laughed.

"Dad, I'm waiting," Addison called from the living room

"Better not keep her waiting." Jessica whispered as I explored her neck with my lips.

The day had been perfect, and the wedding had been wonderful, with minimal issues. I could tell Jessica was tired. The last week had been difficult on her, and she was still recovering from her injuries. On top of the stress of our wedding day, she was also worried about how her business would run while we were away. Handing over control of her business again while we were on our honeymoon was very hard on her. Trust between us had come easy, trust with anyone else would take years to earn.

I slid my hand over to her upper thigh and gripped it. She sat a little straighter in the seat, and I could tell she'd turned to look at me.

"Are you trying to keep me awake?" Her voice was airy and sleepy.

When we finally arrived in Hammond, I checked us in to the hotel and we found our room.

"I'm going to change," Jessica said as she headed to the bathroom. I had other ideas, and grabbed the tie at her waist, letting her shirt fall open.

"Don't change on my account. This view is all I need." Her shirt hung open, and her breasts were partly hidden behind a push-up bra.

Closing the distance between us, I reached out and traced the round arch at the top of her breast, and her flesh immediately broke out in goosebumps. Jessica's breathing changed as I watched her chest rise and fall quicker.

"I've made love to you more times than I can count, but tonight you are truly mine."

I wrapped the ties of her shirt around my hands and pulled her to me. I pushed her shirt off her shoulders, so the sleeves caught on her arms. She was completely under my control, and her eyes were locked on mine.

ROB GUIDED ME BACK TO THE BED AND UNWRAPPED HIS HANDS from the ties of my shirt before he pulled it the rest of the way down my arms. I reached up and grasped the top of Rob's shirt and pulled it open, tugging it off him. Running my hands up his chest, I sighed at the feeling of warmth radiating from him. I didn't think I was cold, but a shiver ran through me.

"What's wrong?"

"Nothing. I was just thinking about how warm you feel and how lucky I am, and it sent a thrill through me. It could also mean I'm cold since your arms aren't around me."

His laugh sent me soaring. Rob reached out and unbuttoned my jeans, pushed me down on the bed, and pulled them off my legs. He chuckled when he looked at me. "Again, no panties? I might have to request it all the time." He ran his hand up my leg and lightly brushed my mound, causing me to inhale sharply.

He removed his hand and stood, dropping his pants and kneeling down over me.

Rob caressed my body, but I needed more than sensual tonight. He was finally my husband, the man I would spend my life with, and I wanted all of him.

I tried to get him to move with more urgency by bucking my hips and reaching for him, but he was in a zone and taking his time.

He finally repositioned himself over me, and I took my

chance. Wrapping my legs around him, I rolled over, so he was now under me.

Rob ran his hand up my stomach and grasped my breast. He kneaded it and pinched at my nipple, which sent thrills through me, and I let my head fall back and enjoyed the sensation.

I didn't stay that way for long because I was in control now. Sitting atop my husband, I realized it was my turn to make him squirm. "Earlier, you were wrong about one thing. Rob Morton, you are mine. Mind, body, and soul."

I shifted and slowly and sank onto Rob, finding him more than ready to join together.

The feeling of being in control was empowering. I shifted my hips slowly at first, knowing it drove him crazy.

"Jessica," he growled, and I let out a giggle.

"Oh, you like it." I whispered as I leaned in closer to him.

"Like might not be the right word for torture." He ran his hand through my hair and grabbed the back of my neck, pulling me closer. "It's my turn to torture."

Before I had a second to process what he said, I was lying on my back again, with Rob over top of me, having never separated from him.

"Now, baby, let me teach you how to torture the person you love." He arched his brow and began moving again. Slowly at first, then he increased his thrusting until it felt like we were on an out-of control-stallion.

It didn't take much time, and I clawed at his back as the waves of pleasure washed through my body. I couldn't catch my breath between the rushes of satisfaction.

CHAPTER 34

"Rob, I have something to ask, and I need you to let me finish before you say anything." I said, looking up at him to watch for a sign that he was listening. When he nodded, I took a deep breath and mustered my courage. "Addison calls me mom, and I absolutely love it. Marrying you months ago was not only a dream come true, but it also made my dream of being a mom happen." I was staring at my hands but made myself look up into his eyes. "What would you think if I petitioned to legally adopt Addison? I would understand if you said no. It's a lot to ask, and could potentially stir up problems, but I want her to know she's, my daughter. It won't matter to me if a piece of paper says it or if Addison only ever just calls me Mom and nothing more. In my heart, she's mine and always will be, but I would love to make it official."

Rob didn't say anything right away, he just sat staring at me. My heart was sinking as the clock on the wall ticked.

"I know it's a lot to ask, and maybe I should have waited until we'd been married longer but…"

He leaned in and kissed me, stopping my words in their tracks, and when we pulled apart, he whispered, "Yes."

My eyes felt like they popped out of my head, and I couldn't help the smile that grew across my face. "Yes?"

"Yes. I've been thinking about it, and I wanted to ask your opinion, but I also didn't want to scare you." Rob's hand caressed the back of my neck, and I relaxed. "I know you love her like she's your own. I don't know what it will require. I'll call my lawyer in the morning and find out." He pulled me toward him, and we kissed again. I never knew I could be so happy. It seemed like the last eight years had never happened. I was always meant to be here with him. Over the years we were apart, I had learned a lot about myself, and there was no way I would change who I am now, but I still had feelings of sadness when I thought about all the time, we could have been a family.

"One thing though. I don't want to say anything to Addison until we have more information. To get her hopes up only to be crushed wouldn't be good for her," I said.

Rob agreed by nodding his head. "I think that's a good idea. She wants so badly to be like all the other kids. She wants a mother." Rob ran his fingers through his hair and let out a slow breath, flopping his head back on the couch. "She used to cry at night when she thought I couldn't hear. I wouldn't have known, but Addison told Kate, and Tyler told me what was going on."

THE DAYS WENT BY, AND I WAITED FOR ROB'S LAWYER TO GET back to us. One afternoon, a few hours after he'd left for work, Rob came flying into the house. "Jessica, can you come to town with me now? I have an appointment with Merrit Hanson at two. He has documents we need to sign so you can start the process of adopting Addison."

After a quick glance at my watch, I fluffed my hair in the mirror and was ready to go. We walked out to the truck hand in hand and both a little nervous.

Half an hour drive managed to feel like an hour and sitting in the waiting was killing me. Finally, the receptionist told us we could go in.

"Rob, it's so nice to see you again. I have gotten so used to doing business with your brother, I wondered if you had run off." Both men laughed, and I stood waiting to be introduced.

"No, I haven't run off. Well, not yet. I would like you to meet my wife, Jessica. Jess, this is Merrit. He's been the family lawyer since his father retired." I stuck my hand out and shook his.

"It's very nice to meet you, ma'am. Congratulations on your wedding. I think beyond the issue you're here for, we'll need to look at updating a few things, Rob. Your will, for one. If anything were to happen before this process is over, we need to put in writing your wishes for who Addison would live with, but for now, please sit."

We took seats in front of the large desk. "I've looked into the custody of Addison, and we're going to need to track down Samantha. While she didn't fight for custody, she never signed parental rights away."

Rob and I looked at each other, knowing this would be ten times harder than we thought if we had to get Samantha involved.

Merrit placed papers in front of us to look at. "These are what she'll need to sign. Termination of Parental Rights. Rob, do you have any idea where she is?"

I looked over at Rob, hoping he had kept tabs on her all these years.

"No, I had been keeping an eye on her, but over the last few years, it seemed silly to keep doing it. She hasn't tried to contact us at all."

Reaching over, I took his hand and squeezed it.

"I'm sure it won't be difficult to track her down again. We'll need to call Bennet and have him put out feelers," Rob said.

Merrit nodded, and it was like I wasn't in the room anymore.

"Who's Bennet?" I asked quietly.

Merrit looked at Rob and then said, "Bennet is the private investigator Brian keeps on staff. He was retained when Samantha needed watching, and he's been used a few times over the last few years."

I nodded and then had a thought.

"If you have a PI, why did you have to go to Montana and sort out Tyler's situation?"

Rob looked at me and opened his mouth to say something, but he didn't have an answer and just shrugged.

"Sorry, Mr. Hanson. You were saying?"

"I'll call Bennet and get him moving."

"This is slightly off topic, but how's the other situation he's working on?" Rob leaned forward and talked quietly.

"Nothing yet. I know he's been working around the clock on it." Merrit leaned back in his chair and folded his hands in his lap. "I won't lie, these cases rarely go easily, but if you can get Samantha to sign these documents, then there will be a court hearing where you can file your petition." He leaned forward again and continued, "A judge will review all the documentation, and usually around four weeks later, depending on the docket, he will come back with a ruling. During that final hearing, he will want to talk to Addison, since she's old enough to express her desire. It will help if you have your entire support system with you that day just to show a united front."

"Well, that should be the easiest part of the entire process. Our family only wants what's best for Addie, and we all know her desire to have a mom who is present in her life," I said as I looked at Rob, who looked comforted by this.

"What else?" He was tense. He gripped my hand as if he thought he would lose me in a sea of people. His jaw was clenched as he waited for the answer.

"Nothing. those are the ins and outs. I know it should be more complicated, or rather, feel more complicated, but when situations get to this point, things are usually cut and dry." Merrit was smiling. "What I see here are two people, in love, wanting to give a little girl the best life she can have. Once we get that signature, I'll try to get things expedited."

"Okay, thanks. When you have my will ready to look at, I'll come back. I need to replace Tyler with Jessica as my beneficiary. Also, we'll need to look at where the assets go in case of my… well… you know."

I was confused by all the legal jargon, so I decided to just ask. "May I ask what should happen to your current assets?" I asked.

Merrit spoke up. "They will be used to keep Addison in the life she is accustomed to. If you are granted the adoption, you will be expected to ensure that happens." The lawyer folded his hands on his lap and leaned back in his chair. As if he thought I would fight that arrangement and ask for Rob's money.

Shifting in my chair, I turned to look at Rob straight on. I held his hand in mine.

"I don't need you to take care of me if something happens. I'm fully capable of doing that on my own. Addie is the one who will need it. I will not be the woman who takes that from her."

Rob looked at me and gave me a half smile. "I hate talking about these things. Jessica and I will discuss it. I have a copy at the house we can look over, then I'll get back to you."

We stood, shook hands again, and then Rob led me out of the office with his hand resting on my lower back.

CHAPTER 35

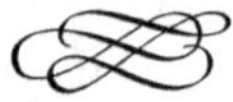

"**C**an I help you?" I asked the woman who had pulled up in front of the house. She was tall and wore too much makeup. Her crimson red hair didn't seem natural on her bronzed skin, and she took the saying "the higher the hair, the closer to Jesus," to heart.

"Yeah, I'm looking for my kid," the stranger quipped as she leaned against her car door.

"I'm sorry. Are you sure you're at the right house? Could you be looking for one of the ranch hands?" I questioned politely, hoping I wasn't offending her.

The stranger let out a shrill laugh. "Not unless Brian is making his own granddaughter do the work around here." Then, as quick as a light switch shutting off a light, her demeanor changed, and a darkness came over her face. "Lady, this is my home, and I'm looking for my daughter, Addie. Judging from that rock on your finger, you're the flavor of the week around here."

Twirling the ring on my finger, I could feel my world spinning out of control. A million thoughts ran through my head, and I couldn't keep them straight. The door opening behind me brought all those thoughts to a halting stop. I spun around and stared into Addie's confused face.

"Addison, darlin', please go inside and call your dad. Tell him we have an emergency." She didn't ask questions, just nodded and turned to go back inside. "Maybe send a text to your grandpa and Uncle Tyler too." Her brown curls bounced as she gave a slight nod and went into the house. Closing my eyes and taking a deep breath, I slowly spun on the heel of my boot to face Samantha. Her face grew redder by the second.

"She's mine, not yours. No matter how long you've been playing house and pretending to be her mom, you aren't. Never will be," she spat out in pure hatred. Unfortunately, that hit a nerve.

"And you think you're her mother? There's a big difference between giving birth to a child and raising a child, lady. I haven't been around her entire life, but Sandra has, and she's given Addie everything you should have given her. Then there's Kate, who has been Addie's rock since she and Tyler got married. It was Kate's arms she cried in when she was teased about not having a mom. Or when she was made fun of because her mom walked out on her. I'm lucky enough to be here now, and I will tell you, Samantha, that little girl in there is my world, and if you think you can waltz in here and take her away, you have another thing coming."

By this time, I had walked right up to her and gotten in her face. Hands flying, fingers pointing, I didn't hear Rob arrive at the house, followed closely by Brian and Tyler.

I felt a slight pull around my waist as I lunged once more, ready to argue, and I turned to see Rob. He looked like he had aged ten years, and I saw a fury in his eyes that I had never witnessed before. I knew he never thought this day would come, and I'm the one who caused it.

"Tyler, call Kate, please. I have a feeling Addie will need to hang out with her for a while," Rob said. The calmness of his voice belied the anger written all over his face.

Tyler nodded and walked away to make his call.

"Dad, check on her, please?"

Brian nodded and walked around Samantha without even acknowledging her. Rob had placed his arm around my waist and stood there staring at his ex-wife.

"WHAT ARE YOU DOING HERE?" RAGE FLOWED THROUGH ME. My hands clenched into fists, my pulse took off, and I was sure my blood pressure was through the roof.

"Like I told her, I'm here to see my daughter." Samantha crossed her arms and waited for my reply. I looked up at Tyler and didn't have to say a word, he was already dialing our lawyer's phone number.

"Samantha, what do you want? You walked out of her life four years ago. There has ample opportunity for you to come back. I never closed that door on you, but why are you here now?" I was trying to keep my voice calm, but even looking at her made me angry.

"Who's she?" The two words flew out of her mouth with so much vitriol it made my stomach lurch.

I looked at Jessica. "This is my wife, Jessica."

"Oh, so this is the Jessica, hmm? The same Jessica you loved more than you could ever love me. The same woman who always stood between us?" Samantha had waltzed over toward her, but I quickly stepped between them.

"Don't make a fool of yourself. You need to leave," I quietly grumbled. What I hadn't expected was the slap across the face that met me when she got close enough.

"You can't bring your floozy in and expect her to take my place."

"Are you serious? Samantha, you walked out. You left us, not the other way around. Never once did I try to keep you from Addison. You did all that yourself. I'm pretty sure the papers you signed when you walked away from her will still hold up in court. You have no right to even see my little girl." I took a quick look over at Tyler, and he nodded. There was no way I could show it, but I was relieved.

"Look, Samantha, I'll talk to my lawyer and find out what's going on and get back to you, but you need to leave." I walked closer to her. "What number can I reach you at?"

"My number hasn't changed." She threw her arms around me and pressed her breasts into my chest. "I always hoped you would try calling, so I never changed it." Her voice was syrupy sweet, and it made my stomach turn. What had I ever seen in her? I was young, in lust, and trying to get over the woman who was standing behind me, watching all this happen. I shook her off and backed away.

I took my phone from my shirt pocket and unlocked the screen. "I don't have your number anymore, and I don't remember it." Watching her eyes change from flirty to forlorn was not something I was sad about.

Samantha rattled off her number, but I really didn't listen. I liked when I told her I didn't remember it. "Okay, thank you. I'll be in touch later. I need to go check on my daughter." Turning, I grabbed Jessica's hand so she would follow. The only thought I had was to talk to Addie.

"Rob, wait… I'll leave if you give me some money. I know your family has always been well off, and the last few years have only increased that wealth, I'm sure. I've been following your business deals." Samantha crossed her arms and smiled slyly.

"I already have custody of Addison All I want is for her to know she has a mother who loves her and wants her." Taking a few steps toward her, I lowered my voice and spoke through clenched teeth. "There is no way I will pay you for my daughter." I turned once more and started to walk away.

"If she is your daughter." My blood ran cold at those words, and I turned back to look at Samantha.

"What did you say?" I hollered as I took a few steps toward her.

"Rob, come on, have you never thought she didn't look like you? You didn't suspect anything when she was supposedly a premature baby who happened to be the size of a full-term baby?"

Samantha's laughter after her confession sent me over the edge. I launched myself toward her and was tipped mid pounce by Jessica hanging on to my arm tightly.

Samantha's eyes danced, and I hated that I'd let her know she'd gotten to me.

"Look, Samantha, I know you hate me, but that little girl in there only wants love. She doesn't deserve this, so if you're lying, I will make it my life's mission to ruin you." I saw red, and all I could focus on was making Samantha sorry for what she was doing. Our faces were inches apart, and I suddenly realized how haggard she looked.

Her life had been hard, but she was the only one to blame for that. She had been rode hard and put away wet for a lot of years.

I felt sorry for the life she'd made for herself.

Her words were full of spite and hate as she said, "According to the birth certificate, she's yours, and to be honest, I couldn't even tell you who her father is."

Jessica wrapped her arm through mine and held on to me. This bit of news changed everything for both of us. All of a sudden, I realized I would not have biological children of my own, and I became acutely aware of the feelings Jessica would have had to come to terms with.

I grabbed Jessica's hand, and we bounded up the stairs. I

heard her car start, and Samantha was gone. I looked behind me and saw my family watching her go. Tyler was still on the phone, and my parents were intently listening to his side of the conversation. They didn't need me right now, but my daughter did.

CHAPTER 36

It wasn't often that a family meeting was called, but I put in an SOS last night and asked everyone to meet at the main house around noon. I hoped Gavin could get here and Naomi was off.

"Hey, bro, what's with the emergency call?" Gavin sauntered into the dining room at Mom and Dads. We hugged, and I looked at my family sitting before me.

"If everyone could have a seat, I'm afraid you're going to need them." I looked at Jessica, who hadn't been able to hide the concern on her face when Addison wasn't around. She tried to smile, but it wasn't very reassuring. "By now, you all know that Jessica and I put a petition before the court to have Jessica legally adopt Addison. Samantha showed up here after a call from her lawyer. She dropped the bombshell that I am not Addison's father, biological anyway."

My mother instantly burst into tears, and I could see anger and sadness growing on my father's face. Tyler put his arm around Kate as she rested her hands on her stomach. Gavin sat staring at me, and Naomi placed her hand on his leg. "Rob, have you ever…?" Gavin's voice trailed off, and I knew what he was asking. He wanted to know if I had ever considered the possibility.

"Honestly, no, never. When we got together, I was hurting, and when she told me she was pregnant, all I was concerned about was the child we were bringing into this world." I looked over at Jessica, and she looked at the floor. Gently, I placed my hand on her shoulder, and she reached up to hold mine. "Addison has no idea, and that's how I want to keep it. For now anyway."

"What's your plan, son? Are you going to find this man?" Dad looked me square in the face. "She's my first grandchild, nothing will change that, and I can't let her go. Rob, she's been ours for eight years. Nothing changes that. She's a Morton, no matter what."

Tears filled my eyes, and I sat down in the chair beside me. "I don't know, Dad." My voice was a whisper, and I dropped my head into my hands. I was worn out.

LATER THAT NIGHT, I WANDERED AROUND THE RANCH ALONE. Jessica stayed in the house to make sure Addison had someone around if she woke up. While she didn't know everything that was happening, she knew enough to realize that Samantha was causing trouble.

"Son, do you need to talk?" I turned around and saw my dad standing in the doorway of his office. While I didn't usually go to him for advice, tonight, he seemed like the right person. Nodding, I turned and followed him into the room.

"What are we doing?" He sat down on one end of the couch and I took the other.

I sighed. There were no words. My entire life for the last nine years had been a lie. "I don't know. She's my daughter, but where do I go from here? What if she eventually wants to find her biological dad? What if she hates me one day because of this? Or worse, what if he wants her?"

There were things in life I couldn't think about, and not having Addison was number one. "She's the only child I will have, and what if she's not even mine?"

"I'm sure you and Jessica will have kids, Rob."

I shook my head. "No, dad, she can't have kids. That's one of the reasons her marriage fell apart. " Running my hands through my hair, I looked at my father. "All I know is I need Samantha to sign those papers so I—we—can get on with our lives and deal with everything else later."

I stood and turned to look at him. "Look, I know we haven't seen eye to eye for a long time, and I'm still working on forgiving you for sending Jessica away, but I want to thank you for what you said about Addison earlier."

Dad moved to my side and lowered his voice. "Rob, you need to decide if you want to find out who he is. You need to think about it and be prepared for anything down the road. Then, we'll be prepared if that man becomes a problem."

I stared off into the dark night, knowing exactly how far it was to my house, the barn, and the corrals. But the one thing I didn't know now was who that little girl shared DNA with. Other than Samantha. in my heart, she was my daughter, and that would never change, regardless of how she arrived in the world. "I know, dad, it's something I've thought of since Samantha showed up here." Turning back to look at him, I said, "I should get home. It isn't fair to Jessica for me to run away. We're supposed to be working on not doing that."

"It's a trait in this family, it seems. Good night, son." Dad patted me on the back, and I turned to head home. But before I took a step, I turned back to him. "You've never run from anything, dad." I searched his face for meaning.

"Oh, son, if you only knew how much running I've done in my life. You would be surprised. Your mother's belief in me was the turning point. I am so glad you boys have found women like your mom."

"Then why did you send Jessica away?"

"Because at that point, you were both dreamers, and I knew the look in your eyes. That day you came to me, I saw me in your face. I didn't think there was any stability in the dreams you spoke of. It pained me to think of you failing, and I knew you had a future here. A bright future, so I thought if I sent her away, you would find your place here. And you did, but I see the damage I caused. You needed to dream, and you needed to go, but I was too selfish to let it happen."

He walked over to stand beside me, took a deep breath, and continued. "I wanted a dynasty, and that meant not letting you boys have your dreams. You were forced to live mine. I wouldn't blame you if you picked up and left. Your mom used to watch Dallas all the time, remember that? I wanted that for my family. Not the dysfunction, but looks like I got that too. Not having a close family of my own, I wanted that for you boys." His voice went quiet stood together.

"Dad, I'm not leaving. We have a good life, and as dysfunctional as we are, there's nothing like being family. Thanks."

"There's no need to thank me. I know what I did was wrong. I see that now. I pushed you boys to be your best and to be the best here, but maybe your best was elsewhere for a time.

"I always wanted a daughter to round out you boys, but your mom had her hands full with you three, so we didn't have another baby. Addison filled that spot in my heart. But it's not just her now. You and Tyler have married women I would be proud to call my daughters. If Gavin gets his head out of his butt, he will too."

I gave him half a smile at that. He nodded, and I walked out of his office. He had a look in his eye that said he was planning something, but I didn't want to know the details. There were some things in life he kept close to the vest, and I had a feeling this would be one of them.

CHAPTER 37

*H*is footsteps up the porch stairs made my heart beat faster. They weren't his usual bounding steps. They were slow and heavy. Closing my eyes, I said a quiet prayer for the words to help him, but I was pretty sure I wouldn't come up with anything.

The door swung open, and his eyes searched the room until they landed on me. His half smile wasn't reassuring at all.

"Hey." I always hated when all people said was "hey." It never meant anything good.

"How was your walk?" I patted the couch beside me, and he walked over and sat down. I placed my hand on his back gently and rubbed it.

He turned to look at me and shook his head. "Well, I ended up in Dad's office talking for a bit. I don't know what he plans to do, Jess, but he's planning something. Part of me wants to know, but I'm pretty sure I can't know." Rob dropped his head into his hands.

I rested my chin on his shoulder. "Let's go to bed. It's been a long day, and I need your arms around me," I whispered, and Rob moved to pull me to him. "Even if we can't fall asleep, lying with you always makes things seem right."

THE DAY WAS LONG, AND ROB HAD BEEN ON THE PHONE talking to the legal team and the Morton private investigator for most of it, but thankfully, we had managed to get Addison off to school with minimal disruption. After what felt like a decade, we went to the main house for supper. We only made it a few feet inside the door when Brian called for us. "Rob, Jessica, I need to speak to you both. Can you please come to the office?" Being summoned by Brian was usually not a great thing, so I looked at Rob as we turned to follow his dad.

"Shut the door, son," he said from behind his massive desk, and we took the seats in front of him. "Look, I know I caused you both much agony with interfering in your lives, and there will never be any way to fix it, but I have this for you."

Brian slid papers across the desk, and Rob and I both leaned forward to look at them.

"Dad, what is this?" Rob picked up the papers and flipped through them. "When did she sign these?"

"I met with Samantha and her lawyer this morning and had her sign them. It was all legal. No bribes, and nothing that could be questioned in court." Brian leaned back in his chair, waiting for Rob to say something.

"I don't know how to..." It was clear Rob was at a loss for words.

"You don't have to. Like I said, Addison is a Morton, and she's going to stay that way."

Rob stood and walked around to his father. Brian embraced his son, and I expected it had been a long time since that had happened last. "Well, we should get back out to supper."

The men stood, but I stayed seated. "Brian, I would like a

word alone, please." I held my tongue but needed to know what he had done. It was better if Rob didn't know.

Rob looked at me quizzically but left the room. Brian took his seat and waited for me to ask my questions.

"What did you do? Don't tell me 'nothing' because I know you too well. There isn't anything you wouldn't do for that little girl."

Brian smiled. "You have me figured out, don't you?" He relaxed back in his chair.

"Don't forget, I've been on the receiving end when you want something to go your way." I arched my brow and waited for his reply.

"Jessica, this doesn't leave the room, you understand?"

I nodded in agreement.

"Keeping Bennet, our PI, on staff was because of her. I always thought she would pull something like this eventually, so I needed to keep an eye on her."

Brian reached down beside him and opened a drawer. He brought out half a dozen big brown envelopes.

Slowly, he began setting photos down in front of me. When I looked at the first one, I saw Samantha stepping into a trailer with some cowboy.

"That one," Brian on tapped the photo, "was Kate's boyfriend at the time. Picture three is a fellow with four kids at home. This one was the one that worried her most."

Brian pulled out another photo of Samantha doing some kind of drug.

"She signed on the dotted line when she saw this. I didn't say a word to her, just laid out the pictures like I did in front of you. I never said a word.

"I knew she would be trouble eventually. Just add it to the list of situations I managed to force my children into. She's been in trouble with the law over the last few years. Not just the drugs, but theft and assault. I told her that if she signed the papers, Addison would never know. The new man she's with doesn't know she has a kid, so I told her I would make sure he found out." Brian looked proud of himself, and I had to admit, it was shrewd to have her lawyer involved so she couldn't go back and claim she was threatened without taking him down with her.

I nodded and said, "Brian, I don't understand why you've made some of the decisions you have for your family, but this is one I can stand behind. Thank you."

We both got up from our chairs, and he nodded in acknowledgment. We stood in silence together for a moment before I turned to leave the office.

Brian called my name just as I was crossing the threshold into the hallway. "Jessica, I know you can't have kids. Rob talked to me the other night after Samantha dropped her news." Brian crossed his arms, but he looked sympathetic.

"Now you know why he can't lose her. It would kill him." My words were quiet and deliberate. Crying in front of Brian was not something I wanted to do, but I could feel my nose tingle and tears fill my eyes. There wasn't much that would crush the soul of my husband, but losing Addison being would.

"He won't lose Addison. Trust me." His eyes bored a hole through me, and there was no need to question the lengths Brian would go to protect Addison and her place in this family. I also knew I would stand beside him if needed.

"I'll do whatever you need. Thank you." I walked out of his office with no more words spoken. On this subject, I understood the man, and I was starting to see what he was trying to do for his sons. Was it always the best decision for them? No, but he did it anyway.

All the Morton boys were home with their significant others. I watched Brian and Sandra bask in the laughter, chatter, and occasional brotherly argument. Even through all the turmoil of the last few days, these men turned into boys, falling back into the behavior of their youth.

Addison had curled up on Sandra's lap, and Kate and Naomi looked like they were in deep conversation, so that left me to slip away from the group.

I walked to the back of the house where Sandra had built a sunroom full of windows and oversized furniture. It was the one place I had always felt comfortable And warm. The rest of the house was so full of stone and wood, I was always chilled.

I sat down on one of the chairs and pulled up my legs, wrapping my arms around them. This wasn't how our marriage should have started. We didn't need all this turmoil. Rob and I deserved to be happy after all we had been through.

The tears fell one by one as I stared out the window and watched the sun set across the prairie. I let my head fall onto my crossed arms and held back the sobs threatening to expose my location.

A large hand snaked across my shoulders and pulled me toward a solid body. I didn't need to look to know who held me. The hand was familiar, and the citrus, lavender, and pine aftershave was one I was intimately aware of.

"You don't need to hide, you know." His whispered words in my ear were soothing.

"I know, but everyone was having a good time, and I didn't want to bring down the atmosphere. Everyone needed a stress relief, so I decided to have mine alone." I wiped my tears with my sleeve.

"Nope, you don't get to do this alone anymore. We're a team, and I want to know when you need support."

I wrapped my arms around his waist and held him like I was holding onto a buoy for dear life so I wouldn't get swept out to sea.

CHAPTER 38

"I don't know what to do. Should I tell her now that I might not be her dad?"

"What do you mean you might not be my dad?" Addison's voice sounded strained. "That's a lie. Why would you say something like that?" in an instant, tears streamed down her face. The last few days were taking their toll. She'd known something was wrong, and now she knew exactly what that was.

"Baby, come here and I'll explain what I know." She slowly walked over and sat down on my knee. I felt like things were going smoothly until I got to the part where Samantha told me I wasn't Addison's father.

She bolted off my lap and down the hall to her room. I followed her, but the lock on the door clicked just before I made it there.

I leaned against the door and hoped divine intervention would give me something to say, but nothing came to mind, so I sat on the floor.

"Addison, I'm waiting here at your door if you want to talk."

There was silence from the other side.

I let thirty minutes go by ,and then I grabbed a coin and unlocked her door. She was gone. Her window was open and her backpack was gone too.

"Addison? Addie, where are you?"

Jessica came running when I started yelling and stopped when she saw the room empty except for me.

"She's gone, Jess. I have to find her." My heart hit the floor, and bile rose in my throat. I ran to the bathroom and lost everything I had eaten so far. When I was sure my stomach was empty, I ran out the door dialing numbers.

"NATE, ADDISON TOOK OFF. CAN YOU TAKE SOME OF THE GUYS and help us look?" My voice was frantic. How could I have let this happen? "I don't even know where to start looking." My voice cracked and tears welled up in my eyes.

"You know the answer is yes. I'll send the guys out and I'll head toward the barn. You head toward Kate and Tyler's, and I'll call Delaney to start heading this way from her place. We'll keep in contact over text." Nate was calm; he was always calm. He knew what to do in a crisis.

Not long after I hung up with Nate, everyone on the farm was searching for Addison. While I looked near Tyler's house, my phone buzzed in my pocket.

GABLES: FOUND HER. SHE'S IN THE BARN

I DIDN'T EVEN REPLY, JUST SHOVED MY PHONE IN MY POCKET and lit out from Tyler's house and headed toward the barn. For a few brief moments, I thought back to the night I'd run away as a child. It hadn't been a nice day like today. Suddenly, after all these years, I knew the terror my parents had felt that night.

I flung the barn door open and heard her soft sobs coming from where Nate was sitting beside her on the stacked bales. Their voices were hushed, but I could hear what they were saying. I stood at the other end of the barn listening to my best friend talk to my daughter much the same way he talked to me the night I ran away all those years ago.

"Nate, he told mom—I mean Jessica—that he's not my real dad. Who is my dad then?" She rested her head on his arm, and Nate shifted to put his arm around her. They'd had a special bond since Addison was born. She was his goddaughter, and he doted on her almost as much as I did.

"Look, I know it's tough, and I don't think your dad ever intended for you to hear it like that, but he's your dad no matter what." Nate stopped talking, and I could tell he was thinking of how to phrase what he wanted to say next. He removed his hat and shifted so he was looking right at Addison. "You know when a momma cow loses her calf or the other way around and we have to pair a momma and baby together so the calf can survive?"

Addison nodded and listened intently to his words.

"That's just like you and your dad. That cow isn't that calf's mom, but that little calf doesn't know it after a few days. That cow looks after that baby just like it was her very own."

I had agonized over what to say to her over the last few days and couldn't come up with anything that made sense. But Nate… he knew exactly what to say.

"So just because you've found out your dad might not be the man who put you in your mom's belly doesn't mean he loves you any less. If I had to guess, I'd say he loves you way more than that."

Addison's sobbing had stopped, and there was just a little sniffle every now and then.

"You know, it's no different than Jessica wanting you for her very own. She's doing everything she can to make you hers. Your dad doesn't have to because he's already on all the papers he needs to be."

Her voice was quiet, and she sounded so little and scared. It took everything in my being not to run over to her, but in this moment, she needed someone to talk to who wasn't me.

"Nate, what if someday he doesn't want me anymore? What if I do something that makes him send me away?"

My own sob caught in my throat, and my tears fell freely. In that second, I knew I would need to spend the rest of my life making sure that little girl knew she was loved and wanted more than anything else in the world.

"Oh, little miss, I've known your dad for a very long time, and there is nothing in this world he loves more than you. There will never be a day he'll want you to go away. You could never do anything that would make him change his mind." Nate gathered up Addison in a hug, and I took that as my opportunity to step out of the shadows.

"Squish, nothing could ever make me want to send you away. I will fight my entire life for you." I had never felt more vulnerable than I did in that moment, waiting for her to decide what to do.

She launched herself off the bales and ran toward me. Grabbing her and picking her up, I hugged her tighter than I had before.

Nate moved toward the door, smiling at the scene before him. We nodded at each other before he quietly exited the barn.

"Addison, I'm sorry you overheard my conversation with Jessica. That was not the way I wanted you to find out. I was hoping to tell you when you were older." I sat down on the bales with Addison still clinging to me.

"For your entire life until two nights ago, I never thought you weren't my biological daughter. Now we know that might be the case, but it doesn't make you any less my daughter. In fact, it makes it even better. Want to know why?"

She nodded her little and looked up at me. Her eyes were as big as saucers waiting for an answer.

"You can pick your friends, and you can pick your nose, but you can't pick your friend's nose."

"Daaaad, that's so embarrassing." She rolled her eyes and giggled before smiling up at me.

I smiled, then ruffled her hair. "But seriously, not many people get to pick their family. We're mighty blessed that we can, Addison. And you better believe I would pick you every time."

"You mean we can pick each other now, like you and I picked Jessica to be my mom?" She looked to me for the answer that made the most sense to her.

"Yes, baby, just like when we picked Jessica to be your mom." She smiled, and the explanation seemed to make sense to her. "So, do you choose me, Addison?"

"Of course I do, daddy." She flung her arms around my neck and squeezed tighter than she ever had before. "We should tell Jessica I choose her too."

"That's a great idea. Let's go find her." I stood, and Addison grabbed a hold of my hand. We left the barn in search of Jessica.

Everyone was gathered at my house when we returned. Addison ran up the stairs and found Jessica immediately. She hopped up on her lap and hugged her. "Jessica, I choose you just like you and Daddy are choosing me. You will be my mom forever?"

Tears flowed down Jessica's face as she looked up at me and smiled. "Yes, Addie, I will be. Forever."

Everyone in the room was crying as they watched the scene unfold before them.

CHAPTER 39

The DNA tests came in the mail, so I handed one to Addison and one Rob. They each had to spit into a vial, which was a hilarious process to watch as they laughed and raced to fill their tiny sample containers. Reluctantly, I accepted the nomination of getting them packaged up when they were done, which made them laugh more. "Eww! Rob, come on! You missed the vial." My face scrunched up when I took his from him. Addison was looking at her dad and laughing at the faces he was making at me

"Hey, you try spitting in that little thing and see how well you do." He crossed his arms and leaned back against the counter.

"Addison didn't seem to have any trouble." I looked at him out of the corner of my eye. He knew I was joking and making Addison feel more like this was a game than it was. "You two owe me a date night after this. Bleh." I turned to look at Rob, who was smiling at me. He mouthed "thank you," and I smiled back at him with a nod.

"Dad, when will you find out?" Addison asked as she walked over to Rob and took his hand.

"It's supposed to take a few weeks, and if there is anything to know, we can decide what to do from there. Do you want to know?" Rob put his arm around her shoulder and waited for an answer.

She looked at the floor for a few moments, then looked up at Rob and shook her head. "No, I don't care. Maybe some-day, but not now. You're my dad and Jessica is my mom and I don't need anyone else."

"Okay." He leaned down and kissed the top of her head and smiled.

"I'm going out to brush down JP." She was out the door and jumping down the stairs in record time.

"I'll send these off tomorrow. What are you going to do when the results come in?" I walked over to where Rob was standing and wrapped my arms around his waist, resting my head on his shoulder.

"I'll decide what to do when the results come in. I would like to stick my head in the sand and ignore it, but we will see." His strong arms surrounded me, and we stood in silence. Something we had been doing more and more in the last week.

He was usually lost in his thoughts and grief. I wasn't sure how to help him but knew this process was something he was going to have to deal with on his own. I could be here to support him, but I couldn't fix this. And then there were my fertility issues staring us in the face once again.

Somehow, he knew exactly what I was thinking and said, "Hey, this isn't your fault. Your situation has nothing to do with this. I haven't once wished we could have our own biolog-ical children since this all happened. It's not even something I want to give brain space to. So I want you to stop."

His eyes told me he was telling the truth, but it didn't ease my guilt about not being able to give him more children. I hadn't felt this helpless since my initial diagnosis.

~

THE WEEKS PASSED, AND I HAD ALMOST FORGOTTEN I WAS waiting for life to change again. We had fallen back into our normal routine. Addison was amazing and never mentioned the test or the events again. Jessica had been my rock, helping me work through feelings and realizations I was suddenly thinking about.

"Jess, what if someday Addison has siblings that came looking for her?" I sat on the end of the bed one night before bed and just stared into the future I imagined. "What if this is just Samantha trying to mess with my head? She would be that low? That despicable?"

She crawled across the bed to where I was sitting and placed a light kiss on my shoulder. Her touch calmed me, sent goosebumps over my skin, and gave me peace. "If she does, then she'll know we're here to support her in any decision she makes." Her hands snaked over my shoulders and rested over my heart.

"Rob, you have to stop asking the what-ifs. It's a never-ending cycle of things you have no control over. She's a smart girl. We'll continue to answer all her questions to the best of our ability, and we'll make sure she knows her decisions supported."

Jessica sat up beside me and gently placed her hand on my cheek.

"If siblings come looking for her, we'll welcome them into our home. They have every right to know her, and I know we'll be happy to have them as an extension of our family."

I moved my hand to rest over hers and smiled. "How did I get so lucky to end up marrying you?"

"Well, to be honest, I settled," she whispered in my ear, and I grabbed her and turned on the bed so she was sitting in my lap laughing.

"You settled? Really? Pretty sure you stalked me for a week trying to get me to notice you again." I slid my hand up her leg, over her round ass, and up into her hair before I pulled her closer to me. "Even if you settled, I'm glad you did."

Our lips met and I laid her down on our bed.

In between our kisses, Jessica whispered, "Settled for the only man I have ever loved." She rested her head back on the pillow and smiled.

The slinky nightgown she wore ended up in a pile on the floor. I loved the way my wife looked before me. Moving over her, I smiled. "You know how to make me want you more every day." I bent down and planted my lips on hers, caressing her breasts until she let her head fall back and ground her hips on my lap.

"Jess, I need you." I slid her off me, removed my boxers, rolled over, and knelt over her. Her lips beckoned me to kiss them again.

I kissed her gently at first, but my need increased, and so did her moans. Sliding my hands down to her centre, I could tell she was wet and ready. Thank God she was, because I couldn't wait anymore. I slid home, groaning at how good she felt wrapped around me.

Jessica's breathing changed almost immediately. Her legs crossed behind me and she pulled me as close as humanly possible. She gasped, and the sound and the new angle pushed her to the brink. After a few more thrusts, she muffled her cry into my shoulder.

Her nails clawed at my back, and it was enough to send me over the edge. I pumped inside her, unable to hold back the flow, wanting to give her all of my love and everything I had.

When I was spent, I collapsed on top of her, letting out a contented sigh.

CHAPTER 40

"Rob, there's an email." I was happy it was raining, and he had stayed close to the house today. He was in the living room, and I handed the laptop to him over the back of the couch. Moving quickly, I walked around to sit beside him.

He sat there looking at the email for minutes that felt like hours before he clicked to open it. "Is the Internet working? This is taking forever. Jess, is the whatever-it-is connected to the computer?" I slid my arm around his shoulder as the web page finally opened.

We both read the email. The person who matched Addison had a public profile, and it was only one click away from being out in the open. "What if I don't want to know?" he whispered his question. I wasn't sure what to say, so I rested my head on his shoulder and waited for him to make the decision.

He clicked on the link, and a name and profile appeared on the screen. The man had blue eyes, much like Addison's, and he was blond with wavy hair.

"I know him." Rob's voice was strong, commanding, and

shocked. "He used to rodeo with Samantha. Team roper, if I remember correctly."

"What are you going to? You can't just call him up and say 'hey, here's the deal.'" I stared at the man looking back at us.

"What else am I supposed to do? I can't play cat and mouse with this man for the next twelve years or until Addison figures out how to hack into my email and contact him herself." Pushing the laptop off to the side, he stood and started to pace.

I watched him walk back and forth in the living room. "Are you planning to walk a hole in the floor? Rob, you don't have to decide this today." I relaxed back into the couch.

Rob stopped walking and picked up the computer. He sat back down beside me and clicked until he found the contact information linked to the man's account and sent an email. "Now we wait. Again."

THE DINER CAME INTO VIEW, AND I WAS SUDDENLY MORE anxious than I had been on the drive over. . What would happen if I continued to drive? If I chose not to have this meeting, would life just be normal? Of course it wouldn't. There was no way I could skip out on this.

The truck, seemingly having a mind of its own, turned into the parking lot and pulled to a stop. I took one more deep breath and got out of the truck and walked into the building. I spotted Tate Riley sitting in the far corner. He was a few years younger than me, and from the look on his face, he was just as anxious as I was.

Forcing my feet to move forward, I got to the table. "Tate, thanks for meeting me." I pulled out the chair and sat as we shook hands.

"Well, there you are, Rob. What can I get for you?" The perky waitress sashayed over.

"Just coffee, please, May," I said.

She nodded and walked back toward the counter. The diner felt like an extension of home and was somewhere I always felt comfortable. Maybe picking this place wasn't such a great idea. It had felt like neutral territory, but now I worried I was going to ruin the memories I associated with this place.

May returned with my coffee and set it on the table before she walked away again. "You didn't seem too surprised when I contacted you." I took a sip of my coffee and looked over at Tate.

"To be honest, I wasn't at all. I had a call from Samantha a few weeks ago. She told me you would eventually contact me." He grabbed his cup of coffee took a sip, waiting for me to respond.

I felt a little stunned. Samantha knew all this time who Addison's father was, and she never breathed a word about it. Part of me wanted to hurt her, a big part of me, but that wouldn't be fair to my daughter.

"What did she tell you?" My voice was a whisper, and I felt like I was holding back the floodgates threatening to tear this man to shreds.

"She told me that Addison was mine, and that we should blackmail your family into paying to keep your daughter. Her exact words were, 'they have our girl, and they think they can keep her. The Morton's need to cough up some dough before I sign her over to them.'" He slumped back in his chair.

I saw red and gripped the cup in my hands so tightly I was surprised it didn't crumble to dust. "Is that why you agreed to meet me? You want me to pay you off?" I clenched my teeth, ready to launch myself across the table.

"No. To be honest, I feel like I'm the one who should be paying you. I don't want to upend my life; it's going pretty well right now. I'm married with two kids and one on the way." He leaned in toward me. His face changed, and I knew he was ready to tell me about his real feelings on the situation.

"I told her that her scheme wasn't going to work. Addison has spent the last eight years in your home, calling you dad, and in turn, you've raised her, taken care of her, but more importantly, loved her like she deserved. Samantha is only looking out for herself and obviously doesn't care about Addison.

"I told her I was happy with my life, and I didn't want Addison ripped away from the only family she's ever known. If you and Jessica are the people I think you are, then Samantha was insane to think I would go along with this idea. Rob, I don't want to interfere, because that little girl is happy." His eyes were sincere, and his hands shook as he brought his cup to his mouth.

"I appreciate your honesty, and thank you for telling Samantha what you think of her. That must have been a diffi-cult decision given the risk to your family. Thank you for protecting mine. If there's anything you need, please let me know." I stood and shook Tate's hand and headed for the door.

I had a lot of information to unpack here, but I needed to talk to my father. As frustrating as he was, I knew the only person besides Jessica I could trust with this was him.

"Hey, Rob."

I turned and saw Tate behind me. Stopping, I waited for him to reach me. "If she comes looking someday, I'll welcome her, but she is and always will be yours."

I nodded in acknowledgment and got into my truck.

There was no polite way to end a meeting like this, so I drove off and left Tate standing at his truck. I knew I should call Jessica, but it would be easier to talk to her in person. My soul felt lighter than it had on the way to town, but this would never be over.

Pulling up in front of the house, I saw Jessica standing on the porch waiting for me. I had to smile. I had wanted to know what having someone waiting for me at home felt like, and with Jessica, I finally knew.

When I reached the porch, she took a few steps toward me and I reached out for her. Instantly, her arms wrapped around me, and I buried my head in her chest.

"I think it's going to be okay. Tate doesn't want to take her away."

Jessica let out an audible sigh, and I felt the air leave her lungs. "So, what now?" Her words were quiet and hesitant.

"We wait until Tate's kids are old enough to come looking for her. Or until she wants to know his family. It's kind of like watching a ticking time bomb, waiting for the explosion."

Jessica's arms tightened around me, and we just stood together in silence. My phone buzzed in my pocket, and I reluctantly let Jessica go to answer it.

Without looking at the screen, I connected the call. "Hello?"

"Rob, it's Merritt. I have some news. The court date for the adoption has been set. Two weeks from today, Addison will officially be Jessica's daughter."

"That's the best news I've heard in weeks," I said. I felt like I could run laps around the ranch. This call couldn't have come at a better time.

"I will see you at the courthouse that morning. Bye."

"Bye, Merritt, and thank you." Pressing end on the call, I grabbed Jessica in my arms and spun her around.

"Rob, what are you doing?" Jessica squealed as I spun her.

"Baby, in two weeks nobody will be able to take Addison from you. In the eyes of the law, you will be her mother."

Jessica's scream would have woken the dead and almost ruptured my eardrum.

"Soon, this will be all behind us. Oh, Rob, this is the best news ever." Jessica wrapped her legs around my waist and held on for dear life.

CHAPTER 41

There were so many families waiting in the hallway, it made me claustrophobic. One family would come out, and another would go in. More seemed to file through the main doors of the courthouse every five minutes. Rob held my hand so tightly I was worried my fingers would lose circulation. Addie seemed oblivious to the tension because she was cooing over Tyler and Kate's new baby, TJ. I watched her, feeling sad that she wouldn't have a sibling to fuss over, but her cousins would be so lucky to have her love on them.

Mom and Sandra were deep in conversation. Brian was talking to someone on his cell phone. Kate and Tyler were trying their best to keep our minds occupied. I noticed a younger man walk up to us, but I didn't pay much attention. The man put his arm around Rob's shoulder.

"Gavin, what are you doing here?" Rob's face beamed, and he finally let go of my hand to hug his brother.

"I wouldn't miss this for the world."

"Where's Naomi? Did she have to work?" I scanned the hallway and didn't see her.

"Now's not the time for that discussion. Today's a happy

day." Gavin's face was pained, and I looked at Rob, who just gave his brother a reassuring pat on the shoulder.

"Morton." A lady in a blue suit with a bun so tight it gave her a face lift stepped out, scanning the hallway as she called.

I looked up at Rob and gave him a tense smile. He winked back at me.

"This has to be good, Jess. I can feel it." His eyes shone, but his smile seemed forced, so as confident as he was, I knew there was a little bit of worry.

Addie walked between us, Rob and I each holding one of her hands as we walked in front of the judge's bench. Our entourage filed into the courtroom behind us and took their seats. The courtroom was quiet, but I felt like I could hear all the nervous energy behind us.

I felt like I could read people, but the judge sat stone-faced. He looked like he could retire at any moment. The glasses he wore were perched on the end of his nose, his hair snow white, and, from what I could see, his right hand, which was turning the pages of our file, was crippled by arthritis.

"Mr. and Mrs. Morton, thank you for being here today. As I understand, Mrs. Morton, you hope to legally adopt Addison Morton. Is that correct?" He pulled his glasses off his nose and stared at me.

Glancing down at Addie, I smiled and looked back at the judge. "Yes, sir, that is correct."

"Now, as I understand, Addison's biological mother hasn't been a part of her life. Is that accurate, Mr. Morton?"

I looked over at Rob and waited for him to reply. "That's right, sir. When Addison was three, her—Samantha—decided it did not suit her to be a mother."

The judge nodded. "Addison, what do you think about all this?"

Addie looked up at me, then Rob, before she spoke. "I don't know Samantha at all. My Grandma Morton was around all the time when I was little. My Uncle Tyler married my Auntie Kate, and she has treated me like a daughter since she arrived on the ranch." Addie turned to look at Sandra and Kate. Her smile spread from ear to ear, and she waved at them.

Both women beamed at her and waved back.

"Mr. Judge, Jessica started dating my dad, and she makes me believe I can do anything. She is there when I get home from school. We do my chores together. She makes my meals and does my laundry. But most of all, she loves me. I don't have to be the kid without a mom anymore because Jessica is my mom." Addie looked up at me with tears in her blue eyes. "I used to get made fun of because my mom didn't want me, but from the second I met Jessica, I knew she did. She didn't even know me, but she loved me." Addie let go of Rob's hand and wrapped her arms around my waist. There was no way I could hold back the tears as I returned Addie's hug.

"In all my years of sitting on this bench, I haven't seen a young lady of nine speak so eloquently. Addison, did anyone tell you what to say here today?" His face was scrunched in a frown.

Addie let go of me and took a few steps toward the bench. "Mr. Judge, nobody told me what to say. You asked me what I thought, and I told you. I don't want any other mom; I just want Jessica." Her hands were on her hips, and I wondered if he had ever come up against a nine-year-old lawyer before.

Addie dropped her hands to her sides. "I just want my mom, Jessica." Her voice was barely above a whisper as she turned to look back at me. Her tears fell, which made the tears I held back flow. There was sniffling behind us too. I didn't care about rules. I stepped toward Addie and took her in my arms.

"Mr. Morton, from what I can see, you provided Addison a wonderful life filled with powerful women for her to look up to." He folded his hands in front of him and looked from Rob to me. "I commend you for that. I think you've added to that strength by marrying Jessica. Not only was she willing to risk her life for Addison's safety, if what I see in this file is accurate, but she has also become a mother overnight and never thought twice about it. You are a very lucky man."

The judge picked up a large stamp and slammed it down on to three different pieces of paper. Then he took his pen and signed in three places. "From the looks of it, this family truly believes it takes a village to raise a child. In all my dealings today, this has been the largest attended hearing." He closed our file and looked at me. "Jessica Morton, I am hereby making you the legal parent of Miss Addison Sandra Morton. From this day on, she is your child."

The cheers and claps behind me began.

I dropped to my knees and pulled Addie to me. I turned to look at the judge through my tears and somehow managed, "Thank you, sir."

He smiled at us and nodded.

Rob had placed his hand on my shoulder, and I stood. We clasped on to each other as tightly as we could.

That night after the celebration was over and we had finally got Addie to sleep, Rob and I lay in each other's arms.

"So, was it worth the wait?"

I looked up at Rob and frowned. "What wait?"

"The wait to be right here, right now. Married to each other and parents to an amazing little girl."

"Yes," was all I could whisper as I pulled Rob toward me and kissed him.

EPILOGUE

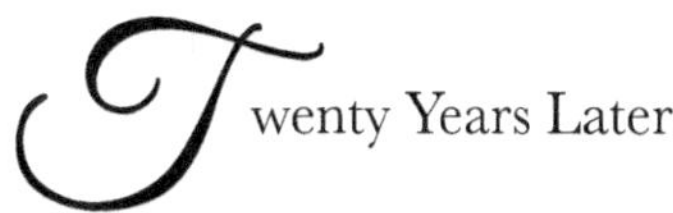wenty Years Later

I watched Rob walk around the yard with Parker, Addie's boyfriend. I didn't have to guess what was going on. I knew. A girl's boyfriend didn't show up at her father's house when she was at work without a reason.

Rob ran his hands through his hair, and I felt like I knew exactly what he was feeling. Biting my fingernails, I waited for him to come back into the house.

Parker's face went from concerned to elated in seconds. Rob shook his hand, and the men went their separate ways. I watched Rob climb the steps and open the door. Even twenty years after marrying him, seeing him walk through the door still made my heart flutter.

"He wants to marry Addison." Rob walked over to the table and sat down in one of the chairs. "I gave him the okay to ask her." His head was in his hand, and there were tears glistening in his eyes. "Jess, how is she old enough to get married?"

I knelt down in front of him and ran my hands up his legs, smiling. "I'm not sure, but we couldn't have asked for anyone better for her."

Rob took my hands in his and leaned down for a kiss. "I know, and I'm glad she'll be close by." His eyes glazed over, and I could tell he was thinking back to all her milestones through the years. "Why didn't I ever think of this day when I imagined her growing up?" His voice was almost a whisper, and I didn't think it was a question he wanted an answer to.

Standing, I walked behind him and wrapped my arms around him, resting my chin on his shoulder.

Parker had arranged to take Addie to the new trapper's cabin. The day of the tornado was one of the first things Addie had told him about, and he wanted that place to have a new meaning for her.

Horses were saddled, the picnic supper was ready for him to pick up, and now Rob and I waited for the couple to come home engaged. I had never seen Rob so anxious.

The week passed, and there was a knock on my office door. "Mom, can I talk to you about the wedding?" Addie walked into my office and sat on the corner of my desk.

"Sure. Have you chosen a date?" I pushed my chair back so I could look up at her.

"No, not yet, but I hope to by next week. I don't know if you remember back when Uncle Tyler and Aunt Kate got married, but you were dancing with dad when I came up to him wanting to go home. You gave me a notebook and told me to write down anything I wanted for my wedding." She handed me a tattered notebook; the cover had been taped back on a few times, and most pages were hanging on by a thread, but she had been writing in it for the last twenty years.

Tears filled my eyes flipping through the book. "I remember. I didn't know you kept it all these years."

"It's one of my most treasured possessions. Now, when can I go over all of this with you? Some of it obviously won't make the cut, but I wanted to see what we can figure out."

Grabbing a tissue, I dabbed my eyes, and we moved to the couch together. I flipped through, seeing some things that were absolutely outdated, but there was more than enough to work with.

One page had a pink piece of paper as a bookmark, so I flipped it open to that page. There before me was a photograph of Rob and me from our wedding day. I hadn't ever seen this picture. We were dancing and looking into each other's eyes.

"I want my day to be perfect like yours." She rested her head on my shoulder. "That day was the best day of my life because that's the day you became mine."

My heart soared. I knew how Addie felt about me, but hearing her say it was always special. We spent the afternoon poring over books and magazines, making notes. By the time Rob and Parker came home from moving cows, we had taken over the kitchen table too.

"Looks like you've been busy."

I looked up from the table into the eyes of my lover and smiled.

I felt like I was a chicken with my head cut off during the months we planned Addie's wedding. As decisive as Addie was, she was also overwhelmed with all the choices she was being asked to make.

on the day of the rehearsal, she was on the verge of tears almost every minute.

"Addie, come here for a moment, please," I called. She quickly came over to the side of the barn where we were decorating. Her eyes were wide, and she looked terrified that I was going to ask her to decide something else.

"You need to go. Have a bath, get ready for supper, and

relax. There's nothing to be done now. Your wedding will be everything you dreamed of. I'll make sure of it."

Addie threw her arms around me and hugged me tight.

I watched her walk to her car and drive off, then I took a deep breath and turned back to where everyone was working like bees getting everything done. A strong hand slid across my back, and I leaned into it.

"Are you going to work through rehearsal or are you going to be my date?"

"I think being your date is more enticing than staying here in the barn." I turned as he wrapped me in his arms. "I guess we better go get ready. Ruby, I'm leaving for a few hours. If you need anything, call me," I called to my assistant as Rob dragged me out of the barn.

"Actually, Ruby, she's not going to be back tonight. And don't call her, just handle things." Rob didn't look back, he just kept walking to the house.

Once back at the house, I looked at the clock, noticing it was much earlier than I had planned to get ready. "Rob, I still have plenty of time before I have to get ready. I don't have time to sit and do nothing."

"Oh, baby, we aren't going to do nothing. I have plans for you that are going to take up all your time." He walked me to our room and closed the door. Making quick work of our clothes and laying me back on the bed, he made love to me.

"Over the last twenty years of our marriage, Jessica and I made each other a top priority. Once Addison's needs were met, we took care of each other. For a marriage to survive, both partners need to fight for one another. The second a couple stops fighting for each other, the relationship you have worked so hard to build starts to crumble. So, Addison and Parker, may you love like no other, fight for each other like you are battling for your lives, and find happiness in the most mundane parts of life." Rob took my hand and pulled me up next to him while he finished his toast to the couple. I had never been prouder of this little family I found. "Addison, your mom and I look forward to watching this new adventure you're starting, but most of all, we love you both."

Tears filled my eyes as Addie embraced her dad. The rough and tough man I had left all those years ago was the most amazing dad to his little girl. I was fortunate that I was able to join their family. Addie wrapped her arms around my neck and hugged me tight. "Thank you, mom, for everything. You have been the most wonderful mother I ever could have dreamed of."

Later that night, we watched the bride and groom head off to start their life together. The day had been amazing, and I hoped it was everything Addison wanted.

The guests trickled slowly off the ranch, saying goodnight as they passed Rob and me.

"Rob, Jessica, I want to thank you for including us on this special day." Tate shook Rob's hand, and his wife, Amber, embraced me. We had settled into a very odd family unit over the years. Tate's kids looked to Addison as a cousin, and she enjoyed spending time with them. It hadn't been easy for Rob when the relationships were forming, but over the last few years, things were good. Tate and Amber even became good friends of ours. We said goodnight and made plans to get together next week.

Rob and I walked home after the party was over and sat on the steps together. "Now what do we do, Mrs. Morton? Our girl has grown up and has someone new to look after her. It's just you and me."

"It hasn't been just you and me for a very long time. I think I'm ready to see what that's like again."

He leaned over, ran his hands through my hair, and pulled me to him. Our lips met, and once again, I was reminded of how in love I was with this man after all these years.

THE ASSIGNMENT

Chapter One

A blue Ford F-350 drove into the yard, and a man about ten years older than me got out. He was tall, with broad shoulders. His chestnut brown hair peeked out from underneath his cowboy hat, and he had enormous work-calloused hands that engulfed mine as we shook hands.

I knew Nate Gables to see him, but I hadn't ever spoken to him. Occasionally, he haunted my dreams on nights when I was lonely. It was going to be strange having someone help out around here without Kate or Tyler being here as well.

Tyler, my sister Kate's husband, must have heard the truck approaching and came walking out of the barn to join us. He was tall, with dark hair and easy on the eyes. I knew exactly why my sister had been in love with him secretly for years. In the back of my mind, I wanted to know what that felt like. He looked at Nate and back at me. "Delaney, this is Nate Gables. Ranch boss at our ranch and the one person I trust completely with this place. This is Delaney. Good luck. I need to get back home. Kate doesn't need to know if there are any problems. I need her resting, so if there are any issues, let me know. Nate, why don't I show you around?"

Life had seemed to settle down after the year we weathered as a family. Who was I kidding? The past year could almost have been described as a train wreck. After Kate and Tyler's marriage, our family and ranch had taken one hit after another, and the whole thing was almost a complete write off. I kept hearing how gracefully I'd handled it all, but inside, I was a cyclone.

Kate leaned on Tyler, Mom leaned on me, and I had nobody. Even before I had broken up with my long-term boyfriend, Jack, I had nobody. I guess you could say I was used to it, but that didn't make it any easier. We had fallen into the too comfortable with each other category easily, and by the time I broke up with him, he was just a roommate.

Back in Austin, I worked day and night hoping to make professor. When I'd heard that the superintendent of the high school I attended here at home was trying to get it back to proper academic standards, I moved home and took the principal position. The job was a welcome distraction from the emotional turmoil of the last year. I had never been the teacher that counted down the days until summer, but this year I was ready for a break.

"Delaney, things here are going to get busy, so Gables will be here full time for now." Tyler had that concerned scowl on his face.

"What's wrong, Tyler? Kate hasn't been around here for days." He was usually happy-go-lucky, especially these days, but this side of Tyler was protective. He was worried.

Tyler turned pale as he told me, "She's struggling, TJ isn't sleeping, crying all the time. She's having a hard time adjusting to being tied to the house and not being able to be out here working. You know your sister, she won't ask for help and gets mad when I suggest anything." Tyler ran his hand through his hair and let out a frustrated breath.

"Okay, well, she's going to rest whether she likes it or not. If Nate's willing to teach me, I'm happy to help. School's done in a week and then I can be here all day." I put my hand on his shoulder. "You need a break too. I don't want you back here until after my sweet nephew is settled and Kate's back to herself. You know I am more than happy to help. I mean, maybe not at night, but if Kate needs a break, you can call me." Tyler's face changed from exhausted to relieved. "I know it's hard with Mom away, but I'm here too."

After a quick tour, Tyler went over a few things he had been planning with Nate, and it all sounded like gibberish to me, but I stood, there looking interested. "I should head home and see how things are. Again, call me if you need anything." He looked from me to Nate, and we both nodded.

"Don't worry, boss, there isn't anything here we—" Gables glanced at me and looked back at Tyler. "—I can't handle." Tyler tried to hide his laugh, but I saw it and frowned at him. The men shook hands.

We watched Tyler drive off. Standing there in silence, I could tell he was looking around and making notes in his head about what needed to be done. I scanned the property, trying to think like him, but I didn't like what he was seeing. There was so much work to be done.

I opened my mouth to say something, but he beat me to it.

"Delaney, I know you haven't done much around here, but that has to change. If I am going to get this place back in working order, I'm going to need help." I hated it when I was talked to like I was stupid. There wasn't a thing around this place I couldn't do. Wanting to do it was a different story. "With your mom gone for the month, I'll stay there. No sense in you changing houses for me."

I nodded. "Fine. When do we start?"

"Now. You'll need gloves, a hat, and you'd better change your clothes. Those shorts and sandals will not cut it."

I stared at him and had so much to say, but words didn't leave my mouth.

"I don't have all day. Let's go." He was gruff, demanding and rude, traits I found annoying, but when they were directed at me, I felt the hair on the back of my neck stand up. I had never been great at taking orders.

Turning, I walked over to my house and changed into jeans and boots. I grabbed Dad's gloves off the counter and went back outside. He started walking, and I followed.

"I know your schedule for the next week is busy, so I won't expect you to be around much, but when school is out, I need you here."

Somehow, it felt like I was the student walking into a brand-new school.

I had to run to catch up to him. Gables had already reached the barn and was headed to work. "Okay, I'm going to treat you like a greenhorn ranch hand. You might not like it, but I don't care." He pointed to the barn, directing my gaze. "So, first get over there and muck the stalls. It looks like they haven't been done for a few days."

There wasn't any point in arguing, so I just nodded and got started. Kate had always had this job. I'd always helped Mom in the house, which usually meant my day was over far sooner than Kate's, and I would dive into a book. Nobody expected me to help with the ranch, and I never tried to help unless they asked.

When the stalls were mucked and fresh straw was ready for the horses, I went out to find Gables. He was out in the pasture working with one of Tyler's new horses. Walking over to the fence, I rested my arms over the top rail and watched him.

He was calm, and his demeanor relaxed. The rope he was swinging made consistent circular motions with the flick of his wrist. He held the lead rope from the horse with his other hand and walked in circles, leading the horse. Every so often, he would make a noise and the horse would jump. Nate's voice was soft, soothing, and the horse would calm down.

He stopped moving and walked up to the horse, wrapped his arm around its neck, and patted it. I could see his mouth moving, but couldn't hear the words. Walking over to the pen's gate, he opened it and let the horse out into the pasture and came toward me.

"Got the barn done?" He was wiping his hands on his pants as he got to me.

"Yep, I did. What's next?" We walked on opposite sides of the fence to meet at the opening.

"Well, I need to go ride and check the cows in the north pasture. Are you coming with me?"

I nodded and walked to the barn to saddle my horse. My cell phone rang and, grabbing it from my back pocket, I looked at the number. Jack's face was staring back at me. I pressed end call and made a mental note to delete his contact later.

Chapter Two

I saddled a horse and waited for Delaney. She was a little rusty saddling her horse, but I didn't want to take over for her. She slipped her foot in the stirrup and threw her leg over the horse's back.

"Well, where are we starting?" she asked as she rode up beside me. "Look, I might not be the best ranch hand around, but I know how to ride." She kicked the side of her horse and was off like a shot. She never even slowed up for the fence. The horse jumped over it. Slowing, she turned back, waiting for me.

Laughing, I shook my head and rode toward the gate. This

was going to be an interesting few weeks, I thought to myself. "Sorry I'm taking the long way around."

"Chicken," she called to me.

Once I rode to her, I had questions. "Where did you learn to ride like that?"

"Kate ran barrels, I rode equestrian. Mom always wanted to jump horses, but back then she did the rodeo circuit. So her dream became mine." Delaney shifted in her saddle and looked at me.

"Don't you ever want to leave the Morton ranch?"

The question I had asked myself quite often when I was younger. "Well, at some point it just became easier than striking out on my own. I came from Montana with the family ten years ago. Walking away from the only place I had ever known in life was scary, even at thirty-three. I took a chance, and the family has always been good to me." I shrugged and kicked my horse to move a little faster.

Delaney took no time catching up to me.

Our afternoon was pleasant, and I was almost sad to see it come to an end. Back at the barn, we brushed down the horses, got them fresh feed and water, and closed everything up for the night.

"You did good today. Tomorrow we will work some heifers and move them to the south pasture." I walked toward the main house.

"Hey, Nate, want to come over for supper?" I stopped and turned. "I would like to, thank you."

"Go get settled in and come over in about thirty minutes?" She shrugged, and I nodded.

Changing out of my dirty clothes, I was ready to make the walk over to Delaney's place.

Knocking on the door, I waited for Delaney. The door swung open, and her smiling face stood before me. Her long curly blond hair was all over the place. It wasn't messy. It was perfect for her.

"Come on in." She moved out of the doorway, and I took a step into her home. It was small, but I should have realized that from the outside. Her home was simple, minimal, but homey.

"Thank you for inviting me over. I hadn't thought much about supper, even though Tyler made sure I had supplies since your mom was gone." Suddenly I felt like I was twelve and meeting a girl for the first time. This was ridiculous. My palms were sweaty, and I was fidgeting with the hat in my hand.

"Here, let me hang your hat up." She reached out, and our hands brushed as she took it from me. I looked up, and she was looking at me. Her smile was infectious, and I smiled back. She turned and hung my hat on the hook beside the door. "Why don't you have a seat at the table, and I will get supper on."

Everything smelled delicious, and even better because I didn't have to cook. Delaney, while maybe not the most experienced working the ranch, knew how to make a person feel comfortable. From what I had heard, she was just like her mom. Nobody had anything bad to say about Julie. She was a wonderful hostess, and her door was always open.

We kept our conversation light, and she was easy to talk to. There was more to her than a pretty face and a bubbly personality. Under everything she showed people there was sadness, maybe even a loneliness, but unless someone sat down with her, they would never know.

"Would you like coffee with your dessert?" Delaney stood and walked into the kitchen. She took a pie out of the oven and set it on the counter. "I made this yesterday and put it in the freezer. I hope you like apple pie."

"My favorite. I will take a coffee, please." I grabbed our plates off the table and walked them over to the sink, then went back to clear the rest of the table.

"Nate, you don't have to do that. Go have a seat."

Delaney's voice was sweet, but I could tell she appreciated the help.

"Nope, my mother raised me better than that, ma'am." Her laugh was light as she handed me the two plates of pie. Then she grabbed the coffee, and I followed her to the couch. "I hope you don't mind me saying this, but I really think people aren't giving you enough credit. You knew what you were doing out there today."

She took a bite of her pie. Somehow, I envied the fork sliding between her lips. Taking a sip of her coffee, she took a deep breath. "It was one of the few things that I had to do growing up. Moving, sorting, and checking cattle were pretty much a family outing. So that's easy for me. The day to day around here, not so much."

Shifting on the couch, she turned and looked at me straight on. Crossing her legs under her, she held her cup as if it was her lifeline. "Supper, dessert, that's my thing. Ask Kate to make a pie? She will call me, and I will do it. You need a calf delivered? Call Kate and she will do it." She gave a slight shrug that I would have missed if I hadn't been watching.

"Well, I appreciate the help." She just about glowed. I wondered when the last time she had been thanked or complimented for her work around this place had been. If I had to guess, it would have been never.

She kept talking, but if they had questioned me, I wouldn't have been able to tell anyone what she said. I was focused on watching her light pink lips moving. As if being pulled toward her, I leaned in, and our lips met. I had never been so forward in my entire life. She froze until I swept the crease of her lips with my tongue. Then she seemed to melt, wrapping her arms around my neck.

It had been a long time since I had held a woman, too long. Before I knew it, she was in my lap. She felt good in my lap, and I tightened my arms around her. Running my hand through her hair, I placed it at the back of her neck and ran my thumb along her skin. She sighed and tightened her arms around me.

We broke the kiss and sat staring at each other. "That was the best thank you for supper I have ever had." Her smile lit up the room and the dark recesses of my heart.

I cleared my throat.

"It was a very good supper and dessert."

She beamed before leaning in and pressing her lips to mine again.

Chapter Three

The kitchen was still a disaster from supper last night, but by the time Nate left, I hadn't cared about cleaning. His kisses were intoxicating. Never in my life had I thought I would end up in the arms of a cowboy. They had always been the men I swore I would never fall for, but there I'd been, making out with one in my living room.

His lips were tender, his hands rough as they had combed through my hair. I could almost feel his strong arms around me all night. Maybe that's exactly what I wanted. Who was I? This was not me. I didn't do things like this. I didn't climb into the laps of random cowboys and make out with them for the better part of the night.

I loaded the dishwasher, washed the pots I'd used last night, and left them to dry on the counter. Looking at the clock, I figured I needed to get out and see what my jobs were for today. What would he be like this morning? The anticipation of seeing him was making me nervous.

Grabbing my gloves, I walked out to the barn. I found Nate in the round pen, working with the chestnut horse again. "'Bout time you got out here, I thought you might stay in bed all day." His surliness was confusing. Had we not less than twelve hours before been making out like teenagers?

"Good morning to you too. I thought maybe you would have woken up on the right side of the bed today." Turning, I headed to the barn.

"Delaney, where do you think you're going?" His gruff voice stopped me in my tracks, and I refused to turn around.

"I'm sure I have to muck stalls or something." I could hear his footsteps coming up behind me.

"Saddle up. We have a fence to fix. I noticed it yesterday when we were out riding." He brushed by me without touching me and kept going.

This is why I steered clear of cowboys. I couldn't believe I let myself get caught up last night. It didn't matter that he was an amazing kisser and I felt safe in his arms. It wouldn't happen again.

Thankfully, I saddled the horse faster than I did yesterday, and I was the one waiting for him today. We rode together to the gate, and I didn't move to open it. He climbed down and opened the gate wide enough to get the horses through. I grabbed the reins of his horse, and it followed me through the open gate. Nate closed it and climbed back onto his horse.

We rode and worked in silence; it was a beautiful day, but I wanted to know what was going on in that head of his.

To say it was a long day would be an understatement. I was hot, frustrated, and confused. He helped muck the stalls when we got back, but again, words were only spoken when the job required it.

There weren't enough happy thoughts when the day was over. I mumbled goodbye as I left the barn. If Nate said anything, I never heard him as I walked home.

There was a knock at the door, and I walked over to it and opened it. I had expected Nate, but Kate stood at my door, eyes red from crying and baby-less.

"Kate, what's wrong?" I asked as I pulled her into the house.

"I think I'm losing my mind, Laney. I haven't slept in days.

Every time I put TJ down, he cries. I'm a terrible mother." She flopped down on the couch and dropped her head into her hands. I walked to the fridge and opened the freezer, grabbed a pint of ice cream and two spoons, and went back to sit with Kate. Elbowing her, I handed her a spoon and held out the ice cream.

"Where's TJ?" Asking this made me nervous. I knew Kate wouldn't do anything, but this wasn't the Kate I knew.

"Tyler has him. I'm sure he went to his parents' place for the evening. He told me to get out of the house. I didn't know where else to go." Her crying increased, and I wrapped my arm around her.

"Have you been eating?" She felt thin, and when she was upset, she would stop eating.

She shook her head. Grabbing the ice cream from her, I closed it and tossed it back in the freezer. I opened the fridge and took out the leftovers from last night. Warming them up, I set the plate in front of her and put the fork in her hand. "Eat. Then we'll talk."

"Laney, this is a pretty fancy dinner just to have in the fridge, and pie?" Her color was coming back around and her eyes started to have life in them again. Kate's sniffles stopped, and she dried her eyes. It was as if she needed to be reminded that she was more than a mother. She went into full-on sister mode.

"I had a friend over for supper last night." I tried to brush her off.

"This isn't just a friend over for supper type of food. Delaney, are you seeing someone? Oh, please tell me Jack isn't hanging around trying to get you back." She set her fork down on her plate, and her eyes bored a hole through me.

"It's not Jack." She looked at me like I was hiding something, so certain I was seeing Jack again. "I had Nate over for supper. Just trying to be nice since he dropped everything to help out around here."

"Nate?" She took another bite of her food and waited for more information.

"Okay, look, we had a good day working, and I figured the last thing he wanted to do was cook supper. So I asked him over. That's all." I sat back on the couch and crossed my arms.

"Nope, that's not all. Your face is doing that thing when you want to say something but are trying not to." She scrunched up her face, trying to imitate me.

"Fine. I hate you can read me this well. We may have kissed." I frowned at her.

"You may have or you did? There is a big difference." Kate set her plate down and grabbed a pillow, waiting for an answer.

"We did," was all I replied.

"Tell. Me. Everything." She squealed and waited for me to keep talking.

"He came over for supper. We had a nice visit and then moved to the couch for dessert and coffee. We were chatting, and he leaned over and kissed me. That lead to a full make-out session well into the night."

Kate had raised the pillow to cover her face, and she excitedly tapped her feet on the floor. "Delaney, that's exciting. Oh, but how were things today? Awkward? More kissing? Well, judging from the fact that you were alone, I'm guessing awkward." She looked at me and waited for an answer.

"Well, we only spoke if he needed to tell me something, and then it was short. I think I did something really stupid, Kate. Look, I knew I should have stopped it, but it was so nice. He was so nice." I wrapped my arms around myself and took a deep breath. "He's the opposite of Jack in all the right ways. He seemed interested in me. Not like interested, interested, he just listened when I talked. Jack never did. He was always preoccupied with something. By the time we broke up, we didn't even say good morning or hello." I had never confided in Kate. We were too different, but right now I needed to talk.

"Delaney, I didn't know things were that bad. Why didn't you ever say anything?" Kate shuffled over and sat beside me. She put her arm around me, and I rested my head on her shoulder.

"I don't know. You were always busy, and then when I came home, all the stuff with Tyler was happening. I didn't want to bring you down. So I just kept it all to myself." One tear rolled down my cheek, and I wiped it away with the sleeve of my shirt.

"You know you can tell me anything. I know we haven't always seen eye to eye or understood each other, but you are my sister. Nobody in the world can ever replace you."

She kissed the top of my head, and I thought that was such a big sister thing to do. "This is silly. You came here wanting to get away from crying, and all I have done is cry and whine about a guy when there isn't anything happening. Besides, he's way too old for me."

"Okay, first, you let me cry, so we are even tonight. Second, I'm an old married woman, so I need to live vicariously through you now. Third, maybe you need a man and not a boy." Her smile was mischievous, and it made me laugh.

Grabbing a pillow, I hit her with it, and that started a pillow fight. We were both laughing so hard when there was a knock on the door. I got up to answer it.

"Nate. Is there a problem?" I asked, gaining my composure.

"No. Tyler just called, wondering if everything was okay. He couldn't get a hold of Kate, and your cell phone is off." He stepped into the house.

"I better call him. Laney, where's your phone? Mine is out in the truck."

"It's in the bedroom on the charger." She walked to the room and closed the door behind her.

"Well, I should head back now that the message is delivered. Sorry to interrupt your evening." He nodded and turned to walk back to Mom's house. I wanted to run after him, but I stood where I was until Kate came back out.

"I should head home. Sandra managed to get TJ to sleep, and he probably needs to eat soon. Thank you for this, I needed it." She wrapped her arms around me.

"You come here anytime and please don't wait so long to ask for help. I am always here, and I will drop anything for you," I whispered. She nodded and let me go.

"I would see what happens with him. The way he looked at you, I can tell there's a spark there. Let him in, Delaney, and maybe chase him instead of waiting for him to chase you."

Closing the door, I sat on the couch. Her words rang through my head. Maybe I should chase him.

Download Delaney and Nate's entire story for free here:

https://dl.bookfunnel.com/9mv3ts68bq

ACKNOWLEDGMENTS

To the five women who were randomly plunked together in a critique group, you are who I was missing in my life. You all make me smile, laugh, and cry (happy tears)! Thank you again for your friendship. You mean the world to me. I can't wait for our next adventure!

Jenni, Amy, and Melissa, you answered my beta reader SOS and helped to make the story stronger by making me see what needed to be changed, moved, or just cut out!

As always, to my little family: Terence, Emerson, and Cassidy. I love you more than you can ever know!

ABOUT THE AUTHOR

Bonnie lives in South Central Saskatchewan in the heart of the Canadian prairies. She's married to Terence, who farms, ranches and is a hunting outfitter and guide in the northern part of the province. Terence and Bonnie have two children. Emerson is six and loves helping with the farm and cattle. Cassidy, who is three, is mom's shadow, talking a mile a minute and loves helping in the garden.

Bonnie has been a Licensed Practical Nurse for the last nineteen years. She's worked in a busy city hospital, managed a long term care facility and is now working casually as a floor nurse to spend time at home raising the kids and helping on the farm.

When she's not writing, helping Terence and keeping the kids busy she enjoys vegetable gardening, tending to her flowers, reading and photography.